Dead Odds

Dead Odds

David Ryan

Greg,

May all your mysteries be easy to solve! Great to meet you.

Published by MacGuffin Publishing
P.O. Box 560776
Orlando, FL 32856, USA

DEAD ODDS
PRINTING HISTORY
MacGuffin edition / December 2018

For more information, address correspondence to:
David Ryan
MacGuffin Publishing
P.O. Box 560776
Orlando, FL 32856
Paperback ISBN: 978-1-7329004-1-7

Cover by Elderlemon Design.
Editing by Richard Shealy and Jim Thomsen.
For more information, visit DavidRyanBooks.com
PRINTED IN THE UNITED STATES OF AMERICA
FIRST EDITION

For Kay and Bit

1

TALLY HANCE CHECKED his watch: midnight. He hoped he wouldn't have to wait two more hours until the bars closed to have his encounter, but that wasn't up to him. Surprise was his friend, and that required patience.

His eyes adjusted to the darkness of Vibe, a club well known by Millennials as a place to drink, dance, and watch. Although it was twenty degrees warmer inside than the windy December chill outside, he left his jacket on, the collar turned up. His black jeans and white, long-sleeve shirt fit in with the crowd, though his age wasn't a match. His college days were nearly a decade behind him.

He studied the men at the bar. No one he recognized. A good start. He started a slow walk around and pretended to look at the bartenders. Every few seconds, he stole glances at the men close by. It took him three minutes to circle the inside. Nothing. He started another lap. And this time was rewarded.

Three-quarters of the way around, tucked into a semi-circular leather-upholstered booth in the corner, sat Sean Riggins with five friends. Three men, three women, all college-aged, all flirting and laughing. A hip-hop beat kept their heads and bodies moving.

Tally realized Sean's male friends were his teammates, football players who, unlike the rest of the students at Orlando University, must not have finals in a few hours. The girl sitting next to Sean looked familiar. *What was her name?* He stared at her for a few seconds, then turned away before she saw him. Tonight he needed to remain inconspicuous.

He made his way out the front door and walked across the brick-paved street to a pizza café, where he bought a slice of pepperoni-and-cheese and a bottled water and picked a sidewalk table. He positioned himself to watch Vibe's front door and wondered how long this would take. He couldn't sit here until the club closed. He'd need to wander and stay close, keep an eye on Vibe.

The hot crust felt good in his hands as he took a bite and promptly burned the roof of his mouth. He guzzled his water, but he knew he was too late. With his tongue, he felt dead skin already coming off. *Small sacrifice*, he thought.

His meal lasted three more bites. Tally recognized the gold long-sleeved button-down hugging Sean's muscular arms and shoulders, a contrast against the rich brown of his skin, as he exited the club and made a right. Tally waited for the others to follow, but Sean was alone. He passed Tally, fifty feet away.

Tally stood and abandoned his meal. From across the street, he paralleled Sean's path to an ATM on the corner. Leaning against a brick building where he could see, he pretended to thumb out a text message while keeping a focus on Sean. If Sean felt he was being followed, he didn't let on.

Sean pulled cash from the automated teller, glanced at the receipt, and started back toward the club. Graceful and athletic, the kid carried more than two-hundred pounds on a frame that stood just over six feet. Not that these were issues for Tally. He was a couple of inches shorter and not as fast as he used to be, but he was stockier than Sean. And meaner. Besides, this wouldn't take long. He expected no fight, no chase. He needed only to pass along a message with a little menace.

Sean retraced his course to the bar. Tally checked for traffic and crossed the street, tucking directly behind Sean and closing the gap quickly. As they approached the club, he made up a ten-foot distance separating them with three quick steps and seized Sean by the arm. "How you doing, Sean? Got a minute?"

Sean protested until he recognized the face. "What the hell, man?"

"We need to talk." Tally steered the taller player past the club to a spot on the sidewalk in front of an empty storefront. It was just the two of them, and Tally faced Sean head-on.

"I don't have anything to say to you. Or anyone else," Sean said.

Tally narrowed his eyes and crooked his lip. "You made promises you need to keep."

Sean backed up and pointed a finger at him. "That's bullshit. All I did, they owe me. They must think I'm stupid. I'm done."

Tally looked around, then threw a hard, quick jab into Sean's stomach. The kid doubled over and gasped for air. Tally followed with a fist to sternum, hard enough to raise Sean upright. "Listen, pal, you'll do what you're told."

He pulled back, surprised that Sean didn't respond with a shove or a bear hug.

Instead, the younger man's face twisted into a pained, questioning scowl. His eyes opened wide, then rolled back. A ploy? Tally wondered. Then

Sean's knees buckled, and his body folded down to his feet. The back of his head bounced off the concrete sidewalk with an audible crack. His mouth gaped open, motionless.

"Hey, hey." Tally bent over and looked into Sean's eyes. Nothing. He couldn't tell if the kid was breathing. Twice on a football field he'd seen a player unconscious. Both times the eyes were half-closed. This didn't look like that.

He looked next to Sean's head and saw no blood. But the kid had nothing, no more fighting for air, no writhing in pain, nothing. Tally reached into Sean's jeans and pulled out the cash spit out by the ATM. He found an iPhone in the kid's other pocket. He tugged on it, but a rubber case caught inside the tight pocket.

Too much time. He left the phone. He needed to improvise.

He stood and waved at a small group of people in front of the bar. "Help! Help me! Somebody call an ambulance!"

A young man with a full red beard ran up and kneeled in front of Sean. "What's wrong?"

"I don't know," Tally said. "He just fainted."

Three other men and two women circled them as the first man checked Sean's breathing and eyes and then started CPR.

"I'm calling 911," Tally said, and walked away from the group and away from the club. After a few steps, he picked up his pace. Fifteen seconds into his escape, a siren shrieked down the narrow street. Help on the way. He sped to a jog to the corner and made a quick right toward the parking lot. The siren fell silent.

His Ford Fusion started on the first try. He felt his heart race as he maneuvered out of his parking space and out of the lot. He sped north out of downtown.

What the hell happened? A heart attack? A stroke? Some weird seizure? He didn't know, and he couldn't explain it, though he knew he'd have to. And soon.

2

CONRAD KEANE AWOKE to a soft knock and the creaking of a bedroom door opening. A small beam of light illuminated the bed, and he blinked the sleep away, remembering where he was: in a guest room that had no clock.

"What's up?" he asked his friend, who also happened to be the father of his half-brother.

Quentin Riggins cleared his throat. "Something's happened. I've got coffee going." Riggins sniffled and retreated, leaving the door cracked.

Keane rolled over and reached for his phone. Four-fifteen. He laid back and closed his eyes. An early December wind whistled around the window frame and blew palm branches against the house outside. He was sure the temperature outside was in the sixties, typical for Boynton Beach, but it sounded like a real winter.

Groaning, he rose and stretched his sturdy, six-foot frame, moving left and right to raise a crack from his back. Today was his getaway day, and his flight back to East Tennessee didn't leave for seven hours. So much for his plan to sleep until seven.

He pulled on last night's jeans and t-shirt, which hung off the footboard, and walked down the hall to the guest bathroom. He closed his eyes as he flipped on the bright fluorescent light, then slowly opened them to assess a night of less than five hours' sleep. A week of South Florida sun, combined with his mostly light-brown hair, gave him a vibrant look. Come tomorrow, his fellow agents at the FBI's Knoxville field office would razz him about his early winter tan. *Oh well*, he thought. The gradual march of gray hair along his temples didn't make him look younger, but it didn't bother him. The crow's feet springing from outside his green eyes did.

He warmed up water in the sink, splashed and rubbed his face and gauged whether this was a shave day. Three days of growth said yes: one more day away from home argued no. The stubble had started to disguise a diagonal, one-inch scar under his chin, not necessarily a deal-breaker. There wasn't much of a story behind it—he'd taken a helmet to the jaw playing high school football twenty years earlier—but that hadn't stopped him from embellishing the truth over the years. It was the only reason he tolerated it, but at least the scar had held its shape. He couldn't say the same for his waistline.

Although he fancied himself as in shape and ready for middle age, whatever arbitrary period that was now, evidence to the contrary was mounting. All his shirts fit tighter than they used to, and his slacks snugged up just enough to display a slight side lop-over and belly paunch. If this kept up, he'd have to lose the extra pounds to pass his upcoming fitness test.

Barefoot, he followed the huffing and groaning of an old-school drip coffee maker through Quentin's sparsely decorated, two-bedroom home for one. The smell of the brew permeated the kitchen, where a single bulb in the stove hood made for a low glow. He found his friend, whom everyone called Q, seated at the head of a table and wiping his eyes with the back of his hands. A cell phone sat in front of him.

"You okay? What's going on?" Keane asked.

Q looked up with red-rimmed eyes and tear trails. "He's gone. They said he's gone."

"Who said? Who's gone?"

"Sean. He's dead."

It took a couple of seconds for the news to register, and it hit Keane like a gut punch. He fell back into a wooden chair next to Q. He tasted bile, and a wave of nausea rolled through him. "What happened?"

Q pointed at his phone. "A detective called from Orlando. She said Sean got mugged around midnight outside a bar downtown. They couldn't revive him."

"Shot?"

"They don't know exactly. They found him on the ground, and they couldn't bring him back. They think maybe he hit his head on the sidewalk, but they're not sure. They don't . . . "

Sean's father couldn't finish the thought and ducked his head into his palms and sobbed.

Keane sat quietly and let Q heave out the loss of his only child, a smart and talented twenty-two-year-old with a future full of career options. There would be no more football, no early graduation, no talk of turning pro.

The coffee machine hissed to a halt, and Keane took it as a cue. Assembling the questions racing through his head—he couldn't stop being an FBI agent, no matter what—he pulled two oversized mugs from the cupboard and filled them with Maxwell House, doctoring Q's with cream and sugar.

Q raised up and stared at the darkness outside the kitchen. He sobbed again. "This ain't happening, man. This can't be happening."

Keane sat back down next to his friend. "What else did they tell you? What did they ask?"

Q cradled his cup. "She wanted to know if I knew about anyone who wanted to hurt him. If he had enemies or anyone who would have wanted to hurt him. I told her I had no idea. She said they didn't know much but that it was early. She said they'd know more soon. But first . . . first they asked me to come to Orlando, you know, to talk about him. And to ID him."

Q broke down again. Eventually he reached for a napkin and blew his nose.

Keane put his elbows on the table and his head in his hands. His heart ached for Q. But his insides started to boil. Yes, this was a tragedy. But something felt wrong.

They drank their coffee and let silence wash over them. Keane allowed himself a few more self-critical thoughts, especially about the past ten years when he and Sean should have shared more than a few weekend visits. He'd wasted so much time. And now there was none left.

Eventually, Keane refilled their cups and slipped into autopilot, thought about what the detective had told Q. *Know more soon* could mean a lot of things. It could mean additional witnesses, video or even preliminary results from an autopsy. The detectives had only just begun. He'd been there.

"They're still talking to witnesses," Q said. "They haven't caught anybody. Seemed like she was in a hurry to get off the phone and get going."

Keane waited.

"She said they were getting security video and that after they saw what was on it they'd probably have a better idea of what happened."

Keane pondered that. If a police officer had volunteered that she had video and witnesses, that was a positive sign. He doubted any detective would lie just to make the next of kin feel better. They were trained simply to say, "I'm sorry," and let that suffice. Maybe there would be a quick arrest.

"Did they ask you if Sean was in trouble, if he had mentioned anything? Something that might have, you know, led to this?" he asked.

Q nodded. "I told them I didn't know anything."

Keane let his professional instincts take over. He focused on the few facts that had been relayed from the police. He wouldn't really know until he saw the file—if he saw the file. Wait, this was Florida, the best open-records state in the country. Eventually, they'd get paperwork.

His memory drifted back eighteen hours. After they finished sweeping and mopping their mother's house, Sean had texted friends and played video games. At this same table, the three of them shared an oversized dinner of barbecue, mac and cheese, collard greens, and cornbread. Keane had insisted on cooking the pork shoulder, and Q prepared all the sides. They'd called their Southern feast an early Christmas celebration, minus any gifts, because they knew they were going back to three separate lives the next day—Sean, the college student, Q, the bar owner, and Keane, the special agent in the FBI.

While they ate, they half-watched Army-Navy football on TV in the adjacent living room. Sean seemed unusually interested in the game. He'd reacted angrily to a fluke fourth-quarter touchdown by Navy, one that had all but assured another Army loss. "I'd just like an underdog to win once in a while," Sean had said, explaining why he'd screamed at the referees on TV.

Then, while Keane washed the dishes, Sean had loaded up his car for the three-hour drive to Orlando. This morning, Sean was supposed to take his first final exam of the fall semester.

"Why would Sean be out so late on Sunday night? Finals start today. Didn't he have a curfew?"

"He lives off campus. They can't enforce curfew for players who aren't in the dorm," Q said. "Why would he be out, man, I have no idea. Why do kids do anything?"

Keane nodded and realized they were both still referring to Sean in the present tense.

Q rapped his knuckles twice on the pine table. "Can you help with this? Can you keep the police honest? Make sure they do the right thing, put in the time to find out who did this? I don't want Sean to become just another black kid who died on the street."

The back of Keane's head tingled, which happened when someone singled him out for duty. "You don't trust the police? What makes you think they need to be kept in line?"

"C'mon, man. It's another black kid dead and nobody knows what happened. That's not exactly an original storyline."

"Let's see what the story is first. Go from there. After that, if I need to keep the heat on, I'll find a way to do that." Keane thought about his boss, about what to say and not to say. After he canceled his return flight home, he'd report his sudden PTO extension. He had shared with his boss about the recent death of his mother in Florida and the need for occasional trips to get her less-than-modest estate probated and settled. The Bureau would understand that part of it. Better that Happy Harding, the special agent in charge, didn't know yet about Sean. Harding would wave him off first thing, and Keane preferred not to disobey a direct order. *Ask for forgiveness, not permission.* If he exerted official influence as an agent, well, he'd need that to stay on the down-low. He put his hand on Q's shoulder as he got up and poured them more coffee. "How long will it take you to line up people to cover the bar for a few days?"

"Not long," Q said. "I can do it from the road."

They finished their coffee in silence. They had a three-hour drive and a world of loss ahead of them.

3

TINA ROSSI THOUGHT it ironic that she'd lived her entire life in a water-logged, creature-filled state and yet despised fishing, hunting, and even lying on a beach. What others called relaxation she deemed boredom. Yet she made a career of the real-world version of a Florida outdoorsman. She fished for information. She hunted killers.

Today the hunter needed eye drops. She had a dead Orlando University football player, no good suspects, and only a couple of witnesses, neither of whom qualified as solid. The three women and two OU players hanging out with Sean Riggins at the club provided little help. Even the girlfriend, a pretty, petite junior at OU, described Riggins as a college student with no enemies or even an ex-girlfriend. They'd dated less than a year, and they didn't live together.

Rossi pinched the top of her nose. The fluorescent lights in the detectives' room at the Orlando Police Department did their job too well. Four hours of glare from her computer screen pushed pain into the front of her head. Another rewarding day on the job.

Rossi had been a homicide detective for nearly five years, and all her friends still imagined her life as one gun-filled car chase after another. In truth, going blind from grainy video was far more representative of her life. She squinted at black-and-white images and jotted down tag numbers. *Is that a J or an I? Is that a 5 or an S?*

Rossi shut her laptop and unclipped her jet-black hair, letting it tumble behind her. She leaned back and closed her eyes. Just a fifteen-second nap would work.

"Perfect timing." Detective Bob Thomas dropped a DVD on her desk as he sat down across from her. "More video."

She let the chair rock her back upright. "I can't wait."

"What have you got so far?" Thomas loosened his tie and opened up his laptop.

"The ATM video has Riggins taking out money, looks like ten twenty-dollar bills, right after he left the club," she said. "So right before he died. He counted the money, put it in his pocket, and headed back in the direction of Vibe. . . . you got any eye drops?"

He lobbed a tiny bottle of Refresh drops at her. She flushed her eyes and blinked. She placed the bottle on her desk. She had a feeling she'd need them again soon.

"Riggins didn't have any money on him," Thomas said. "Somebody was watching him." He held up his own disc. "Maybe we'll get lucky."

"There's always that. How long are these?"

Thomas queued up his video. "They're all an hour. They start right before the assault and end about fifty-five minutes after that. You can see a few of our witnesses on there."

"And the suspect?"

"He's there, too."

She ejected the ATM video and put in the new one. The camera was fixed catty-corner from Vibe, west of the front door. Designed to document the comings and goings of residents and visitors of a recently constructed condo complex, it captured the final moments of a college kid who lived twenty miles away.

Riggins came into frame first, pushed ahead by the other man. There was a quick conversation: not pleasant, not violent. His back to the camera, the other man did most of the talking. Got into Riggins's face.

They knew each other. No one would let a stranger get this close.

A couple walked by, from the right to left, but neither person reacted as if danger were imminent. *It wasn't a loud argument.*

Half a minute in, the shorter man threw a surprise punch, then another. The second blow looked particularly power-packed. Riggins collapsed like a tall building coming down on itself. He landed hard on his left side, facing away from the camera, his head bouncing off the concrete. Start to finish, it took forty-six seconds.

"Jesus," she said, and watched the white man look around, take Riggins's money, and finally look for help. And then he slipped out of frame. "Look at this."

Thomas stopped his video and stepped around behind her. She rewound and re-started the video, and they watched it together twice: first at normal speed, then slowed down.

"House of cards," Thomas said. "It's pretty rare to take a shot to the midsection and not get up. I don't even know what to make of it. You get hit like that, you get a broken rib maybe, but you don't die."

"Skull fracture?" she said. "A lot of force when his head hits the sidewalk."

"He'd have bled. It's possible he got a brain bleed. I've never seen one, but would you go out just like that? One minute you're here, the next you're dead?"

She agreed. Not much made sense. She'd witnessed nonsensical violence—and the aftermath—but this was downright strange. The medical examiner expected to find an enlarged heart and possibly evidence of drug use or a genetic defect.

None of those factors would work a prosecutor into a lather, but she didn't worry about that. The ER doctor had said it was likely a heart attack, and she could only argue, "Who the hell dies of a heart attack at twenty-two?" The kid had had an altercation, but no evidence existed of a weapon. There was no mess, no blood, no broken bones. The kid had no bullet holes or stab wounds. She'd collected witnesses, but no good ones.

They'd already run the 911 calls, which provided little help. Three people called in, two women and a man. All of them sounded concerned but not panicked. To them it looked like someone had fainted.

Two people heard the dead kid arguing with another man but neither knew why. The kid was black. Witnesses said the other man was white. One Good Samaritan reported the white man said he was going to get help. The man never returned. No one saw any blows struck, just one man trying to help another early Monday morning—not a crowded time downtown.

Rossi said, "At least we have a robbery charge."

Thomas tapped the back of her chair. "We may get more, assuming we find him. He sucker-punched Riggins twice, and the kid crashed. It shouldn't have killed him but it did."

"They argued, but we're going to need more than this."

"More than what?" Sherman Beale asked.

Rossi looked at the bright-eyed face of the chief of detectives. "More than what we have."

Beale half-smiled. "I need you two for a minute."

They followed Beale back to his office, where his charcoal-gray suit coat hung on a rack behind his desk.

"Close the door," he said. "Sit."

Rossi followed Thomas into the boss's office and shut the door behind her. They sat side by side in front of the chief's large oak desk, which was littered with reports, manila folders, stray papers, and dozens of yellow sticky notes.

Everything about Beale was red: bright hair muted only by the start of gray at the temples, a button nose with a rosy tip, cheeks that looked like they'd been scrubbed by a Brillo pad. They looked particularly raw today. Beale ran a hand through his hair, one of his tells. This wasn't good news.

"Where are you two on the football player?" Beale asked.

She looked at Thomas. He nodded ever so slightly.

"Looking for more witnesses," she said. "Chasing down leads from video. We'll get there. We're waiting for more video to come in. We don't have any DNA yet, and there's not much there. We don't know why the kid died. The ME has a couple of bad-heart theories. Those would fit with him getting hit in the chest."

Beale looked at Thomas. "You have an opinion here?"

"I think it's possible this was a guy wanting to settle a score, and the situation went bad," Thomas said. "Witnesses confirm what we see on video, that the attacker was built like a football player. Broad shoulders, plenty of muscle. This probably wasn't random."

Beale put his hands together as if in prayer and buried his chin in them in thought. "So, you're guessing."

Rossi uncrossed her legs and sat up for the oncoming battle. Thomas said nothing and waited out Beale, who wasn't known for his patience.

"This kid was an NFL prospect," Beale said. "The media's going to eat us for lunch if we screw this up. So, you two have clear objectives. Solve this, and don't drop the ball. Find the guy in the video, lean on him to get some answers. Get a story to feed the media. You've got a week."

She sighed. Seven days wasn't realistic, especially on this case. The university's penchant for red tape and politics would eat into their time. She and Thomas needed immediate luck.

"That's fast," Thomas said finally.

"There's no sense in wasting any time in here." Beale rose from his chair, signaling the end of the discussion. "You already know the mayor is fond of OU's president. Understand?"

Too many outside voices, Rossi thought, but nodded. They left Beale to his politics, and Rossi checked her watch. She needed to learn more about Sean Riggins. What had he done to deserve this?

ROSSI WATCHED TWO more hours of post-attack video from various city-owned cameras before random images clicked into a pattern. "I have something." Thomas looked up from his computer screen but didn't answer. "I've got a white male with the same color jacket as our guy. Same build.

He's walking the right direction, from the area of the bar. And I've got a partial plate."

She read out four letters, two shy of the normal letters or numbers from most Florida license plates. "It's a specialty plate, too. An OU plate."

Like many states, Florida had turned to vanity license plates and specialty plates to raise tax revenue. Virtually every major special-interest group, from golfers to hunters to fishing enthusiasts to right-to-lifers, enjoyed its own tag. So did every college and university in the state. They were an administrative pain in the ass. But they often made police work easier.

"See what you get," Thomas said.

Rossi punched the letters into the database kept by the Division of Motor Vehicles. She found four OU plates that were a match or similar. She cross-referenced the plate registration names against information in the DMV's driver's license database. "Got something." She made two printouts and spotted one name. "David William Hance of Orlando. Twenty-eight years old. White. Five-eleven, two hundred-twenty pounds. I'm running his record." She wrinkled her brow.

"And?"

"His name sounds familiar, but I don't know why." Rossi stopped typing and closed her eyes to get a break from the fluorescent lighting in the detectives' room. She heard Thomas, oblivious to everyone else, working a slow *tap, tap, tap* on his keyboard, the hunt-and-peck method in full swing. She leaned back and thought about Sean Riggins. On campus, he was a star. Popular, even envied. But universally beloved? She didn't know, at least not yet. Local sportscasters were calling him an NFL prospect who never lived long enough to get his big break. How was David Hance connected?

Her desk phone chirped in bursts, an internal call. She picked up and on the other end she heard, "Detective, there are two men here asking for someone working on the Sean Riggins case. One's the father."

"We'll be right out."

She caught Thomas's attention. "Our dad's here, and he's got a friend with him."

"A lawyer?"

"Aren't you the optimist?"

4

KEANE STUDIED THE obligatory bulletin board of most-wanted suspects by the Orlando Police Department as he and Q waited for the detectives assigned to Sean Riggins's case. The roster of the accused: six murderers, two rapists, a child molester, and a kidnapper, all men. Only the rapists surprised him. Two was a small number, from what he remembered of Florida. He'd grown up near Fort Myers, on the west coast of the state. Since landing in law enforcement, he'd made a point to keep an eye on the state's crime statistics. Florida rarely disappointed. It always led the country in something.

Keane looked at the dates on the criminals sheet. Only one was more than two years old. *A good sign for OPD*, he thought.

A thin, silver-haired man with a badge lanyard approached them with a short, well-figured detective who wore her dark hair in a tightly constructed bun.

She offered her hand to Q first. "Mr. Riggins? I'm Detective Rossi. This is Detective Thomas. We're investigating Sean's death. We're very sorry for your loss. Your son was a valued part of the university and the community. We talked to the paramedics, and we know they did everything they could."

"Thank you. I'm sure they did," Q said.

Rossi turned to Keane. "And you are?"

"I'm Sean Riggins's brother," he said. He caught the detectives' confusion as they looked at each other, trying to connect a black victim, a black father, and the third-wheel white man in front of them. "Technically, half-brother. Same mother. Different father, obviously."

"What's . . . the age difference?" Rossi asked.

"Eighteen years," Keane said. "Mom and I were a pair until I went to college. And after that, she and Sean were a pair. She was a single mom twice. Raised us both on her own."

Rossi and Thomas nodded at him, digesting the odd family construction. "Let's find a place to talk," Rossi said. Thomas led them to a conference room while Rossi split off.

Keane let Q take a seat at one side of the table, and he took one ninety degrees to the left, facing the door. If the meeting turned into a formal interview, he preferred not to let the detectives stage Us-vs.-Them seating, with Q and him on one side of the table, Thomas and Rossi on the other. Thomas sat next to Q and across from Keane. When Rossi rejoined them, she brought with her a case folder and a small, clear plastic bag. She took the last chair across from Q and next to Keane.

She collected their cell phone numbers and slid Q a paper to sign, a release for Sean's belongings. She unsealed the bag and dumped out keys and a wallet.

"This is all I can give you right now." Rossi slid paperwork across the table.

Q scanned the release form and handed it to Keane. "I can't take his clothes? Or his phone?"

"I'm sorry," she said. "Not until the case is finished."

"That'll be when? Next week?" Q asked.

"We'll push, but every case has its own timeline," Rossi said.

"Aw, who are you kidding? You guys will never solve this. I know how this works. Just another dead black kid."

"Mr. Riggins, we're working very hard. We have every intention of finding out what happened and bringing someone to justice if the circumstances warrant it."

"What do you mean, 'if circumstances warrant it'? He was killed."

"I'm sorry, but the coroner thinks Sean may have had a heart defect or a condition that left his heart vulnerable. We're investigating, and we're talking to witnesses, but it's certainly possible this was an accident. A one-in-a-million situation."

"They tell you to say that in the police handbook? 'One in a million'?"

Thomas leaned toward Q. "Mr. Riggins, this is hard, and you don't know us. But trust me. This has our full attention. We're looking at this closely. We want justice."

"We'll see about that."

Keane looked at Q. "Let them do their jobs. If this drags on, we'll deal with it then." He caught Rossi and Thomas glancing at each other, but they let his not-so-veiled threat go unchallenged.

"Mr. Riggins, what can you tell us about your son?" Rossi asked. "From what we know so far, he was an excellent football player, an exemplary student. We know he was popular. But what don't we know? We need to fill in those gaps. I know I've asked you this already, but have you been able to think of any reason why someone would want to harm your son?"

Q stayed silent.

"If you know, tell her," Keane said.

Q took a deep breath. "I don't know. I surely don't. I mean, I only saw him with all his friends on the team, and they were all pretty close."

Keane sat quietly while Rossi and Thomas ignored him and focused on collecting details from the father of a victim. He'd done it a number of times himself. It was expected.

He listened to Q paint Sean as a son with a bright future and as a college student without an enemy. He described a young man with a banker's brain for business who possessed charm equal to his athletic ability and who could persuade teammates to follow him even when they might have preferred otherwise.

Keane silently wished he had a father who could tell his story so eloquently and forcefully. He had no memories of his father, who died before Keane reached his second birthday.

After twenty minutes, the detectives paused to look at their notes. Keane asked, "What can you tell us about how Sean died?"

Thomas nodded at Rossi, who said, "There was no blunt-force trauma, no lacerations or stab wounds. Sean did have a bruise on the back of his head, probably from when he hit the sidewalk after he collapsed. She looked at Q. "What do you know about your family history of heart disease?"

"No history of it," Q said.

Thomas picked up with the rest of the ME's preliminary report: "No obvious indications of any other ailments. He had an elevated blood-alcohol level, point-oh-seven, not legally intoxicated. The ME will do an autopsy, but the full tox screen won't be back for a few weeks. We're looking for anything else you can fill in."

Q shook his head. "He was a physical specimen. He was healthy."

"During the altercation, your son was struck twice, once in the stomach, once in the chest," Rossi said. "We think it triggered his heart stoppage. We think—"

"Do you have a motive?" Keane asked.

Rossi grimaced at the interruption and shot him an irritated look. "Sean had just gone to the ATM before he was accosted. Video shows he withdrew about two hundred dollars. Whoever did this took the money."

"You're saying this was a mugging that escalated?" Keane asked.

"Usually during a mugging there's a gun or a knife involved. We have no evidence that this was the case. This doesn't seem to be about money. We think the money was just an opportunity of chance."

"Then what is the motive?"

"We don't know yet."

"You don't know much."

"Listen—"

Thomas held up his hand and cut Rossi off. "We don't know as much as we'd like. That's why we wanted to talk to Mr. Riggins." He turned to Q. "If we had answers, you'd have them. We're after the same thing you're after."

The four of them sat in silence for several seconds before Rossi started again with Q. "Your son, he had expensive tastes."

"How so?" Q asked.

"His furniture is quality stuff. He's got a state-of-the-art big-screen TV and a closet full of expensive clothes and shoes. I have to tell you, Mr. Riggins, I don't see many college students with such nice stuff."

"Is that right?" Q said. "You don't have any fraternities here, fraternities with boys from well-off families?"

Thomas cleared his throat. "Mr. Riggins, we're looking for things that are unusual. And this is unusual. It's not bad, it's not good. It's just out of the ordinary. We're not making any judgments whatsoever. But anything you can tell us helps. Because—"

"Because you don't see many black kids with money, is that it?" Q banged the table and shook his head.

"We don't see many college students, period, with all that. A lot of them have nice TVs, because it seems like they all want to play video games. We do see nice stereo systems, surround sound and all that. A few have had nice wardrobes. But not too many of them—I'd say hardly any of them—have nice furniture. It's just not something they care about. And none of them have all of the above. But Sean had it all."

Q studied Thomas for a few seconds and scooted back up in his chair. "Whatever Sean wanted, I got for him, okay? Like you said, he was a good athlete and a good student. Made the dean's list almost every semester. I rewarded him for everything he accomplished. It kept him motivated."

"You bankrolled him."

"No, but if he needed something and I could afford it, I got it for him," Q said.

"What do you do for a living?"

"I own a restaurant."

"You must do well."

"I'm good at what I do," Q said.

Rossi looked at her notes. "Your son, he was on full scholarship? All expenses paid?"

"Not all of them. They cover tuition, housing and almost all the food. They don't cover spending money."

The detectives probed for details about Sean's finances, and Q said he gave his son cash every month. "It was probably a couple hundred dollars. What he did with it, I don't know. I got the impression it was for pizza and fun. I never really asked."

Keane raised his hand like a schoolboy. "I have a question." All three of them turned to him.

"Yes?" Rossi asked.

"You made an observation about Sean's lifestyle, the things in his apartment. I assume you collected what you thought was important. I'd like to see the inventory sheet."

Rossi and Thomas picked up on his language and glanced at each other. She then produced a paper that listed everything they'd confiscated from Sean's body, residence, and SUV, which was discovered in a downtown garage. Keane studied the list: From Sean's apartment they'd taken a Dell laptop, bed sheets and a bedspread, some dirty drinking glasses, and whatever paperwork they found. No bank statements were listed. If Sean banked solely online, which was likely given his age, his records were probably all electronic too. He knew it was unlikely that the detectives had accessed them. Which meant Rossi wasn't confirming information. She was fishing.

"The video you have. Who does it show attacking Sean?" he asked.

"We can't see his face," Rossi said. "We can get a basic body type and age, but we don't have anything solid on that yet. But we're confident we'll have an ID soon."

"White? Black? Hispanic?"

"Likely white. Shorter than Sean but maybe thicker in the chest. A man who looks like he could do damage with a punch."

Keane surveyed her face. She didn't give away much, but he was now certain the detectives hadn't interviewed the person who slugged Sean. They were still looking. This was the soft-shoe, so he spun the conversation. "How many other cases do you have? As of today?"

Rossi's face flashed confusion. Thomas said, "Three. We always work a few at a time. But those cases will not influence this case. We're engaged on this case, and we'll work it with our best effort, I promise you."

"I know you will. The media's already all over this." Keane smiled and turned back to Rossi. "When can we get into Sean's apartment? Start cleaning it out?"

"Any time," she said. "We're done with it."

"Great. We have a lot of things to get done. I'm sure you know how long the list is."

She nodded. "Anything else?"

"Sean's car. When can we get that?"

They made arrangements to pick up the SUV, and Rossi circled back with questions about Sean's friends and family, teammates and coaches. Again she asked about conflicts.

"I don't know of any," Q said. "Everybody got along with him."

She turned to Keane. "What about you? Can you shed any light here?"

Keane rubbed his chin and thought for a few seconds. "Not really. I wasn't close to Sean."

"What does that mean exactly?" she asked.

"Just that. We were a generation apart, and except for sharing a crazy but hard-working mother and the fact that we both saw football as a way out, we didn't have much in common. Our mother . . . encouraged the divide, and after a while I quit fighting it. I lived in my world, Sean lived in his. We traded emails and text messages every once in a while, but that was about it. I saw him play football once a year, sometimes only on TV, but I have no idea who his friends were, much less any enemies."

Rossi nodded. She looked at Q and then back at Keane. "Do you or Sean have any more siblings? Are there any more living relatives?"

"There's nobody on their side," Q said, motioning at Keane.

"My dad died when I was two," Keane said. "When my mom died a couple months ago, I had no more living relatives. At least, not as far as I know."

"I don't have any other kids," Q said. "Sean was it."

The detectives looked at each other, said nothing, and concluded the interview. As they walked to the lobby and handed out business cards, Thomas asked, "How long are you planning to be in town?"

"We'll probably leave right after we clean out Sean's apartment," Q said.

"If you think of anything that might help, we'd appreciate a call."

Q nodded, but Keane answered. "You'll be the first to know."

5

TEDDY SIMPSON HAD no idea what had happened downtown, but he aimed to find out. He'd make sure to punish whoever was responsible for Sean Riggins's death. Looking out of his pristine Orlando University office at a crystal-blue fountain below, he used the contact list from one cell phone to find the number to dial with a second phone he'd picked up that morning.

He wondered how many other college presidents used throwaway cells.

Tally answered on the third ring, sounding like a man who hadn't slept in days.

"Where the hell have you been?" Teddy bellowed. "I've been trying to reach you for hours."

Tally sounded confused. "It's you. You got a new number? Your name didn't come up."

"What the hell happened?"

"How should I know? He took a punch and just fell over."

"Wait. You did this? You hit him?"

Tally's voice went up an octave. "You wanted me to give him a message, right? I gave him the message."

"Unbelievable. You were supposed to scare the kid straight. You fucking put him in a box."

"It just happened," Tally said. "We talked, I said what I needed to say, delivered the message, and he just . . . collapsed. The TVs all say he had a bad heart. They talked to the doctors. How was I supposed to know he had a bad heart?"

Teddy absorbed Tally's explanation and understood all he needed to. He'd just called the killer. He rolled options through his head like he always did and realized this was bad on every level. No scenario played out well for either of them, although all of Tally's were worse.

He sat back in his leather chair and whispered into the phone, "If they catch you, you're going to prison for sure, son. Jesus, those boys in Starke are going to love you."

Tally gasped. "Prison? I didn't kill anybody. What the hell?"

"You heard me."

"Man, this is bullshit."

Teddy pictured Tally pacing and rubbing his hand through his buzz cut, which he did every time he got nervous. "You need to think about leaving Orlando and never coming back. At least not for a long time."

"I can't do that," Tally said.

"You want to live? Don't let the police find you. They're going to pin this on someone. Might as well be the person who actually did it. Or the person who was right there. You see what I'm saying? Don't even worry about getting yourself a lawyer, son. I don't know if anyone can help you at this point."

He heard Tally moan as he hung up. He'd have to get him a lawyer if the police found him, but his lawyer would make damn sure Tally took a deal without revealing anything important. He didn't need Tally talking to the cops or anyone else.

6

KEANE UNDERSTOOD INSTANTLY why the detectives had questioned Q so hard about Sean's belongings. He decided after one look at Sean's apartment that his brother had enjoyed a life Keane had never seen in a college student. At least, no college student this side of a drug dealer.

"You paid for all this?" he asked Q after taking in a forty-two-inch TV, a micro-leather couch, matching recliner, and a coffee table with matching end tables. Best Buy meets Scan Design.

"A lot of it," Q said.

He wandered through the small living and dining areas and into the kitchen. The police and crime-scene techs had left their usual trail. The residue of fingerprint powder coated doorknobs, the refrigerator and every flat surface. He found the same residue in the bedroom, which was spacious enough to fit a queen bed and full-sized desk and leave walking space.

The cops had stripped the bed of its sheets and cut a swath of fabric from a small stain in the mattress. They'd also vacuumed the tan, short-piled carpet: basic forensic and DNA profiling. The oversized bathroom, unlike the rest of the unit, cried *college student*. White tile all around with sporadic mold, and mildew spots staining grout lines in the shower. Any excess hair on the floor had been swept away. More DNA.

Sean's walk-in closet was awash in designer jeans, dress slacks, button-down dress shirts, and golf shirts hanging over nearly twenty pairs of dress shoes and signature sneakers. None of the short-sleeved shirts carried a school logo, a wardrobe staple for any college athlete. Keane thought: *Clotheshorse*. And then: *Money?*

"You got anything?" Q asked from the other room.

"Not much," he said, and turned his attention to the desk. Two small, stand-up photo frames were set up so that whoever sat at the desk had an up-close view. One held a picture of Sean and Q side by side, both of them beaming. It looked like the photo had been taken outside a stadium after a recent game. The other frame contained an image of Sean and a cute college-aged woman with light brown skin and long dark hair. They had been captured outdoors, at a picnic or a party. They looked relaxed in shorts and t-shirts, and they looked happy.

He pulled open a desk drawer and discovered that any papers that had been there were now gone. Police left only a set of ear buds, a white power cord, and a white power adapter. He powered up a wireless black desk printer/scanner but failed to find the last document that was scanned or printed.

Disappointed, he back-tracked and looked for anything he might have missed. In the kitchen, he pulled open drawers and found uninspiring flatware, knives, a few pots and pans. One drawer had Scotch tape and to-go menus. Vito's, Papa John's, Domino's, Olive Garden, Pita Pocket, and Huey Magoo's, a mix of chain restaurants and local fast-food joints.

Q asked, "What are you looking for?"

"There's no speaker for music. Or a stereo system."

"You ever heard of an iTunes? You know, on your phone?"

He ignored the question and double-checked the police inventory list. There it was. A Dell laptop. And a power cord. But no docking station and no other electronics.

"There's another laptop out there," he said.

Q frowned. "How do you know that?"

"The laptop they took was a Dell. Those have black power cords. Every other cord in Sean's desk is white, not black. Apple computers and devices almost always come with white cords. And the printer in there"—he pointed to the bedroom—"is a wireless printer programmed to print from a Dell and from a MacBook. The police don't have that computer." He held up the paper as if presenting evidence to a judge. "If we assume Sean never had to replace a power cord, there's a computer missing. So where's the MacBook?"

AN INTERCOM INTERRUPTED Teddy Simpson's coed watching. The massive fountain below his office window was the most iconic symbol of student life on campus, and it was also a magnet for undergrads when the sun was out. They came in droves throughout the day for a central spot to read, text, nap, or talk. Watching all the action was Teddy's secret pleasure, a readily available and welcome diversion.

His secretary's voice squawked, "The detectives are here." Ten seconds later she ushered in a tall, thin man with a silver crew cut and a pleasing-looking woman with dark eyes and pinned-up black hair. Teddy thought for a second he recognized her, though he wasn't sure from where.

"Detective Tina Rossi," the woman said as she stuck out her hand. "And this is Detective Bob Thomas."

He shook their hands and offered soda, coffee, or water. They said no, and he motioned them to an oblong mahogany table.

"Mr. Simpson, we wanted to let you know we'll be spending time on campus talking to a number of people, probably most of them in the football program," Thomas said. "Any help we can get lining up interviews would be appreciated."

"Certainly," he said. "Anything you need."

"For starters, we'll need someone to coordinate interviews."

"A person you trust," Rossi said. "Preferably not in the athletic department."

"We'll handle it," Teddy said. "Talk to Nancy on the way out."

"Perfect," Rossi said. "We'll start today, but we'll be back." The detectives stood to leave.

Teddy stayed seated. He'd sat through so many power meetings during his days in Tallahassee that he knew whoever acted the contrarian in the room often secured more valuable information. "Can you at least give me an update on where things are? Do you know what happened?"

Rossi sat back down and looked at Thomas, who followed suit. She said, "We're investigating. We have video and eyewitnesses, but it's early. We still have a lot of ground to cover."

Teddy twice rapped the knuckles of his right hand on the table and thought about the morning news. Riggins's death was the day's top story and figured to stay there for a while. "What do the video and witnesses tell you? Was it an accident?"

"Too early to tell," Thomas said. "We think Riggins could have been targeted. That would make it . . . not an accident."

"Targeted. Jesus. By who?"

"We don't know. That's why we're here."

"And you think our players and coaches can help you with that?"

The detectives looked at each other and then back to the president. "We hope so," Rossi said.

Teddy nodded. "As I said, we'll help any way we can."

"Good, because I had a quick question for you," Rossi said and looked him in the eye.

"Oh?"

"What was Sean Riggins's reputation around campus?"

He paused and scratched at an imaginary spot on the table. "He was well-liked. He was a kid with an NFL future who went to class and wasn't a prima donna. What wasn't to like?"

"How well did you know him?"

"I'd talked to him. I shook his hand a couple times after games. Great player. Smart kid."

"How smart?" she asked.

"If he didn't make it in pro football, we thought he'd make a great assistant coach one day. He loved the game." Teddy shrugged. "I think he just wanted to play football. I never spoke to him about his future."

The detectives stood for the second time and thanked him for his time. He walked them out, closed the door, and heard them consulting his secretary.

TEDDY PUNCHED FOUR digits on his desk phone. Duke Childress picked up on the second ring, and

Teddy didn't bother with a greeting. "There are two of them. They're on their way over. Give them whoever they want."

"Who do they want?" Childress asked.

"They didn't say, but I imagine you're on the list."

"Any players?"

He raised his voice loud enough to make a point but not enough to escape his office. "Goddammit, just handle it." He hung up before the coach offered a response, cursed to himself, and dialed an off-campus number from memory.

"The police are on their way to talk to Duke," he said.

On the other end, Don Henson groaned. "That's too fast. What do they know?"

"They've got something, but they're not saying what. Said the players could help them."

"You need to put an end to that. Get the players lawyers. Then call the mayor. Get him to lean on the police a bit. Surely all the money you contributed to his campaign still counts for something."

"Too drastic. It'd cause too much attention." Teddy had no idea how much attention it would cause, but he was certain the police would look unkindly on any attorney intervention. It would beg the question of guilt. It would be overkill in an investigation that might never get off the ground. Besides, if he needed to play that card later, he'd remind the mayor who helped him get elected.

"You're willing to risk it?" Henson asked.

"They're fishing."

"You'd better be right."

Teddy placed the phone in its cradle. Henson hadn't put up a fight. Central Florida's most notable car dealer promoted a public image of "your place for a friendly face and four wheels." The truth was, the man was a greedy, intolerant son of a bitch who disliked not getting his way. He was exactly like the scumbag state legislators Teddy had manipulated for twenty years.

He sighed and turned back to the coeds.

7

Rossi pitched her plan to Thomas on the quarter-mile walk from the president's office to the football complex. OU's campus carried all the signs of a modern university. A semi-organized maze of old and new buildings was attached by sidewalks and occasional swaths of grass. Parking lots took up much of the landscape.

They passed two of the dozen parking garages scattered throughout the acreage. Designers spruced up the natural appeal with a liberal planting of palm trees, tall grasses surrounded by pine straw mulch. But Rossi knew from experience that trekking from building to building here was less about the visuals and more about the day's heat index. Today's temperature was in the fifties. They wouldn't arrive sweaty.

"I want to talk to the coaches and have you talk to the players," she said. "I want the coaches to underestimate us, which they definitely will if I'm alone with them. I think the players will be more nervous with you. Then we both make a run at the head coach."

"That'll play," Thomas said.

Rossi hoped for meaningful details from three specific assistant coaches: the man who recruited Sean out of Boynton Beach, his position coach, and the team's defensive coordinator. She didn't count on much. She had done her homework and was already playing in her head the directions she would take her interviews.

Their stroll ended in Duke Childress's office, where two twenty-something office assistants smiled at them and a third, who looked to be in her fifties, was all business. "We're ready for you. I just need to know who you want to talk to first."

"The president's office called with the names?" Rossi asked.

The woman nodded.

"I'll need one room for the coaches. Detective Thomas will need another room to meet with the players. We'll finish with Coach Childress."

The assistant, wearing the same khaki pants and white polo shirt as her colleagues in the outer office, walked them down a hallway and presented each of them with a small meeting room.

"Any order for these interviews?" she asked them.

"Whatever's convenient," Rossi said. "We'll let you know when we're done with one and ready for another."

FOUR HOURS LATER, Rossi checked email on her phone while she waited for her partner to finish. A short, slender, muscular student with a stylish t-shirt and jeans hanging below his waist emerged, followed by Thomas. The young man looked scared but ignored her as he started texting. He walked past without a word, head down.

Thomas stretched his arms above his head and rubbed his back. "How'd you do?"

"Learned a few things," she said. "They all loved Sean, just like the dad said. The background is he came from a single-parent household, and the surprise is the dad's still around. His mom died about three months ago, and now the dad gets to be a parent." She put her phone away as they started out the door. "Coaches said he was a type-A—a good leader but stubborn. He'd talk back to coaches, yell at them in practice and in games."

"You can get away with it if you're good. Did anybody say he had friends in high places?"

"Not really. Why?"

"One of the other linebackers made a comment that if Riggins got into trouble, he'd get taken care of. Said, 'Somebody would bail him out.' I pushed him, but that was all he gave up."

Rossi frowned. Sean didn't have an arrest record. That was one of the first things they'd checked. "Bailed out" had to be a euphemism. "I need to talk to two more players: Darrell Dubrow and Johnnie Jones. They roomed with Riggins before this year."

"Now?"

"Soon. I want to think about what we just heard. Now we need Childress."

Rossi put on a polite smile for Duke Childress, as the football coach motioned for them to sit in chairs in front of his desk. They shook hands and sat, and she noted his near-professional tan from five months of standing in the Florida sun watching practice. His skin tone and a loose, boyish haircut gave the coach the look of a younger man, and she caught him staring as he leaned back in his well-worn leather chair.

"I know you," Childress said.

Rossi nodded. "Before I made detective, I used to work security detail here on game days. I had the sideline."

The coach squinted at her as if he were trying to force a memory. "Hopefully we didn't run you off."

"I got promoted."

Childress nodded. "What can I do for you now?"

Rossi and Thomas gave the coach basic facts from their interviews but nothing that hinted at suspicion. They enjoyed tag-teaming interviews, each playing off the other. They often played good cop/bad cop, a cliché constantly played out on TV but one that nevertheless worked in real life. They'd learned how to reveal a small fact in the course of questioning, and that one detail often led to verbose answers and explanations from the next person in front of them. This time, the coach echoed what his assistants gave them and professed to know nothing about Riggins's life without a jersey.

Half an hour in, Childress leaned back in his chair. She realized he was comfortable and not at all aggravated by their presence or their questions.

"How much of a pain in the ass was Riggins?" Rossi asked. She saw a brief flash in the coach's eyes, but it evaporated as quickly as it arrived.

"He wasn't at all," Childress said. "I don't know where you got that idea."

"Your coaches say he was damned smart. But it seems like he was so intelligent, he kept the coaches on their toes. Or is that wrong?"

"If you told him something, he remembered. If you backtracked, he'd call you on it."

"Like what?" Thomas asked.

Childress shrugged. "If you told him the sky was blue and then one day you tried to say it was a little gray, he'd call bullshit on you."

"How about a real-world example?" she asked.

"You just couldn't lie to the kid, okay? Some of these kids, you have to lie to them to motivate them. Tell them if they play well on Saturday they'll be a starter the next week. Riggins, he took you at your word and expected you to live by it. Those kind of players carry your water for you, so you don't try to bullshit them."

"But you said you sometimes didn't shoot straight with him."

"There's a time to salute and keep marching." Childress leaned forward in his chair. "We don't have time to explain every decision."

Rossi looked at her partner and gave him a look that said *Your turn*. Thomas caught her eye and looked back at Childress. "Tell us, who didn't like him?"

"Everybody on offense."

"Why's that?"

"He'd play full-speed in practice. He hit them, and sometimes runners and receivers don't want to get hit by their own guys."

"Anyone else?"

Childress shook his head. "Not that I know of."

They questioned the coach for another twenty minutes, Rossi and Thomas getting a handle on Riggins's friends and rivals. Not much about Childress had changed since the days when she spent time close to his football team, she thought, except that having a succession of winning teams again three years after nearly losing his job seemed to have hardened him. The business of college sports.

She head-motioned Thomas that she was done and stood to face Childress. "We have a few more people to talk to tomorrow. We'll follow up with you."

The coach stood but did not offer a hand. "Anything you need."

WALKING THROUGH THE lobby, Rossi pulled Thomas down a back hallway.

"I thought we were done," he said.

"I promised you video," she said. Midway down the hall, a sign next to a closed door said VIDEO SUITE. She knocked twice and stepped inside.

A diminutive woman with caramel skin and shoulder-length black hair spun her chair away from a quad of computer monitors and looked back at them. She stood but rose barely to five feet. *She's a pixie*, Rossi thought.

"Can I help you?" the woman asked.

Rossi introduced herself and Thomas with her badge. "We're talking to people about Sean Riggins."

"Oh," the woman said. "There are people here who knew him a lot better than I did. I hardly knew him."

"And you are?"

"Alicia Arsenault. I'm the assistant video coordinator."

"Perfect," Rossi said. "We're looking for practice video." She looked at the monitors beyond the woman. Each displayed one full-screen shot of a football game, and each shot was different.

"Practice video? Have you ever seen it? You can't even see faces."

"We'll see."

Arsenault was right. Several years ago when she got to know the assistant coaches through her security detail, Rossi talked one of them into showing her practice video. Her attractiveness had gotten her noticed—and special attention—and she wondered what kind of video that coaches spent all those hours and days watching.

The video was completely unlike what fans saw on TV. It was void of graphics, time, score, down and distance, and also sound. Camera angles were also different. There was one from the end zone, which she learned that the coaches loved because they could view the entire field. Even the side angles were long-distance. With each view, assistants could watch the same play over and over and watch the actions of all twenty-two players on the field. Offensive coaches graded their eleven players after each practice, defensive coaches graded their eleven.

Today, Rossi didn't care about any grades or even any actual practice video. She said to Arsenault, "It's okay. The president promised us we could have whatever we needed. Plus, we're not taking anything with us. We just need to see one video. Can you put up the fight video?"

"What fight video?"

She gave Arsenault a look that said *I know, okay* and waited. This was another benefit from her security days. Her friendly assistant coach had once cued up a fight video for her when he thought a date might result from it. Now her time investment might pay off.

Arsenault bit her lower lip but turned without a word and opened a sliding tray beneath the countertop. She pulled out a DVD and slid the disc into the computer.

"You don't have this on the server?" Rossi asked.

Arsenault shook her head. "Not this. Not anymore."

On her far left monitor, a wide-angle view from above the practice field opened up. Almost instantly, two players dressed in practice gear—full pads and helmets —began teeing off on each other.

The scene went on for another fifteen seconds before coaches rushed in to stop matters. Then the image changed. Two new players, smaller but no less angry, delivered punches to each other. Again coaches separated them. The clip ended and a third one began.

This time, a fight between a running back and a linebacker started after a particularly nasty block on the linebacker's knees. The running back fought even worse than he blocked.

Thomas shook his head and looked stunned. "How long does this go?"

"Maybe twenty minutes," Arsenault said. "This is everything since August." She swiveled her chair around to capture their reactions, then spun back.

"How many fights did Sean Riggins have?" Rossi asked.

"I don't know for sure. Maybe three or four. Everyone has one sooner or later. That's just the way it is."

"Four seems like a lot."

"Older players have more. They like to toughen up the freshmen and sophomores."

"How many did Riggins have recently?" Rossi asked.

The younger woman fell silent, then said, "I could get in trouble."

Rossi spun her chair, bent down and looked at her face to face. "We're the police. If you get in trouble, it'll be with us."

Arsenault's lower lip trembled. "Sean had a fight recently, but it's not on here. It was after practice. In the locker room."

"Who was he fighting?"

"Darrell. Darrell Dubrow."

"What was it about?"

Arsenault shook her head. "Don't know. I only heard Darrell started it, and Sean finished it."

She asked Arsenault to find practice video of a Sean Riggins fight. There were three of them, one from early-season practice and two late in the season. Rossi asked Arsenault to identify the players involved, and one of Riggins's three incidents was with Darrell Dubrow after a collision that looked avoidable but that Dubrow seemed to want to make happen.

"Did these guys hate each other?" Thomas asked.

"They're best friends," Arsenault said. "Sometimes they just . . . get into it."

They watched Riggins's three on-camera fights again before Rossi handed Arsenault her contact card and said thanks. "Don't worry. We were never here."

Outside as they walked to the car, Thomas asked, "How'd you know about the fight video?"

"I used to work game-day security on the sidelines here when I was coming up," she said. "One time, there was a fight between two players. One guy got his helmet pulled off. All the OU players were into it, and one of them said, 'That'll make the video.' I asked about it."

"Someone admitted it?"

"One of the assistant coaches. To him, it was no big deal. Like everybody keeps fight video. I think they show it to the players after the season for comic relief."

"You knew Riggins would be on it."

"Like she said, almost everyone gets into a fight. This time of year, practically the whole team's on that video. I was hoping we'd see a trend. The locker room fight, we just got lucky."

Thomas stopped and grabbed Rossi by the arm. "Dubrow was with Riggins at the bar when he died. The interview notes of Dubrow didn't mention anything about him and Riggins not getting along. Plus, I think they actually did get along. You don't go out to a bar like that with a small group if there's someone you don't want to be around."

"Okay, they had a fight, patched things up, were still friends. And no one on the scene the other night had any reason to suspect otherwise. What now?"

"It's probably nothing," Thomas said. "But he's got to explain it."

8

KEANE STOOD BACK as Q knocked on the apartment door. A mocha-skinned, college-aged woman answered, and she lost control as soon as she saw them. Sobbing, she stumbled across the threshold, grabbed Q around the neck and held on as she heaved for air. He let them have their moment.

"Why? Why? Why?" she cried as Q whispered into her ear. When they released after a full minute, she sniffled and removed black-framed glasses to wipe her puffy eyes.

Q motioned her inside. "Tiff, this is Conrad Keane. This is . . . this is Sean's brother. Connie, this is Tiffany Lewis."

Keane nodded at her. She studied him, looked back at Q, and then back at him again. "I don't understand. How . . ."

Keane stepped forward and grasped one of her hands in both of his. "It's okay. I'm sure Sean didn't talk about me much. It's all right. I'm so sorry about Sean."

"I guess I should be telling you that," she said. "It sucks." She retreated to the couch with a box of Kleenex. An oversized V-neck t-shirt covered up black sweatpants as she tucked her legs beneath her.

Keane looked around and took stock. She'd decorated her apartment from Target—same as him—but her mixed wall art blended well with framed photos of her family on the walls. A thirty-six-inch flat screen sat on a stand.

A small, pressed-wood bookcase held a handful of textbooks in the middle. Two framed pictures sat on top. One was a snapshot of Tiffany with an older woman and a male who looked to be in his mid-twenties. He guessed her mother and an older brother. The other, clearly snapped on high school graduation day, was of Tiffany and the same older woman arm in arm. A backpack leaned against the bookcase.

All in all, her second-floor apartment represented the college experience of his memories, certainly more than Sean's. He pulled in a plastic deck chair from an adjacent eating area and was delighted when it didn't collapse underneath him. Q sat next to her on the couch.

"Are you taking Sean back home?" she asked Q.

Q nodded. "They're doing an autopsy. When that's done, yes." He paused. "Do you have anything in his apartment you need to get back? We're going through it—what's left of it. The police already took what they wanted."

Tiffany shook her head. "I didn't stay over that much." She sniffled and started crying. They waited her out, and Keane took the lead. "How long did you and Sean go out?"

She gave him a blank stare. "Since the spring. April."

Almost nine months, he thought. It was long enough to know a few secrets, maybe not long enough to know them all.

"Is there a chance Sean left a few belongings here that we should know about?" he asked. She shook her head and looked at Q. He caught the tell that she was hiding something. "We need to find Sean's other laptop, the MacBook. It wasn't in his apartment."

"Did you look in his car?" she asked.

"The police have his car, but they don't have the computer. I don't even think they know about it. But you know about it."

She shot him an angry look. He said, "Please get it."

Q held his hands up and pushed them toward Keane. "Hey, man, there's no need to be like that. She wants the same thing we want."

Keane nodded at Q, then looked back at Tiffany. "Then she'll help us get there."

Without a word, she got up and disappeared into a bedroom. She returned with a white laptop and presented it as if it were radioactive.

Keane took it and leaned it against the chair. "Why did he need two laptops?"

Tiffany sat back down and shrugged. "He said it was for backup. He said he had a laptop that crashed last year, and they had to wipe out the hard drive. He lost everything he had on there."

"He backed up everything on this?"

"I don't think that's what he meant by backup. He just wanted to have a computer that worked. He said he couldn't be without one."

"So this one and the Dell . . . different computers but the same programs, same files? That doesn't make sense. Most people are one or the other. Mac or PC."

She pursed her lips and hesitated. "He used the Dell for school. He got it from the athletic department free. This was his personal computer."

Keane considered the arrangement. "And he didn't have a dedicated hard drive here for backing up both computers? Or any flash drives?"

Tiffany gave him a poker face. "He said he had it all backed up, but I never saw where."

"Do you know when Sean got his flat screen?"

Her eyebrows shot up. "His TV? He bought it himself last spring, after spring practice."

Keane blinked. "He bought it?"

"At Best Buy."

"That's about a thousand-dollar TV. Where did he get the money?"

She shook her head. "Two thousand. He got it on sale. He put it on his credit card."

Q interrupted, "And I helped him pay the bill."

He glanced at Q. "Did he tell you he was buying it or did he tell you after he bought it?"

"He—"

Tiffany broke in. "It was his present to himself. He'd finished his last spring practice, and he said he wanted to celebrate. He said, 'After next season, the next time I work out will be for money.'"

Q scooted up on the couch and looked at Keane. "He used to talk like that, but he was going to get his degree."

"He thought he'd get drafted." Keane said and turned to Q. "Isn't that right?"

"Third round. Maybe second," Q said, "if he didn't get hurt." Q faced Tiffany. "What did the police ask you?"

"They haven't been around," she said. "I talked to them Sunday night, the night, you know . . . but not since then."

"What did happen?" Keane asked.

She told them about the six of them, three football players and their girlfriends, eating and drinking downtown, having a good time. They all drank too much, and it got late. Sean had excused himself, and they all assumed he went to the bathroom. When he didn't come back in fifteen minutes, she went to the bar to find him. Then she sent Darrell Dubrow into the men's room.

When he wasn't there, she walked outside. That's when she saw the paramedics and Sean on the ground.

"Then they just took him away," she said. "We got to the hospital, he was already gone." She broke down again. "The police wanted to know what everybody heard and saw, but we didn't know anything."

Keane thought about her story. It made sense and gave him context. The police could be right. It could have been a robbery gone bad. The hour, the location, the unpredictability of human interaction all made random possible. Or not.

It didn't explain how Sean ended up dead. He grabbed the MacBook off the floor. "One last thing. You guys were out late for a Sunday night. You all had school the next day?"

Tiffany nodded. "I don't know why the guys wanted to go out, but they did. They were celebrating."

Keane chewed on that. "Celebrating what?"

"I don't know. They still had to take their finals. And after that they had practice before they could go home for Christmas. But they were really happy."

KEANE AND Q followed the secretary into a spacious, sunlit office, where a short, rotund man with a deep tan welcomed them with a somber look. Teddy Simpson's dark suit, white shirt, and crimson power tie gave credence to his solemnity.

"Come in, come in," Simpson said. The president came around the desk and gripped Q's hand and bicep. "I'm very sorry for your loss. Sean was a terrific young man, and we're all deeply saddened by this. He made this campus better."

"Nice of you to say," Q said.

Keane shook the president's hand and instantly felt as if he'd agreed to buy a new car—a nice one. *This guy is an operator.* He took in a space separated into distinct quadrants. A standing area where they were worked for greeting and mingling. The area to their left held a mid-sized conference table and chairs. To the right was a sitting area with a leather couch and cushioned chairs placed in a small rectangle, an Oval Office look without an eagle-adorned carpet. The fourth area featured the president's desk and work area. Keane noted that a small bar sat closest to the desk.

"Please, sit," Simpson said, and directed them to the couch and sat in a side chair. He looked straight at Q. "It goes without saying that whatever we can do for you, we'll do. Just ask. I've already been approached by people who'd like to help out paying for the funeral, once you decide the details."

Q cleared his throat. "I don't even—"

"That's kind of them," Keane said. "Why would they do that?"

"Like I said, Sean meant a lot to us around here. And they want to help."

"If they really want to help, they'll help the police find people who know what happened and why. We can pay for a funeral. We can't get people to speak up."

Simpson sat back. "If that's what you really want, we'll get the word out."

Keane leaned in. "Do that. Also, is there anything you can share about the night Sean died? Anything you've heard?"

The president shook his head. "You probably know more than we know. There don't seem to be any answers. It's just such a shame."

"Sean was mad about something," Q said.

"Pardon me?" Simpson asked.

"I said Sean was mad. He wouldn't say why, but whatever it was, it had him all twisted up."

"And you think whatever angered him up . . . led to what happened?"

Q shrugged. "Couldn't tell you. We saw him the day before, and everything was good until it wasn't. We'd had a nice Saturday together. He was going to stay through Sunday, but then all of a sudden he decided to drive back Saturday night. Said he had to get back here."

The president looked at Keane as if to ask for further explanation. Keane remembered Sean's emotional reaction to the Army-Navy game but gave Simpson a non-committal expression. *You tell us.*

"I have no idea about any of this. I don't know how you'd find out such a thing," Simpson said.

"I'm sure we'll figure it out," Keane said. "Like you said, Sean touched a lot of people around here."

The president nodded slowly, stood, and started walking them to the door. "Please let me know if there's anything we can do to help you get through this."

Keane studied Simpson's expression and figured the man was an expert at conveying sincerity. "Help us find the right answers. You do that, you'll help."

"I'll do what I can. That's a promise."

9

KEANE HAD ASKED for two single rooms with kitchenettes and told Q he'd pay for both. He threw a six pack of Coors Light in the fridge and fired up the coffee maker as soon as he tucked his suitcase away. Eventually he'd need distance from Q to ensure he had space to think and work without interruption, but now they were in his room taking the first crack at Sean's second laptop. The smell of dark roast filled the room as the MacBook booted up.

"You think you can get in?" Q asked. "I'm pretty sure Sean password-protected everything."

"Only one way to find out."

Q was right. The laptop was locked up tight. After several failed login and password combinations, Keane booted up his own laptop and opened up the FBI's best password-cracking software. Two hours, and six cups of coffee later, the MacBook surrendered. He stared at Sean's password: FBIman1978. He admired its simplicity and that it had no obvious connection to Sean. He was also struck by its symbolism. He was an FBI man born in 1978, and Sean knew it.

Eyes wide, Q looked at him. "Ain't that something?"

FBI protocol dictated copying all the files first in case a Trojan horse was programmed to eat data and files upon opening. But he wasn't on FBI time, which cut both ways. In reality, he wasn't supposed to use Bureau software unless he worked on an assigned case. He'd been in the bureau long enough to know its IT resources were focused on catching terrorists and not on monitoring borderline actions. He, like other special agents, performed background checks on would-be boyfriends and girlfriends all the time. Nothing was ever said.

Keane compiled a list of the most recently accessed files and internet sites and worked through them, ignoring music files.

"What are you trying to find?" Q asked.

"Nothing specific. I'm just poking around to see what there is to see."

Keane found three dozen websites bookmarked in Sean's browser. Many were predictable. Sports sites. Orlando University's athletics site. A few porn sites. A bank site. Others he didn't recognize.

Unwilling to add any history to the computer, he used his own Dell to peek into the unknown websites. A handful of them were gambling sites. Three of them were anti-tax sites. Among them, one was a business. The other two were blogs, individually run and written sites about how best to avoid sending money to the IRS. If Sean was the budding businessman Q said he was, he'd been getting a head start.

Then he toured the internet for all of Sean's bookmarked sites. The gambling sites were foreign-based, hardly a surprise given the appetite for gambling in the United States. Half the sites called out to online poker players. The other half beckoned sports gamblers. He felt his stomach roll.

College athletes were hounded never to gamble on sports.

Next he went through photo and video files. The JPEGs were mostly of teammates and girls. Nothing unusual there.

"Looks like a big dead end," Q said.

Keane nodded. "Maybe. But we're not done yet."

Sean's videos were more revealing. He'd surreptitiously taped a few postgame locker-room scenes, a handful of post-game speeches by Coach Childress, and post-game celebrations with teammates. There were clips from parties and two short ones of Tiffany making pouty faces. Kids.

Finally, Keane dug into Sean's saved documents. There were more than a hundred highly organized files, and most appeared to be for various business classes. Many looked as if they'd been created by him. Others were templates, probably downloaded.

"Nothing but schoolwork," Q said.

Keane pressed on. He started with a spreadsheet called CONTACTS and found an orderly collection of names, email addresses, phone numbers, and land addresses. They were of friends, teammates, coaches—people pertinent in one way or another to Sean's life.

Each document showed more than a hundred entries alphabetized by name. He scrolled and recognized only a handful of names. He saw that an overwhelming number of contacts had email addresses ending in OU.EDU, confirming an affiliation with Orlando University.

The one he recognized first was noted simply as DAD. Next to the entry was Q's address, cell number, name of his restaurant, and two other phone numbers.

Looking over Keane's shoulder, Q said, "That's the landline to the restaurant. And the fax line. Which I don't use anymore."

The next entry was another surprise: it was him. In the column titled WORK, Sean had typed, FBI. Keane's direct work number, cell number, and email address at the Knoxville field office were listed, contacts he'd given his brother three or four years before. Sean had never called him or emailed him, but they'd texted each other in recent months, starting when their mother acknowledged she was dying of lung cancer.

He scrolled through the rest of the spreadsheet. He saw a line for PRESIDENT, no formal name. Two phone numbers were listed, as was an email address. The address indicated whoever the "president" was he wasn't affiliated with the school. It was a personal address and an ominous one at that: Bigstick1955@aol.com.

The last thing that caught his attention was a series of innocuously designated contacts at the bottom of the spreadsheet. They weren't in alphabetical order or any order, as far as he could tell. There was a designated contact at First Bank, but the rest of the entries were accounts, log-ins, passwords, and personal identification numbers for bank, email, and other internet accounts. It was hardly the smartest way to hide passwords, but he was grateful for the shortcut.

"Bless you, Sean," he said aloud.

"What?" Q asked.

"Sean left a roadmap."

"To where?"

Keane kept scouring the file. "To whatever his life was." He opened another spreadsheet called PLAYER.XLS and found a list of names. There was no header and there was only one column of information, one that started with Jeff Adams and was followed by more than three hundred other names. The list was not alphabetized and seemed to be in random order.

"Anybody here you recognize?" he asked.

Q peered over his shoulder, and they scrolled up and down for a few minutes. "I see three or four guys on the team, but other than that . . ."

Keane closed the file, made a global file search for the word *Childress* and found the coach's cell number in another spreadsheet. "I think just about everybody who's not a freshman has the coach's number," Q said, answering Keane's question before he could ask it. "Pretty sure the coach has everybody's number, so if he called, you'd save it."

The rest of the spreadsheets, about two dozen of them, proved cryptic. Files were named by initials and contained only numbers. No headers, no explanations, just a handful of columns and a couple hundred rows.

It took nearly two hours to march through each spreadsheet. He detected patterns but couldn't determine what they were. He was certain that several rows contained the same information with the exception of only one or two numbers. And a handful of the rows were also nearly identical to those in other files.

Keane rubbed his eyes. "This is strange." There was a master file here, but where?

He backed out of the spreadsheets and instead looked at the file names. They were identified by two or three letters. AK was one. TL was another. SDN was a third. But the initials meant nothing to him. He crossed-checked the file names against the names on the football team roster and against coaches' names. No good.

Keane spun and looked at Q, who backed up a step. "What the hell was this kid into?"

Q shook his head. "Your guess is as good as mine. All this stuff looks like gibberish to me."

Keane turned back and created a separate folder on his flash drive and dragged all the mystery files into the folder. Including the spreadsheet with just the names, they had an even two dozen. He shut the laptop and closed his eyes. He needed the puzzle to work his brain over until an answer arrived. It would happen eventually.

"Now what?" Q asked.

Keane smiled. "Now we play."

Using Sean's files as a guide to his personal accounts, Keane navigated to various websites, typed in usernames and passwords, and dove in. He started with three bank accounts, went to three credit accounts, and then hit Sean's PayPal account. Soon, he felt more cast off from Sean than he ever had. Sean had died with nearly eighteen thousand dollars sitting in his checking account.

"This is unbelievable," he said. "Did you know about all this?"

Q shook his head slowly, as if in a daze. "Never knew, never knew . . ."

The totals in the accounts didn't make sense, but they explained how Sean paid for his lifestyle. The SUV, the luxurious sofa, a state-of-the-art laptop and TV—Sean had more than enough money to pay for all of it.

"Good God," he said. Sean had almost as much money in the bank as he did. He found the last transaction Sean made, a two-hundred-dollar withdrawal from an ATM on Church Street.

"This is craziness, man," Q said. "This can't be right."

Keane kept moving through the account. It showed no regular deposits, but the ones that did post were big: five thousand here, three thousand there, two for four thousand, all in the past two months. He surfed a bit more and learned they weren't really deposits at all but transfers from a PayPal account. He opened up Sean's PayPal account and found transfers that matched the ones on the bank account. He also found corresponding PayPal deposits from another unidentified PayPal account.

He sighed. "This isn't going to be as easy as I thought."

"What do you mean?" Q asked.

"I don't have subpoena power. I can get everything we see here, but this will only give us part of the money trail. All this money, this is just conversation. The real stuff is where it comes from—and why." He paused and looked at Q. "You understand what this is, right?"

Q said nothing.

Keane pointed at the laptop. "That's motive."

KEANE LOGGED OUT of the bank account and typed *Blindside.com* into the browser. He assumed it was a football site because *blindside* was a word every football player understood. It was the side of the field to anyone's back. For a defender, there were few better moments than rushing in from behind and planting a shoulder into the kidney of an unsuspecting quarterback. For the defense, only good things happened from such hits.

Blindside.com wasn't a football website. It was a gambling site. Keane peeked back at the spreadsheet at Sean's logins and typed in the one for that site, then the password.

Welcome, Mr. Riggins, read the greeting on the top left of the screen. Just below the greeting was a listing of Sean's account totals.

It read $86,560. They both stared at the number, the buzz from the hotel room heater providing the only sound.

"Holy shit," Keane said.

Q hopped up from behind him and stared at the home page. "I don't know what the fuck I'm seeing. This is crazy, man. What the hell's going on?"

Keane knew but said nothing. He clicked on different links associated with Sean's account and confirmed his suspicions. Sean had been betting on football games, college and NFL.

He couldn't find a listing of Sean's wagers, couldn't see if he'd committed the cardinal sin of betting against his own team. If he had, that would lead to another set of clouds in an already murky young life. Possibly another motive.

Keane stood and turned and looked at Q. "Answer me straight. Was Sean shaving points?"

"No, no," Q said. "I don't think he was even doing what you're thinking he was doing. This is all a mistake." He pointed at the laptop. "That can't be right."

"I can guarantee you it's right. And with the money that's flowing through here, people are going to think Sean was on the take and fixing OU games. And if that was the case, I can assure you he's not dead because he happened to run into the wrong person on the street."

Q rubbed his face and braced himself on the kitchen counter. "This doesn't make any sense."

"I'll tell you what doesn't make sense. Having eighty-six grand in a gambling account and eighteen grand in a checking account—and you're a fucking college student. And you know what else?"

Q looked at him but didn't respond. Instead, he shook his head.

"It makes no sense that he actually *had* money in the bank. Because you know what happens with gamblers? They lose. That's how most of them end up with broken ankles or in the river. They owe money they can't pay. And here we have Sean, who's dead, and he *had* money—a lot of money."

They looked at each other for several seconds before Keane sat back down. He worked through the Blindside account for five more minutes, then surveyed the website's About Us page. The business behind the site was located in Costa Rica, a noted home for offshore gambling operations. They were legal for almost every user on the planet. The exception was the United States. By letting Americans win and lose money online, the company was violating U.S. law. So were any U.S. residents who gambled through the site.

Q grabbed a beer out of the refrigerator and took a seat on the couch. "What are you going to do with that?"

Keane looked as his friend and grimaced. "I'll use it for leverage, but eventually I'll have to give the computer to the police. I can't withhold it."

"Can't you just smash it up and throw it into a Dumpster?"

"If nobody knew I had it, that might work. But you know. Tiffany knows." He shook his head. "And I know. I'll have to turn it in."

Q took another hard pull from his beer. "I'd never say a word."

10

TEDDY LET THE Glenlivet chill for five seconds before he poured it down. He kept the liquid on his tongue, savoring its warming properties, a celebratory salute before a lingering swallow. On a brief phone call, the mayor had sounded confident, although the police desperately wanted to find the last person who talked to Sean Riggins.

Teddy's partners called for updates every hour. He'd shared the good news that the police were running their investigation through him, but they were nervous. Detectives on campus questioning players and coaches made them vulnerable. They'd railed that he wasn't controlling the situation, that the local media smelled blood.

Hair-sprayed reporters had turned his campus into a shark pool. One of the partners suggested it was only a matter of time before CNN and the other national networks showed up with their satellite trucks and towers of klieg lights for prime-time updates. When the university communications director alerted him to the impending blitz, Teddy ordered him to rope off one-quarter of a paved lot on the southeast side of campus, a mile's hike from the athletic complex. OU would welcome the media with their own parking spaces, and Teddy would play the blowhards like a six-string. Briefings four times a day, just before the noon, five, six, and ten o'clock newscasts. He would give them nothing, but the illusion of so much access meant more than actual news. As short-term media strategies went, this was a winner. He found reporters even easier to manipulate than politicians.

"Fucking amateurs," he said, and poured himself another shot over ice.

He read over the printout he'd made after talking to the mayor. His quick research on Quentin Riggins and Conrad Keane gave him a couple surprises.

The mayor had said Keane, the white man, claimed to be Sean Riggins's half-brother. That meant the connection was probably the mother Sean had mourned just before the season started. Teddy remembered Childress filling him in, though he hadn't listened at the time.

Quentin Riggins, the father, owned a restaurant in South Florida. His police record showed a three-year-old DUI and a ten-year-old arrest for marijuana possession. Both had been pleaded out.

Teddy picked up his new cell phone again, redialed the same number he'd been dialing off and on for three hours. Again it went straight to voicemail. "Fucking Tally," he said, and hung up. Help was on the way, but he needed to hear that Tally was already running. He poured himself another Scotch over ice, adjusted a home stereo system to light rock, and watched a meaningless West Coast basketball game on ESPN. Half an hour later, precisely ninety minutes from his call to Montgomery Services, his doorbell rang.

"You look wonderful," Teddy said to Valerie as he opened the door. He spied a crimson Toyota Camry, her Uber ride, pulling away on the street. Then he looked back at her. She wore a long black

Vera Wang with an open back. Her shoulders were covered by a black shawl. Her long, straight, raven-colored hair flowed down her back.

"Well, thank you," she said and walked past him as he held the door open. Her ginger-spiced and musky scent, like everything else about her, thrust him into emotional submission.

Teddy closed his eyes and breathed through his nose, slowly closing the door. "I have a delicious red for you," he said.

"Sounds lovely," Valerie said, giving him the shawl. Teddy guessed she was in her mid-thirties—he had never asked and never would—but, with taut skin, no sign of sun damage, and deep brown eyes, she looked ten years younger. Plus, at almost six feet, she stood at least three inches taller than him.

She stood behind Teddy and rubbed his neck and shoulders with long, firm fingers. "Let's go listen to some music," she said, using their little code phrase. She disappeared down the hallway to his bedroom. He uncorked a Pinot Noir and poured them each a glass. He was happy at least one person had answered a call tonight.

KEANE STUDIED THE late-night menu amid a mix of over-caffeinated college students and families with kids as he fended off Q's complaints.

"We could have done better than this," Q said. "You afraid to do a little investigating? Hell, if we drove around for twenty minutes, we'd find a nice place."

Keane ignored the grease on his laminated menu. "What's nicer than dinner at Denny's? It's downright American. The coffee's almost as good as Dunkin' Donuts."

"Hardly," Q said and dumped more cream into coffee that was now more white than black.

Q appreciated simple and easy, a place where the owners were family and the profits stayed local. That was where he liked to spend his money. And that was what he owned. His restaurant and bar, The Tides, was one of those places. Q, who had never been married, bought The Tides nearly a decade earlier after working on a commercial fishing boat and then for a fishmonger.

His prep skills got him off the sea full-time, and his cooking savvy gave him the confidence to try the restaurant business. He could scale and filet a grouper in a minute, and he had no issues cracking oysters. Then, after he positioned fish for display in the cooler, he whipped up homemade fish dips, crab-and-shrimp stuffing, remoulades, and marinades to sell with the fish. They grew to be popular, allowing the owner to raise the price and carve out a brand not as a fish seller but as the local seafood expert.

Q glanced around the inside of the chain eatery and matched his sour face with a headshake, but Keane had no intention of letting his friend get comfortable. This was the second of several tasks Keane had for himself tonight, and he'd have to push hard to get them done. They'd already picked up Sean's Honda Pilot from the police impound. The rest of his chores didn't include Q.

Keane excused himself and walked to the back bathroom. He returned to find Q wiping his eyes. Q ducked his head and sobbed quietly. Keane waved away a smiling, brown-haired waitress who ventured over with more coffee.

Q looked up and started another anecdote about Sean. That's what the day had been, one story after another, almost as if Q stopped talking about his son, people would forget.

Keane leaned in. "We need to talk about what's next. About how I'm going to find out what really happened."

"All I want you to do is to make sure they get the guy who did this."

"I'm not the police."

"Just you being there, they'll have to respect you."

Keane shook his head. "Doesn't work that way." Cops detested FBI agents, even ones on extended leave.

He caught the eye of the waitress he'd sent away. No grin this time, but she poured them a final refill of coffee, and Keane asked for the check. He thought about what he was about to do, knowing that without Sean, Q's world had become narrow. Three months ago he'd lost the only woman he'd ever loved—no matter that it had been unrequited for years—and now he'd lost his only child.

Keane had met one of Q's sisters before, long ago in Fort Myers, but had no idea if that sister was still alive. Or if Q had any other living relatives. Q did have his business, but from what Keane had witnessed, the business needed upkeep, which meant money, and that Q needed more manpower. He considered that Q might not be up to the task of keeping both The Tides and himself afloat.

After the waitress dropped off their bill, Q asked, "How much do you think the cops know about the gambling?"

"I don't think they know anything. Otherwise, they would have asked about it. But they'll figure it out soon enough."

"Maybe if they catch the guy who hit Sean, they won't worry about it. They'll be happy enough to put someone in jail for what he did to Sean."

"You ever see a dog willingly give up a bone? If the cops see a chance to arrest more people for crimes that are related to Sean's death, they'll do it—assuming there aren't any politics involved. If there are, there's no telling what'll happen."

Q added another creamer to his coffee. "They don't have the other laptop. They might not ever see it."

"They'll see it," Keane said. "I'll have to turn it over to them soon enough. I'm already in deep shit for not turning it over already."

"You could throw it in a Dumpster five miles from here, and they'd never find it."

"I don't have a choice. I have to turn it over. That's the law."

"I'd never tell if you didn't," Q said. Keane said nothing. "So you're taking the laptop in?"

"Right after I download all the data. Otherwise we won't know for months what all is on there, and I don't like flying blind. So you go home, and I go poke the bear."

Q stopped drinking and set his cup down hard. "You're kicking me out? Sending me back home? I thought we were doing this."

"We were. But you've done your part. Now I'll do mine. You've got things to take care of. Go do that, and let me do this. It's what I do. It's safer this way."

"I'm ready to take this where it needs to go. I can do what I need to do from here."

"This is not penny-ante stuff. This is a lot of money, and whoever's behind this, they're not screwing around. I'll grant you that I think it's possible that what happened to Sean was an accident." Keane lowered his voice. "Whoever did this, if they'd meant to be a hardass, would have used a gun or a knife or both. Regardless, Sean's dead, and there's a reason. So, no, you're out of here. I'll take care of this."

Keane expected more of a protest but didn't get it.

"If you fuck up, you're going to lose your job," Q said.

Keane laughed. "We'll see. The federal government is more forgiving than you think. I mean, Hoover used to wear dresses, for God's sake."

"You call me when you know something. You have to keep me up to date."

Keane reached for the check and pulled out a twenty and a ten to cover the bill and tip. "I can do that."

They walked to the Honda, now Q's. They gave each other a firm handshake, and Keane pulled Q into a hug and slapped his back.

"Go home, and do what you have to do. I'll figure this out."

11

AFTER ALL THIS time, the man didn't know where Tally lived. But he damn sure knew where the idiot worked.

He drove eight miles north of Orlando to Fern Park, a suburban hometown to strangeness. Jai alai, greyhound racing, and all-nude strip clubs thrived there. So did dozens of upper-middle-class neighborhoods, a few of them gated.

Getting an up-close look at cleanly shaved women proved an unspoken, but especially unbeatable, marketing plan for both the unincorporated town and the Jaguar, the club that employed Tally Hance.

Tally had any number of places he could go for help, but he could turn only to a few places for money. Among the options, the Jaguar club was the most likely.

The man pulled into the parking lot and found an empty space in the club's side lot several spots away from an overhead light. Tonight, darkness was a welcome friend. He calculated there was video inside the club. He didn't see any cameras in the back. From here he could see most of the rest of the parking area and the front door. He backed into the space and tilted his seat back for a long night.

Rossi's memory improved with Google. David William Hance was Tally Hance, which she confirmed unofficially by comparing Google images to his registered driver's license photo.

Internet searches brought up a PDF of an old OU football media guide. As soon as she saw Hance's black-and-white head shot in the guide, more images of him came back to her.

From her days running sideline security, she remembered David Hance. She found an online bio, and it clicked that no one called him David. Teammates and coaches called him Tally because his hometown was Tallahassee. The vignette claimed Hance was a decent-sized linebacker who started a handful of games one season, mostly when teammates were injured and couldn't play. Rossi remembered him as a mediocre defender who was too slow.

She ran a criminal background check on Hance, and it came back surprisingly clean: no driving offenses and only one significant incident, a dropped assault charge from a strip club in Seminole County. She looked through the electronic case file to see if he'd been arrested because he was a bouncer who'd gotten too rough with a customer. She checked the date: last year. A tingle ran up her back through her neck, the rush of threading a needle.

Hance liked to throw a punch. And Hance and Riggins were connected through the OU football team. Hance was old enough that he'd never played on the same OU teams as Riggins, but she knew football players were like fraternity brothers. Once in the club, always in.

This was their guy. They'd have no trouble securing an arrest warrant for the assault on

Riggins. They'd need to work a bit harder for grounds to inspect Hance's residence and car.

"Who do you like for a search warrant?" she asked Thomas.

He looked up from his laptop across their desks, then looked at the office clock. "When in doubt, go with Crowley." Judge John J. Crowley wasn't the most investigator-friendly jurist in Orange County, but he did harbor a reputation of erring on the side of law enforcement. "It's not too late, so he's apt to not turn on us for bothering him."

"I'll type if you call," Rossi said.

Ninety minutes later, they held two warrants for Hance, each bearing the robust signature of Judge Crowley. Rossi double-checked her vest and her Glock. She didn't like surprise night-time visits. Darkness was only a cop's friend if night-vision goggles were in play, which was rare. This wasn't one of those times.

Hance wouldn't expect them, but they had no idea if he was armed, dangerous, or even alone. For all they knew, he'd be surrounded by friends and family—just enough people to make arresting him problematic. They weren't even sure if he'd be home. She thought they might end up chasing him down at work.

She prepared for the worst and tugged the strap on her vest. It snugged around her midsection. She gave herself a slight nod. Ready.

ROSSI AND THOMAS pulled in front of a two-story wood-frame house a mile north of downtown. They got no help from a dead street light or an unlit porch light. Thomas knocked three times, called out, and knocked again. No one home. Rossi nodded at the head of the tactical team.

"Just hold on," Thomas said. He produced a zip tool and credit card. "If the deadbolt's not turned, we can make this simple."

The deadbolt wasn't turned. He worked the card and zip. Ten seconds later, he pushed the door open.

Thomas went in first, flashlight working, and they both called out again for Hance. They moved through three rooms and heard only the crickets outside and the hum of a refrigerator icemaker. Rossi flipped on a light. They cleared the rest of the house, and Rossi hustled to the bedroom.

"I think we just missed him," she said. "It's still humid in the bathroom, like he just took a shower."

She wandered from room to room and evaluated their suspect. It looked as if Hance lived alone, and a quick sweep turned up multiple ID badges for OU events. They were all recent, which made it more plausible he knew Riggins. Her neck felt funny again.

They searched his dresser, nightstand, closet, shelves, bathroom, and kitchen. There were no signs that Hance smoked or used drugs. There was no beer in the refrigerator, nor was there any bar.

"This is some clean living," Rossi said as she looked under the sink. "It looks like his only bad habit is he doesn't make his bed in the morning."

After ninety minutes, Rossi dropped the search warrant on the kitchen counter for Hance to find when he returned, and the detectives left with nothing in hand.

"I never thought I'd say this to you," Thomas said, "but let's go check out a strip club."

12

THOMAS PARKED ILLEGALLY in front of the Jaguar as Rossi counted her cash. Not that she would need it. "I can't remember the last time I was in a place like this. Maybe three years?"

"Long time," Thomas said. "You've had a higher class of criminal recently."

She cackled. "Yeah, right." The truth was, the areas where most of their suspects lived had houses with security bars. In most of those neighborhoods, a strip club would be an upgrade.

They got out of their car and approached a cute, blond, muscle-bound doorman. They held up their badges. Rossi said, "We're looking for David Hance. You might know him as Tally."

Blondie pursed his lips and gave a slight nod. "I know him, but I haven't seen him. He's been sick."

"He's not working tonight?"

Blondie shook his head. "Feel free to look for yourself."

"Thanks. We will."

Blondie held the door open for them, and Rossi turned back to him. "Stay here. And stay off your phone. We wouldn't want to have to subpoena your records."

Blondie held up his one free hand. "Whatever you say."

THE CLUB SMELLED overly clean and scented, a cross between Pine-Sol and Dior.

"At least the music doesn't suck," Rossi yelled at Thomas. Classic rock was never bad, even if the volume hurt. She maneuvered around a couple of cocktail waitresses in black fishnet stockings. None of the customers noticed them. They cast their attention on a naked, cavorting Latina dancer on stage.

A quick walk-through proved Blondie right. They'd missed Hance at home. Now they'd missed him at work. Thomas yelled over the music, "Let's make sure."

They moved to the bar, where Rossi laid down a twenty-dollar bill. It caught the attention of a lone bartender, a tall, doughboy with a shaved head and tiny barbell in one eyebrow. She could envision him playing an amateur metal band. She ordered two club sodas. When the drinks arrived, she held up a second twenty with her badge.

She motioned him forward and leaned in. "When's the last time you saw David Hance?"

He backed up and pulled the twenty from the bar and the one from her hand. He leaned forward again. "Tally? About half an hour ago. He was here for about five minutes. Walked in, walked out."

"Who did he talk to?"

The bartender looked around the club and nodded his head at a fully dressed blonde woman in front of the stage. The woman sat by herself at a two-top, where she seemed entranced by the moves of the on-stage dancer.

They wound their way to her. Rossi plopped down in the empty chair, startling the woman, who wore jeans and a thin black blouse over a tight black tank top. She looked to be in her early thirties, though a deeply tanned face made her look older. Rossi thought: *off-duty dancer.*

Rossi showed her badge again as Thomas pulled up a chair from a nearby table. She rubbed her ears, hoping to dim the screams of AC/DC, and Thomas launched in with a shout. "How often do you come here on your night off?"

"At least one too many times," the woman yelled back. "What do you need?"

"Tally Hance. Do you know where he is?"

She shook her head. Rossi shot a look at Thomas, and he nodded. Strippers rarely cooperated with cops, most of whom saw the job as a marketing tool for prostitution. They sometimes opened up to female officers one on one. Thomas got up and took his club soda back to the bar as "Back in Black" gave way to Billy Joel's "Uptown Girl."

Rossi drew herself close to the dancer. "What's your name?"

The woman gave her a poker face. "Destiny."

"Your real name. And I don't want to walk you backstage to pull your ID."

The woman rolled her eyes. "Carla. Carla Young."

"Okay, Carla, I'm Tina. Tell me: Are you dating David Hance? Tally?"

Carla gave her a confused look. "What? No. He works here. That's it. He's a nice guy. A lot nicer than most of the others around here." She looked around as if she were concerned about an eavesdropper over the blaring music.

"But you talked to him when he was here a little while ago?"

Carla nodded.

"Why you?"

Carla weighed her answer and said finally, "I owed him. He loaned me money a few months ago when I was running low."

"You never paid him back?

"I did, a couple weeks later. I was returning the favor."

"What favor?"

"It was his turn to need money."

"How much?"

"More than I had. He wanted a thousand, more if I had it. I only had five hundred."

"You gave him five hundred dollars? What for?"

Carla shook her head. "Sounded like traveling money."

"Why sounded like?"

"He said he needed to get away. Figure some things out."

"Is he in trouble? Is somebody looking for him? Is he short on money?"

Carla let out a laugh. "Honey, we're all short on money."

"Okay," Rossi said. "Where's he going?"

"He didn't say. I know he's got family in the Panhandle, but he hates it up there. And they don't really have any clubs like this up there, so he wouldn't get a quick job. Maybe Miami or Fort Lauderdale. Maybe Daytona. If he really wanted to get away, maybe Atlanta. I honestly don't know."

Rossi moved her chair a couple inches closer and looked Carla in the eyes. "What else? There's something else."

The stripper shrugged. "He just said he had to get away for a while, and it sounds like it'll be a long while."

"How so?"

"Because he said, 'I don't know when I'll be around to pay you back.' He said he *would* pay me back, but he wasn't sure when. I believed him. I trust him. But now I'm not so sure."

"Really? Why?"

"I don't know why he's leaving town, but it must be pretty bad if you're here."

Rossi ignored the implication. "Did he look scared?"

"He was a little wired."

"Coke? Speed?"

"Not like that." Carla paused. "Well, maybe speed. Or Adderall. Maybe just a lot of Red Bull. He was ready to get out of here."

"What do you know about him?"

Carla shrugged. "He keeps to himself, but he likes to work out. He likes his body."

Rossi walked Carla back through her story and poked around for more details about Tally. His support system seemed to be his connections at OU and the Jaguar and none with family. That was problematic. Family was always the best place to start an investigation. Leverage was much easier.

"One more thing," Rossi said. "I need his cell number."

Carla made a face but dug into her purse for her phone. She scrolled through her contacts and recited a number. Rossi wrapped one of her cards in a twenty and handed it to her. "We can help you if you help us."

Carla looked at the money and stuck it in her purse with her phone. "Gee, thanks."

When they were out the door, Thomas banged his hand on the car roof as he climbed in. "He's in the wind. We may have missed him for good."

Rossi didn't disagree.

THE MAN CONGRATULATED himself on a good plan. He'd had a tension-filled evening, but he'd been able to manage that. All in all, everything was under control. And tonight, Tally showed up for work like a dog coming to dinner. The bouncer had parked in the back and entered the Jaguar through the back door.

But to his surprise, Tally emerged from the club ten minutes later. It hadn't given him time to prep a mobile GPS device and snap it under Tally's red Honda Civic, so Tally drove away clean. Now he tracked the bouncer the old-fashioned way. And got lucky.

After twenty minutes on back roads, Tally pulled into a 1950s wood-frame house. The man slowed and drove past, catching the Honda's taillights down a gravel driveway that wrapped behind the home. He stopped at a cross street, jotted down the address, and decided he needed to act quickly. No telling how fast Tally was moving. Or what the kid was up to.

Two miles away, he found a 7-Eleven and parked at the gas pump. He bought a plastic gas can and a liter bottle of Sprite, and he gave the male attendant seven extra dollars, enough for two gallons of gas.

He found a spot to park on a dark street two blocks away and lugged the gasoline and Sprite to the back of Tally's house. He opened the Sprite, dumped it into the gravel, and left the empty soda bottle and the nearly full gas can next to the back stoop.

As he walked around to the front of the house, he pulled the Taser from his windbreaker, checked that it was fully charged. The front porch light was off, though he'd be lucky if it stayed that way. He pulled his baseball cap low on his head. Ignoring the doorbell, he knocked on the wood door. He turned his face away from the peep hole.

"Who is it?" Tally asked from the other side.

"UPS," he said.

"Yeah? You sure you're not back with another search warrant?"

He heard the deadbolt unlatch. The door cracked open. He braced on his left leg and jammed his right heel into the door just left of the knob. Age-hardened oak cracked against Tally's forehead and drove him backward into his living room. He darted through the opening and discharged a Taser against Tally's neck.

"Ahhhhhhh." Tally's head bobbed as twenty-thousand volts surged through him. He fell backward on the hardwood floor, writhing and jerking as the electricity finished its job.

The man found a faint pulse on Tally's neck, but it didn't concern him. Tally wasn't going anywhere. He searched the bedroom and found a duffel bag packed with clothes and a shoulder bag with a laptop, miscellaneous papers, and five hundred dollars in twenties. He slung the bag over his shoulder and moved through the house, riffling through a makeshift desk in the living room and through drawers in the kitchen.

He unclipped the barbs from Tally's neck and rolled up the wires. He stuffed the Taser in the duffel and set the bag on the back stoop. He retrieved a gas can and a propane-grill lighter. Then he collected the Sprite bottle.

Inside, he found Tally conscious but still unable to move. He flipped Tally over onto his stomach and whispered into his ear, "You didn't leave me any choice."

With his left hand he held the green plastic bottle. With his right he put the muzzle of a nine millimeter against the bottle mouth and touched the bottom to Tally's head. He pulled the trigger. Tally's body rocked. Blood pooled on the floor.

He left the bottle in the curve of Tally's lower back and doused the bottle and body with gasoline. He splashed gas around the living room and into the bedroom, leaving most of the front of the house untouched. He poured a path of gas to the back door and left the gas can and bottle inside.

Blue flames started with the second flick of the lighter, and Tally caught fire with a WHOOMPH. Three-foot tall yellow flames moved from the body to the gas-doused floors. As soon as he closed the back door behind him, he heard the crackling of soon-to-be-destroyed floors.

The man hustled around to the side of the house and walked normally back to his car. He put the nine millimeter under his seat and got moving. He checked his rearview. Nothing. Good.

He started the car and gave one last look. Through the trees two blocks away, he saw the house start to glow. Tally living so close to downtown probably meant a fast response from the Orlando Fire Department. Firemen might save the house. They wouldn't save its resident.

He pulled the car out slowly and made two right turns to head back toward town.

Half an hour later he sat alone, sipping bourbon over ice. From the back of his mind, he remembered Tally saying something about a search warrant. He rolled that around for a few minutes and wondered what the cops might have. *Doesn't matter much now*, he thought. The police had gotten close, but not close enough.

He smiled. Keeping the gun was the right move.

Satisfied, he poured himself another glass. Two hours later, he was sound asleep.

13

FOR THE SECOND time in twelve hours, Rossi rode as Thomas drove them to Hance's Colonialtown house. The stench of burned wood hit her before she saw the fire trucks and the half-dozen neighbors gathered across the street.

The two-story house stood, thanks to the brick and concrete that made up its first floor and foundation, but its flat white exterior was charred black on one side wall. Paint peeled away from the cinderblock. Part of the roof had collapsed, and parts of the second floor were now the first floor.

"It was almost gone by the time we got here," the fire chief said. "The house was divided into two apartments. The woman living upstairs was damned lucky. She went to bed early, around ten, and her fire alarm went off around eleven thirty. She and her cat barely got down the fire escape. But the guy downstairs, we found him as soon as we got in there. He looks like he was gone before the fire. He's got holes in front of his head and in the back. Guessing in one side, out the other."

"You ID him?" Rossi asked.

"We're just assuming it's Hance because that's what the neighbor said. I'm sure the ME will figure it out. But if your guy lived on the bottom floor, he's either dead or not around. Either way . . ."

"You got a cause?"

"It was torched. Fire marshal and the arson guys are on their way, but there's not much to figure out. Total amateur job. You can smell the gasoline. The guy was probably covered with it. And by the looks of it, the floor and walls too."

"If the body's here, we'd like to see it," Thomas said.

The chief pointed to the medical examiner's black van. "Be my guest."

The ME's assistant, a diminutive man with thinning light brown hair and a brush mustache, handed them masks and opened the door. The smell of charred flesh and bone wafted out.

Rossi covered her mouth and nose and climbed in. She knew cops who listed burned bodies as the worst of the worst parts of their job, but the experience never bothered her. Bodies were bodies. What stuck to her soul were emotionally damaged survivors.

They climbed up, and the assistant handed them blue rubber medical gloves. The body was on a stretcher covered by a white sheet. She pulled the sheet back to reveal the remains of Hance: an unidentifiable black mass with two pea-sized holes in the forehead. Thomas rolled the body to the side. Two nickel-sized holes showed them the exit wounds.

"Probably nine-millimeter," Thomas said.

They thanked the chief on their way out and agreed to split up to find witnesses. An hour later, they had nothing concrete. One man thought he'd heard two cats fighting. Another heard cars driving by around midnight, but that was a common occurrence, and he hadn't seen anything.

On their way out of the neighborhood, they stopped at two nearby convenience stores. The on-duty managers said they hadn't seen anyone filling up five- or ten-gallon gas cans recently. But one had started his shift at five a.m., and the other began hers at six a.m. Rossi got the names of the managers they had relieved. She'd pull the outside video if the case ran cold. She left her card and rejoined Thomas.

"Pretty convenient, this fire," she said.

"Not for us," Thomas said.

He was right. Riggins was connected to Hance, and neither would ever talk about it.

KEANE HAD NO chance to talk with Duke Childress if he arrived later than eleven o'clock, the secretary had told him, and he believed her. Knowing coaches and their compulsion for punctuality, he arrived at nine forty-five and walked outside the athletics complex for an hour.

Sean had spent the better part of three years walking these sidewalks amid patches of soft Zoysia grass that would hold its color during the winter. He found himself among students of many ethnicities either on their way to a fall semester exam or celebrating the end of one. A few cruised past him on long skateboards. Others walked fast or slow.

When he circled back to the football building, he came face to face with a makeshift memorial, a white-carnation wreath placed next to an eight-by-ten photo of Sean, the flowers and picture leaned up against the light brick façade and were surrounded by hundreds of other flowers and cards. *Everyone knows.*

Keane walked inside, self-conscious about the fading stain on his shirt where he'd dabbed water to erase a salsa stain. It was barely detectable on the white polo shirt. All things considered, it meant nothing, but it irritated him nonetheless.

A full-faced brunette in her early forties came around her desk to greet him. "Can I help you?"

"I called this morning," he said. "I was hoping to see Coach Childress."

"You're here about Sean," she said. Not a question. "After you called I told Coach Childress you might be coming by. He wants to see you."

She turned to a mahogany door, knocked softly three times, and slipped into a dark office. He saw part of a wall-sized movie screen with a football game playing on it before the door closed.

A minute later, the woman was back at the door, holding it open for him. "Coach Childress will see you."

The lights had been undimmed. Whatever game had been on the screen a minute earlier was gone, replaced by an OU athletics logo beamed from an overhead projector. He laughed to himself. Childress had no clue where Keane's college allegiances were, and the coach wasn't taking any chances about a strategy leak.

Childress stood. Light bounced off his short-cropped hair that had started showing silver. His height helped offset the start of a thickened midsection and allowed him to wear his khakis and white OU polo well. "It's good of you to stop in," the coach said, motioning to a chair in front of the desk without offering a handshake.

He sized up the man against his official bio. Despite being relatively fit, Childress looked in dire need of a long nap. Crow's feet, accentuated by tanned but sun-beaten skin, brushed back from his dark eyes.

Papers and stacks of manila folders covered his desk. A remote control rested on top of the folders.

"Always working on a game plan, huh?" Keane asked, nodding at the laptop.

"If there's a game, there's a game plan," the coach said. "Especially for a bowl game."

"I prefer a true playoff," Keane said. "Nothing like winning a real national championship."

"You played?"

"Georgia Southern."

"You won more than one," Childress said.

"Two."

"Linebacker? Or tight end?"

"Safety," Keane said. "You didn't need as much speed back then."

"I'll bet you were a hitter. You've got the shoulders."

"It was easier back then. Teams didn't pass the way they do now. Most of the time, all I had to do was tackle."

Childress laughed. "It wasn't easy then, and it's not easy now. People just pay more attention. Too many media people and too much social media. Your coaches never had to worry about you getting on Twitter."

"Nah, just beer and girls."

"The good old days," Childress said. He lowered his voice. "I talked to the equipment manager, told him I'd send you down to see him. The police took everything from Sean's locker, but we can get you an extra game jersey if you want."

"His dad will want it. It'll mean a lot."

"It's a damned shame what happened. If there's anything you need, just ask."

"There is one thing. I'd like your opinion. Could Sean have gone to the next level? Was he good enough?"

"NFL? Maybe. He didn't have the size the pro scouts like, but he had the speed and the smarts.

I've always said you can't be an idiot and play in the NFL but as long as you have speed and a few tools, your smarts can get you into a huddle."

"What did the scouts say?"

"They liked him. They wondered if he was a little headstrong, but they liked his frame, his quickness. They saw that he could think on his feet. They loved that."

"But?"

"It's the same thing all over. At the end of the day, those guys all look at their stopwatches and height and weight charts. It's all about the numbers."

"Why headstrong?" he asked.

"Hell, because he was. If Sean thought he could do something his way, he did it that way."

"That's not usually the way to make your coaches happy."

"We had our moments," Childress said. "There were times he was challenging to coach. At the end of the day, though, I was always happy I had a playmaker on the field."

He nodded. Childress was no different from any college coach in any sport. They were whores for talent, the same as admissions officers at Ivy League schools who bent over backward to find high-school students with straight As, high standardized test scores, good looks, and one-of-a-kind personal stories.

"Who didn't like Sean?"

Childress shrugged. "Who said somebody didn't like him?"

"He was attacked, Coach."

"We heard it was an accident."

"Maybe. The police aren't sure. They're pursuing this as something other than an accident. Maybe even as a murder. So who?"

"No one here that I know of."

"You're telling me you had a star player everyone got along with? Even though you and I both know that Sean was the kind of guy who liked being the center of attention and didn't mind that other people knew it?"

The coach's brown eyes narrowed. Predictable. Few coaches tolerated unwanted detours, even in conversation.

"We keep people in line pretty good," Childress said. "You get a swelled head around here, you're likely to get it knocked off."

Keane smiled. "I think you just made my point. So who decided to knock off Sean's swelled head?"

The coach leaned forward. "You'd have to ask the police. That's their job."

"Coach, I'm not trying to be an asshole. Sean's dad was hoping I could get some answers."

"I don't have any answers. I have just as many questions as you do."

"Like what?"

"I want to know why he went outside alone. I tell my guys to practice Noah's Rule: Two by two. Never go out alone at night."

"Why would you preach that? It's not like they're women alone in a strange place."

"If there's two things I know, it's that nothing good ever happens after midnight. And whatever does happen, you're always better off having help or having a witness."

"Who should have gone out there with him?"

"Darrell or Johnnie. Same as always."

"How many regular students did Sean hang out with?"

"I'm not the best person to know that." Childress looked at his watch. Keane knew despite the subject matter, the coach was in football mode, already thinking about his next appointment.

"What kind of privileges do you give your best players?" he asked. "Or your seniors?"

"What do you mean?"

"You know what I mean. How do you play favorites?"

"You mean, 'Was Sean one of my favorites?' He was a hell of a player. He meant a lot to me, to everyone, to the school."

"What did you do for him? What did everyone else do?"

"What do you mean 'do'?"

"C'mon, Coach. Did you make sure he got good grades? Did you make sure he made his car payment? Did you make sure he had spending money?"

The coach rapped his knuckles on his desk. "I don't know what you think you know, but whatever it is, it's wrong. We don't play that kind of shit here."

"Tell it to the media, coach. You don't get players like you have and keep them without taking care of them in ways that, shall we say, the school president doesn't know about."

Childress jabbed a finger in his direction. "We win fair and square here. No shortcuts. No bullshit."

"If you say so."

"I say so because that's the truth. You got anything else?"

"Yeah. Who was paying the kid?"

"That's it." Childress stood up.

"Coach, the kid was flush." Keane looked around the office. "He had nicer furniture than you do. He had money everywhere. Somebody was taking care of that."

"Ask his father."

"I have. He admits he bought some of it. But not all of it. Not by a long shot. You know what I think? I think maybe somebody else was paying for it. And maybe that person decided he wasn't getting back what he was paying for. And that person got mad."

"You've got a wild imagination."

He laughed. "Maybe. Maybe not. But I'm going to find out what happened. And why. You can count on that."

"Are you done?"

"I'm just getting started. So are the police. They're poking around. The detectives I met, they're going to get the answers they need. And you already know that I know how college football works."

"What's that supposed to mean?"

"It means don't get too cute and think you're smarter than everybody who walks into your office."

Childress hiked out of his chair and flicked the back of his hand at him. "We're done. Get the hell out of here."

Keane started his retreat. "My pleasure. Thanks for the time."

He smiled at the secretaries and chuckled on his way out the door, pleased with his antics. He'd gotten under the coach's skin, and it hadn't taken much.

TEDDY PICKED UP his cell phone on the second ring. "What?"

"We have a problem," Duke Childress said.

14

ON HIS WAY out of Childress's office, Keane thanked the secretary. "He said the equipment manager has a couple things of Sean's to give me. What's his name?"

"Jimmy Wyndham," she said. "Second hallway, down on the left."

He found the equipment room and Jimmy Wyndham inside it. The room had an old-fashioned Dutch door, top and bottom split. The top half was open, allowing anyone to see inside. Keane rapped on the shelf as he opened the bottom door and walked in. He closed the door behind him, and as he turned a slim, tanned man in his early fifties appeared from behind a tall row of lockers.

"Can I help you?" the man asked.

"You can if you're Jimmy," he said.

"I am," Wyndham said. He wore khakis and an OU polo that were identical to Childress's, plus white sneakers. His lower lip appeared swollen, but this wasn't the result of an altercation. A chunk of snuff, the Southern man's security blanket, peeked out, contrasted by stained teeth.

"I'm supposed to pick up Sean Riggins's things. Coach Childress said you had them together."

"Well . . . the cops already took them. Not sure why they need dirty shoes and used shirts. But hang on."

Wyndham disappeared between rows of lockers. Keane heard a door unlock and unlatch in the back. Wyndham returned carrying a small stack of t-shirts and two jerseys under his arm, one white and one red, the school colors.

"Coach said you could have whatever you wanted," Wyndham said. "I didn't think you'd want the socks."

"Good call," he said. "What time's practice?"

"Pretty quick. Coach don't like if we're late."

"Gotcha. Hey, thanks for this. It'll be nice for Sean's dad."

"No problem. Sean was a good kid. Good player, too. We'll miss him."

"Hey, before you go. Sean's dad—well, all of us, really—we're trying to make sense out of all this. You hearing anything?"

Wyndham shook his head. "Guys on the team go out all the time. Every now and then they get into scrapes and fights. But nothing like this."

"No gossip among the guys on the team? I played college ball. I know if there's anything going on with a football team, there's two people who know: the trainers and the equipment managers. So I wondered."

Wyndham squinted and took two seconds to size him up. "Police have been around, but they're not talking. You're talking to them, right? They talk to the family?"

Keane rolled his eyes as dramatically as he could. "Not as much as you'd think."

"Yeah. Assholes." Wyndham smiled and looked for a reaction.

Keane smiled back. "I know what you mean."

"Yeah, well, I haven't heard anything."

"Thanks anyway. Say, is there a back door out of here? I think I parked on the wrong side of the complex."

Wyndham walked him past lockers and shelves and finally to an outward-opening metal door. He pushed it open, and sunshine poured in. "Here you go."

He let the door click shut, waited ten seconds, and then tried opening the door from the outside. Locked. He made a mental note, got his bearings, and walked around the building.

His Ford rental listed slightly to the right, and as he got closer he saw why. The right front tire was flat. He knelt down and inspected the sidewall, where a clean, two-inch-wide gash presented itself. He thought, *sharp knife*.

15

SWEATY AND FLUSHED, Keane spotted Rossi on the far side of El Cerro sipping iced tea through a straw. The Tex-Mex restaurant was one of only two lunch places the hotel desk clerk had recommended, and it had the bonus of being a stone's throw from the OU campus.

"I already ordered," Rossi said as he sat down. "You're late, and I'm hungry."

"Donut tires don't go on as quick as they say," he said. He caught her staring at his starched white shirt. He looked down and grimaced at smudge spots. "I'll be right back."

When he returned from scrubbing his grease- and rubber-soiled hands and toweling off his face, he gulped half his water.

"Thanks for meeting me," he said, but he was met with a glower.

Rossi leaned across the table. "Screw thanks. How'd you get my cell number?"

"You want a good answer or an honest answer?"

"I want the right answer."

The truth was, he'd called in a favor to get her number. He'd debated whether to call her directly or go through the police switchboard, figuring correctly she'd react to an outsider invading her private world. And he'd called it mostly out of curiosity to judge her reaction. He hadn't meant to anger her. That he'd miscalculated.

"When you met with Q and me the other day you had your phone in a hip holster, and I could tell it was an iPhone. I have contacts at all the phone companies, including AT&T. I reached out and asked for a favor."

"You called AT&T and got my number? Are you fucking kidding me? You realize you committed a crime, right? Violated my right to privacy, among other things."

"I didn't commit anything. There's somebody at AT&T that might have a problem, though."

"FYI, pissing off your local detective isn't the way to win friends and influence people. Just so you know."

He liked her attitude, mostly because he'd have had the same reaction, except maybe more profane. Now he had to tip-toe. His little investigation would get much easier if she were inclined to help him in any way.

"My apologies," he said. "I didn't want to be blown off. If I thought you'd drink something stronger, I'd buy you a top-shelf margarita."

"Maybe next year."

She drank the last of her tea and looked around for their waiter. Then she withdrew the straw, sucked in a couple of ice cubes and loudly crunched them.

He winced. "That's bad for your teeth."

"So my dentist tells me."

Now he leaned forward. "Where do things stand on Sean's case? What can you share?"

Rossi spit an ice cube back into her glass. "You figured you could buy me lunch and get me to tell you about an investigation? It doesn't work that way."

"I'm not asking you to open your book. I just want to know if you have a suspect or if an arrest is imminent. Hell, give me a sound bite. Can the OU community feel safer if you confirm that there's not a maniac out there stalking football players?"

She stared at him, and he realized he'd slipped. Most people asked about the investigation or case. He'd said "book." Book was cop talk.

"You're on the job," she said.

Hell's bells. Had he wanted to tell the Orlando police he was FBI, he'd have done it days before. Since then, he'd pondered whether to come clean, but he'd decided against it. He was tired of being tired. And after only a couple days in Orlando, he was weary again.

"I'm not," he said.

"No? What are you?"

"Off the job."

"You were a cop? What are you? Who are you?"

He took a deep breath and tried not to show it. "Not a cop. Federal agent."

She smacked her hand on the table, startling the diners around them. "You're fucking kidding me!"

"I'm not."

"Jesus almighty. You're FBI?"

He did his best to soften his face and not smile, anything to neutralize her growing ire.

"Show me."

He pulled his credentials from his back pocket and opened the leather holder as he laid it on the table. She looked at the badge and stared at the photo ID.

She started with "unbelievable," then interrogated him until lunch arrived, and he obliged with a short version of his history. He skirted his family life and focused on his career path. Four years of corporate law until his student loans were gone and his brain was numbed by greedy clients and greedier partners. He turned to the FBI and was surprised when it said yes. He mostly chased high-level pot dealers and white-collar criminals around eastern Tennessee, southern Kentucky and Virginia, and western North Carolina. On the rare occasion that terrorism came into play, he'd get plugged in, usually executing search warrants.

"And you go after muggers in Orlando," Rossi said.

He shook his head. "Your job, not mine."

"Yeah, right," she said. "You're going to try to help the father and then you're gone?"

"You'll find who was responsible." He paused. "I want to find out why."

Rossi shoved the basket of chips at him. "We do that, too, in case you didn't know. You assholes are unbelievable. Just waltz in and push everybody to the side." She jabbed her fork at him. "Every damn time. But you have no standing."

He looked at his half-empty cup. "I never pretended to. The only real crime I need to investigate here is the person who's calling this iced tea authentic."

"It might be the water. It's not the best around here." She turned serious again. "I'm not sure you're ever going to find the answers you're looking for."

"Why is that?"

"First, I need to know where you were two nights ago."

"Where I was? Am I a suspect?"

She shook her head. "You know how this goes. Just answer the question. Two nights ago?"

He looked across the table at a woman who needed sleep and normalcy. He decided to give her the benefit of the doubt and take her at her word.

"I was in my hotel room," he said. "I was there all night with the TV on and working on the computer."

"What kind of work?"

"Research. Isn't that what you do?"

She ignored him. "What about the father? Mr. Riggins?"

"What about him?"

"Was he with you?"

"He's back home, planning a funeral. What are you getting at?"

"I just want you on the record."

"Now I am. What's up?"

"You carry a standard FBI-issue Glock?" she asked.

"Not right now, but that's my usual," he said. "Why?"

"What about nine millimeter? You have one of those?"

"I've been known to have one in my possession. If I didn't know better, I'd think you suspected I'd committed a serious crime."

"I can't tell you anything more. I just thought you'd like to know that we think we got our guy."

"And yet no press conference. No media splash."

"Don't worry. It's coming. I'm sure of it."

"You're kidding. When?"

Rossi shrugged. Now she'd revealed too much, and her silence was confirmation. It was a minor detail but telling nonetheless. Rossi was on the young side as detectives went, early to mid-thirties, and he could tell she was sharp. And a touch emotional.

"I didn't hear about an arrest," he said.

"We haven't made one."

"Didn't hear about a police-involved shooting, either."

"House fire just north of downtown. Our suspect died in the fire."

"That's quite a coincidence. What aren't you saying?"

When Rossi went for more chips, he said, "Don't tell me your fire victim was shot."

"Geez, you might have a future in law enforcement."

"Who was it?"

"We're pretty sure it was the person who accosted Sean Riggins. A former OU football player named David Hance."

"What would have been his motive for going after Sean?"

She shook her head. "Still looking into it."

"Why do I think you're not going to get much time for that? As much attention as Sean's death is getting, there's got to be pressure to close the case and move on. I have to believe nobody wants to open a can of worms."

Rossi didn't answer.

"That's what I thought." He'd seen these politics before. Cops rarely got a chance to pat themselves on the back on the local news. Too many of their TV appearances involved answering for one misstep or another, real or perceived. This case was sure to give Rossi and Thomas heartburn. And he could make things worse for them if he dug in and got stubborn.

"What's next for you?" she asked finally.

"Not sure," he said. "I've already upset the football coach and local police. That's enough for one day."

Rossi leaned in. "Childress? You talked to Childress?"

"Of course. I had to give him a chance to tell me how great Sean was."

"Childress is slick."

"He's also up to his hips in shit."

Rossi tilted her head. "What makes you say that?"

Keane chuckled and studied her expression: nothing. "I think you know already. Quentin Riggins is a hardworking, upstanding father. Owns a bar and grill in a town full of bars and grills. His place is nice, but it's not a well-oiled moneymaker like your favorite chain. And it's not high-end. I don't know how much you know about the restaurant and bar business, but it's a tough way to make a living. Margins are tight, employees are undependable, and customers move from place to place, depending on what's trendy."

"I know all about restaurants. My folks own one, and I worked there for years. What's your point?"

"Q tells everyone he bought Sean everything he needed or wanted up here, but my guess is that's all bullshit. He probably paid for a few things, but he didn't buy that kid a big-screen TV or half the clothes in the closet. He damn sure didn't pony up for that SUV."

"His name was on the title," Rossi said. "If he didn't pay for it, he probably helped."

"Maybe. He likes to talk big, but he's not made from cash. Unless he went into hock to pay for all his kid's luxuries, which I doubt, then someone else was doing the job for him."

The waiter picked up the last of the chips and left a bill sitting on the table. Rossi nodded at the check. "That one's yours. For the cell number."

He picked it up and studied it. He pulled a twenty dollar bill from his wallet put it down with the tab. He used a salt shaker to keep them together. "That's a bargain."

They walked out of the restaurant and peeled off in opposite directions. Rossi stopped and walked back toward the off-duty federal agent.

"If you weren't close to Sean Riggins, why do you care so much?" she asked. "I mean, I told you we have the guy who was responsible, but you're digging in for the long haul. Which, by the way, I strongly advise against."

He shrugged. "This is what Q wants."

"That doesn't hold any water. Doesn't matter one bit. Surely you know this. But you're, what? Going to put yourself on the line for the father of a victim. Why? I know you're related to Sean, but . . . are you related to Quentin Riggins?"

Keane laughed. "In an alternate universe maybe."

"What does that mean?"

Keane took a deep breath and let it out as he considered how much to share. "Before Sean was born, Q wanted to marry my mom. He was head over heels for her. When she got pregnant, he really wanted to marry her. And he wanted to marry her after Sean was born and every day since then. He'd have married her right up until the time she died. But it wasn't what she wanted."

"Okay, but the two of you?"

"Even though he never got what he wanted with her, Q still treated me like gold. When I was young, just out of college, he was a smart sounding board about life. Later, we just became friends. He hasn't had the easiest life, and I help him when I can. Let's just leave it at that. And right now, he needs help."

Rossi held up one finger to make a point. "I need you to mind your manners here."

"Meaning what?"

"Meaning the Orlando Police Department knows officially there's an FBI man in town poking around in one of our cases unofficially. Don't stick your nose in a place where it could get cut off."

"And?"

"And you tell us anything you come across."

"You'll share too?"

"No guarantees."

"What if I say you're full of shit?"

She arched an eyebrow. "You probably don't want to test that. I'm serious. Don't fuck around on this. You're not exactly on my good side here, pulling the shit you've already pulled with us. You don't want to get on my bad side."

"Yeah," he said. "I might have to pay for dinner *and* dessert."

16

Rossi met Thomas at the football office, where this time Duke Childress's secretaries greeted them absent smiling faces. The eldest of the three glanced at a clock on the wall and said, "You're early. But we're ready for you."

She knocked twice on the interior door and opened it without waiting for a reply. "They're here," she said.

A tall, pale man in a pinstripe blue suit emerged, followed by a slightly shorter and much younger black man. The man in the suit extended his hand and delivered a business card to each detective. "I'm Arthur Chance, the university's general counsel. I'll be sitting in to help Mr. Dubrow."

"Darrell, you're good with Mr. Chance as your attorney?" Thomas asked.

Dubrow nodded.

Thomas opened his palm to the secretary. "Lead the way."

Everything about Chance was slender, from his nose to his stomach to his long, narrow feet wrapped in black Johnston & Murphy wingtips. A full head of brown hair with only wisps of gray completed the contrast.

Rossi sized up Dubrow at five-feet-ten, not counting the three inches of height from his hair.

His slim waist, highlighted by skinny jeans, and a tight-fitting gray t-shirt, gave him a compact look. She'd Googled him this morning, and he was considered OU's top defensive back. But for her and Thomas, Dubrow's skills mattered little. They were banking on him knowing details about his former roommate that no one else did.

They followed the secretary to the same meeting room where Rossi interrogated players and coaches two days earlier. Thomas and Rossi sat on one side of the white Formica-topped table, Chance and Dubrow on the other.

The detectives ran through the basics, honing in on Dubrow's relationship with Riggins. They'd been roommates for three years, starting with their freshman year, but seven months ago Riggins had moved out on his own.

"He was dating Tiffany and wanted more privacy," Dubrow said.

"A lot of privacy, apparently," Rossi said. "They didn't live together."

Dubrow shook his head. "Tiffany said her mom would freak out if she moved in with Sean. With any guy."

"I finished school almost twenty years ago, but every college student I ever met either lived at home or had a roommate. Yet Sean lived alone."

Chance cleared his throat and leaned in. "Student-athletes who are on scholarship and have the ability to live off campus receive a housing stipend from the university. That offsets the cost."

"True," Rossi said. "But most athletes still like to team up with one, two, or three roommates so that some of that stipend is left over after they pay rent. It's basically income."

"That's permissible," Chance said.

Rossi turned back to Dubrow. "How many roommates do you have?"

Dubrow looked at the attorney, who said, "You can answer."

"One," Dubrow said.

"And how much of that university money do you have left over each month?"

"About seven hundred."

"What's the rent?"

"Eighteen hundred."

Rossi did the quick math. "So you get $1,600 a month from the school, and nine hundred of that goes to rent. So if Sean was pocketing any savings from the stipend, it wasn't much."

"I don't know what—"

"Darrell doesn't have that information," Chance said. "I'm sure somebody at the university could help you with that."

"We'll find it," Rossi said. She reached out in Dubrow's direction and put her hands on the table. She looked him in the eyes. "We were told that a few days ago you and Sean had a fight in the locker room after practice. What was that about?"

Dubrow shifted in his chair. "It was nothing."

"If it was nothing, you might have yelled at each other. But you went at each other," Thomas said. "So it wasn't nothing."

"Aw, Sean made some comment about my girl, said she'd be dumping me soon for somebody else. Which she won't. But I didn't like it."

Rossi looked at Thomas and back at the young man. "You got into a fist fight over something he said about your girlfriend?"

"He said some things he shouldn't have said."

"And yet a few days later, you and your girl end up going out with Sean and his girl and with your friend Johnnie and his girl. That was a pretty fast apology."

"Like I said, it was nothing," Dubrow said.

"We heard you and Sean fought more than once. That you always patched it up but that you guys were always at each other. That seems like a weird relationship."

"You never met Sean."

Rossi scooted up in her chair. "Okay. So tell us about him. What do we need to know?"

Dubrow first looked at Chance, who nodded an okay, then lightly rapped the bottom of a fist on the table, as if he were drumming through his thought process. "He was intense, you know? He wanted to win every game, and he personally wanted to make sure he played the best he could. He never wanted people to say he didn't play hard enough. You know that type of person, right?"

"We've seen it," Thomas said.

"Yeah, well, Sean took it personal when people around him slacked off. He didn't like that at all."

"How did he not like it? What would happen?" Rossi asked.

Dubrow shrugged. "He just . . . called them out. He'd yell, or grab a guy's jersey or facemask. He was more like a coach than a player."

"We heard that sometimes he'd treat the coaches the same way. Yell and even get in their faces."

"Yeah, it happened. He'd do that. Like I said, he was intense, even during practice."

"What else would you two fight about besides a girl?"

"Oh, man." Dubrow's eyes grew wide, and he looked around the room before answering. "Mostly . . . football. Usually he didn't think I was playing hard enough."

"Were you?"

"I thought I was. But Sean, he'd get on me even if the coaches weren't yelling at me. That's what I mean when I say he was like a coach."

"So girls and football," Rossi said. "Nothing else?"

Dubrow looked up at the wall behind her. "If there was, I don't remember it."

"Because usually when someone has a temper and is as emotional as everyone says Sean was . . . they usually get emotional about any number of subjects, not just one or two in particular."

Dubrow stared at her as if he were unsure what he was supposed to say.

After several seconds, Chance asked, "What else can Darrell help you with?"

Rossi picked her second priority topic for Dubrow. "Tell us about Coach Childress. What's he like to play for?"

Dubrow sat back in his chair and looked up in thought. Finally: "He's great. He's hard on us when he needs to be, but he only wants the best for us. And the team."

Rossi nodded and went through the rest of her Childress questions, but Dubrow towed the company line, giving answers to each query that were sure to make the coach happy if he were there listening. Rossi was sure Chance would provide a blow-by-blow to Simpson, and possibly Childress, of everything being discussed. She figured Dubrow knew it, too.

After twenty more minutes, Rossi thanked Dubrow and said goodbye.

When Dubrow left, Chance closed the door and said, "You had asked for Johnnie Jones, but he's not available today. We'll need to reschedule. We can do that now or later. Your choice."

Rossi looked at her partner, who said, "We'll get back to you."

"I DON'T BELIEVE Dubrow," Rossi said as she and Thomas walked to the car. "Maybe that locker room fight was about a girl. And maybe they argued with each other all the time about football and girls. But there were other things, too."

"That's what I think," Thomas said. "We'll find it."

BEFORE TEDDY SAID hello, Don Henson delivered his news.

"Our problem is handled."

"Which problem? Handled how?"

"There was a rental-house fire in Colonialtown this morning. One of the tenants died. His name was Tally Hance."

Teddy processed how his friend knew this fact before he did. "That's . . . a tragedy. That's amazing."

This was the best news of all. Tally had screwed up a give-him-a-message meeting with Sean Riggins and killed the kid. That mistake brought the unwanted eyes and attention of the police, a situation that had no upside. Action was needed.

Their group huddle the day before delivered a series of options. They talked about payoffs, blackmail, the promise of a job far away, but they hadn't settled on one.

Now, improbably, Tally was dead. And dead by accident. Another accident. What were the odds? He'd have to replace Tally with some other loyal foot soldier. Finding a loyal acolyte might be problematic, but it beat having their little business broken up. Or, worse, having it discovered.

"How did we get this lucky?" he asked.

"Yeah, luck. That's what it was," Henson said.

"What else would you call it?"

"I'd say people make their own luck."

"What are you saying?"

"I'm saying Hance made his bed. We had a situation, and now we don't. We move on."

"You did this?"

"Don't be ridiculous. But we couldn't agree on a solution, and now we don't have to."

"This is crazy. This is—"

"Teddy, shut up. Not on the phone. Let's deal with the facts and move on."

He was speechless. Henson was a ruthless businessman and power broker. He wrapped disarming charm around both qualities to make himself presentable, but everyone who dealt with him knew he was about getting a job done. He was one of the most successful car dealers in the South, a man who had no trouble making hard decisions. But firing general managers was a long way from murder.

"Do you have someone else in mind?" Henson asked.

"What?"

"A replacement, Teddy. Do you have one for Hance?"

"I will, don't worry."

"I'm not worried anymore, Teddy."

He cut Henson off by hanging up and tossing the phone onto his desk. The crawl of an oncoming headache pinched his eyes, and he yearned for a Scotch. How had he ended up here? He was a fundraising machine destined for a gubernatorial run in one of the most corrupt states in the country.

It was a shoo-in. No one cared about his dalliances or his addictions. He'd lobbied for men substantially sleazier than he was. Besides, he was unashamed of his desires.

He made the short drive home and splashed three fingers of Dewar's into a glass. Tally Hance dead. He'd deserved to be punished, for sure. But this? How did Henson do it?

A wave of sadness washed over him. He recalled the totality of his relationship with a big-hearted country boy who wasn't terribly bright but was blessed with ideas and a penchant for sharing them. It was Tally who tipped him off to an impending raid of the strip club, Tally who escorted him out the back door in time, and Tally who ushered him in and out on his later trips to the Jaguar.

Tally passed along the blueprint for the side-business successes he, Henson, and the others enjoyed. Teddy took the plan and put the people together, rewarding Tally with a small position just outside the inner circle. Tally ran his errands, happy to be associated in any way with wealth.

He loved Tally for his loyalty. Tally did anything Teddy needed him to do, usually without question. Teddy hoisted his glass in a quiet salute and drank down his Scotch.

17

ROSSI AND THOMAS punched away on their laptops creating more paperwork for the Hance homicide file and whatever Sean Riggins's file was called. They had plenty of suppositions, guesses, and suspicions. They had advanced both cases, but typing out witness summations was a necessary pause. They had to get the paperwork out of the way before they could get on with the next step. Which was to uncover exactly what Tally Hance did when he wasn't protecting strippers into the early morning hours.

Alicia Arsenault had told her Tally was tight with the football coach. Carla Young, the dancer, had mentioned Hance also had enjoyed a friendship of sorts with Teddy Simpson. That left room for a lot of follow-up. A plus B plus C didn't prove a connection to OU or the reason the detectives were now producing homicide paperwork. But it seemed likely.

Neither of them knew what to make of Hance's connections to the university. Why would any college team allow someone employed by a strip club to work closely with college students? Even if half the strippers were OU coeds?

She considered the possibilities, and they were as lengthy as the imagination. A pipeline of easy, not to mention titillating, part-time summer jobs for players. Or access to adventuresome dancers and cheerleaders, tomorrow's star strippers. Or access to untraceable cash, brought in a dollar at a time. Hance could have bartered any of them to football players or would-be players. All of these reasons served as viable sales pitches to high-school athletes looking to trade football stardom for a good time on campus.

She turned to Thomas. "When do you want to go back to see the president?"

"Right after we talk to the football coach."

ROSSI THANKED CHILDRESS for seeing them and took a seat next to Thomas at a small, empty table in the coach's office. She noted Childress's amusement with them had ended sometime after their previous meeting. She opened her notebook and laid it on the table.

Childress abandoned the pleasantries. "What's up?"

"Something we want to clear up," she said. "There's a kid who played here for you a couple years ago. David Hance."

"Tally?" Childress said. "Wasn't all that good."

"How so?"

"Too slow. Not the sharpest tool in the shed, either. We never had any problems with him, but I don't know if he graduated."

"You stay in touch with him?"

"He shows up at practice every now and then, says hello."

"Just shows up? What's 'every now and then?' "

Childress scratched his face and thought about it. "Once a week, maybe once every two weeks. We have an open-door policy for former players as long as they left on good terms. And he did." The coach paused. "What's he got to do with all this?"

"Probably nothing," Thomas said. "But we're sorry to have to tell you he died in a fire last night."

"Fire? The house fire near downtown?"

Thomas nodded. "Hell of a way to go. That's awful."

"When did you see him last?" Rossi asked.

"Maybe a month ago," Childress said. "He came to practice."

"Besides other players, who else comes to practice? Friends of yours? Friends of the program?"

"All of them. Mostly, it's former players who still live close. They get off work early, show up to watch an hour of practice. They all wish they were still playing."

"And the others?" she asked.

"Boosters come by. People who give money expect more than they used to."

"Like what?"

"Access. They want to tell their golf buddies, 'Yeah, I went to practice last week and talked to Coach.' That kind of thing."

"I didn't know that was such a big deal."

Childress shrugged. "Seems to be. Pain in my ass."

She gave him a curious look and he bit.

"It's like recruiting," he said. "These boosters, all of them want to be treated nice, be told they're special. You know who's special? The guys that give six and seven figures."

"Who are those guys?" Thomas asked.

"It changes all the time. I don't keep track."

"But you screen who gets in and who doesn't, right? You don't let just anybody in."

The coach shrugged. "We have a security guard, but it's not like there's a lot of people who show up, you know? We ask people to call ahead and let us know they're coming. Some people, we know who they are. They don't have to call."

"Such as . . ."

"Former players and boosters, which I told you. The president. His friends."

"Like?"

"Don Henson. He tags along."

"The car dealer? That Don Henson?" Rossi asked.

"That's him," Childress said. "He handles the courtesy cars for the staff."

She made eye contact with Thomas and tried not to give Childress a tell. Henson had a big bankroll and a shady reputation. "Who else?" she asked.

Childress ticked off half a dozen names.

"Would any of these guys have a reason to have David Hance in their company? To have any association with him?"

"What kind of association?" Childress asked.

"Any work or business? Any connection at all?"

"No idea. The kid played for me several years back, and he lived here in town. How he paid his bills, I couldn't tell you. But I do know he doesn't run with that crowd."

"Wait. You don't know what he did?"

"Should I?"

"No one told you he worked at a strip club?"

Childress shook his head and chuckled. "I hope he wasn't a dancer." He walked them through a list of people who showed up at practice. They ranged from academic administrators to tutors to the occasional player's girlfriend. If Tiffany Lewis was one of the girlfriends, Childress didn't know it.

Rossi changed subjects. "Tell us about Darrell Dubrow and Johnnie Jones."

"Not bad players," Childress said. "They're young, still learning. Off the record, they do what they're supposed to do, go to study hall, go to class. They struggle at times. I don't think they care that much about school, only that they have to do certain things to stay eligible. I don't think they're dumb. But they're not . . . motivated by school. It's not their priority."

"Their priority being football," she said. "Why did Dubrow get into a fight with Riggins recently?"

Childress shrugged. "Could have been a lot of things. Maybe Riggins hit him too hard the play before. We used to have to tell Riggins to lighten up in practice. His motor ran hot most of the time."

"The fight didn't happen on the field. They got into it in the locker room after practice."

"I wouldn't know."

Rossi coughed out a laugh. "We both know you run a tight ship. You know everything that goes on in your program. Your staff keeps you informed."

"Once upon a time, maybe," the coach said. "There's too much to keep up with. It used to be you had to know who all the girlfriends were. Now it's girls and boosters and social media I'd need ten more compliance officers to know everything. Nobody wants that, especially me."

"Because some things you just don't want to know."

Childress nodded but said nothing. The conversation swung to the non-players and then back to Hance. Despite his lack of football acuity, Hance had earned decent grades. He didn't cause problems and did what he was told. Once in a while, he surprised the coaches with his play. Plus, he seemed like a nice guy. It wasn't hard to understand why Childress wouldn't mind Hance coming to practice.

"My coaches told me to keep an eye on him because they thought he was fooling around with steroids," Childress said. "He liked to lift weights. If you say he was a bouncer, I guess that would make sense."

"You think he sold steroids to players?"

Childress shot her a mean look. "That . . . I would have known."

Rossi made a note of the coach's emphatic reaction and decided to fan his coals. "What about something else? Weed? Or maybe something stronger?"

"Lady, have you ever seen a great athlete who smokes that stuff? It ain't exactly performance-enhancing."

"That's not a no," Rossi said.

"Jesus Christ. Okay, no. No, no, no!" Childress slapped the table so hard that her notebook jumped up and re-settled in place. "Are we done?"

Rossi met the coach's glare. "We are. For now. Thanks for your time."

18

THEIR SECOND MEETING with Teddy Simpson was more formal and more hastily arranged than the first. The foursome included Chance, the general counsel, whose trimness and height presented a stark contrast to the shorter, rotund president. They all shook hands and sat at the president's conference table.

Rossi had insisted Thomas run this meeting so she could take the measure of Simpson. She wanted to focus on answers and reactions more than questions.

Thomas skipped over most of the details of both cases and stuck to the basic frameworks. There was a fire, Hance was dead, and they believed arson played a role. Thomas made no mention of bullets or homicides other than they had good evidence that Hance was involved in the death of Sean Riggins.

"Are you serious?" Simpson asked.

"Yes, sir," Thomas said.

"So the investigation about Sean Riggins, that's over?"

"Not quite yet, but it's getting there. We have a few loose ends to tie up."

"Loose ends?"

"For instance, we learned that you knew David Hance."

"Knew him pretty well," Simpson said. "He didn't do anything to distinguish himself as a football player or a student here, but he loved the university. Loved the football program, especially."

Thomas coughed and shot a glance at Rossi. "Mr. Hance hardly seems like a typical friend of the university."

"*Typical* being a friend who gives us money? He wasn't. Not at all. I mean, he was a bouncer at a strip club. But as I said, he had an affinity for the university."

Rossi interrupted them. "You know what he did?"

"Sure," Simpson said. "He helped me out of a jam there once."

"At the Jaguar?" she asked. "What kind of jam?"

"The Casselberry cops busted a drug dealer there one night, a regular customer, and supposedly he was dealing in the club. Sold to one of the bartenders and two of the girls who worked there. I picked a bad night to be at the club."

Rossi tried not to look surprised at Simpson's wild left turn. "You were at the club the night they arrested the dealer?"

"Like I said, bad night. But it could have been a lot worse. Tally got a text, and the next thing I know, he was rushing me out the back door. I mean, I wasn't doing anything illegal, but the last thing I needed was my name in the paper, even as a witness."

She couldn't believe what she was hearing, especially in front of his attorney and two detectives. She snuck a look at the attorney, who looked amused and not a bit surprised.

"After that, you owed him," Thomas said.

"Hell, yes, I owed him. I was more than happy to pay that debt."

"What form did your gratitude take?"

Simpson chuckled. "Access, mostly. I made sure the athletic department didn't require him to give a lot of money to get the football tickets he wanted. Where he wanted, I should say."

"You took care of him."

"Sure did. I'd do it again."

Thomas said, "How close to him were you?"

"We weren't close. I knew him. Did favors for him. He did favors for me."

"More than just the one."

"Sure. You know, I have been back to . . . where he worked."

Thomas cleared his throat. "Even after the raid."

Simpson nodded. "For business, mostly. Occasionally we have a patron who has . . . well, I think you know where I'm going."

"Oh, keep going," Rossi said.

Simpson furrowed his brow and slowly shook his head. "Every now and then, I have occasion to be at the club. If I knew I was going, I'd call Tally to make sure he was going to be there when I was. And we'd talk. I'd get a free drink or two."

"What other favors did he do for you?" Thomas asked.

"He took care of me or my friends when we needed a little extra attention."

Thomas turned his head. "Attention?"

"Call it VIP treatment. We didn't wait long for our drinks. And he'd make sure the dancers paid us regular visits."

"Visits. That's what you call it?"

"Just dances. Nothing else. My friends all do pretty well for themselves. If they need those kinds of favors, they can get them from a much more . . . sophisticated source."

Thomas continued lobbing questions at Simpson while Rossi sprinkled in a few of her own. If the president had dealings with Hance other than what he'd just described, he didn't admit them.

"And you don't have any notion of who might have wanted him dead?" Rossi asked.

"None," Simpson said. "Can't imagine why anyone would."

"Quite possibly to cover up the fact that he was exceptionally close to a university president."

Jolted, Chance came halfway out of his chair. "Whoa, whoa! That's an unfounded accusation. The president isn't accused of anything. Or is he?"

"He's not," Thomas said. "But let's be clear. Right now we're working on the notion that Tally Hance was responsible for the death of one of OU's football players and that Mr. Hance then came into focus as a target. Possibly, so that he'd never have to talk about Sean Riggins or the university or the school president that he was so fond of."

"Or a hundred other reasons that have nothing to do with the university or Mr. Simpson," Chance said.

"These cases are connected, and we're going to solve them. If certain facts about Mr. Simpson's life away from the job become part of the case, well, we don't want that to happen any more than he does."

"But you'll use it, and what's more—"

"If you have more questions, ask them," Simpson said. "I'll answer whatever you ask. You're not going to embarrass me. Hell, I told you about the strip club. The bottom line is, I didn't do anything wrong. I don't know how much more plain I can make it."

Rossi moved them away from the subject of Simpson as a suspect. "Exactly how close was Tally Hance to the football program?"

"He came to all the home games. And he'd make a road game or two a year. I'm sure he would have wanted to go to the bowl game."

"Was he close to Coach Childress?"

"He played for Coach Childress. He liked Coach Childress. How close they were, you'd have to ask Coach Childress."

She was certain Simpson knew they'd just talked to Childress and what was said. She wondered if the president would share this conversation with his coach.

"You hired Coach Childress?" she asked.

"A year after I got here," Simpson said. "We needed a change. And it's worked out. He's had a couple of lean years, but we're much better now than when Duke first got here. We have more to do, but I can't complain about where we are."

"No problems with players?"

"There are always problems with players. Just like there are always problems with fraternity houses. And business majors. And art students. They're all kids, Detective."

"Okay, but nothing in a pattern that made you think you might need to change the leadership?"

"Nothing like that."

They talked for ten more minutes, but the president had nothing more of substance to offer. He'd given them enough already.

ROSSI COULDN'T HIDE her surprise. "Can you believe what he said? All that stuff he admitted? About the strip club and how he met Hance and how close they were?"

"I believe it," Thomas said.

"Why wouldn't he deny everything and just do damage control?"

"Because he's smart. If he admits what he knows is true—and maybe he thinks we know more than we do at this point—he keeps the power."

"How do you figure?"

"You've heard about PR people, even at law enforcement agencies, talk about 'controlling the story' in the media? You throw a fact out there that you want to talk about before you get asked about it. That way, you're not in a position of looking like you're on the defensive about the thing you *don't* want to talk about. You make the other person react to you."

"Of course. But I've never seen it to that degree. That was wild."

"It's the same principle. It's leverage. If the president admits his screw-ups, his failures, it makes it hard to use them against him. As long as he doesn't rack up a DUI or diddle a kid, he can probably get away with a little misbehavior as long as it's all in the open."

She rolled that around. "I'm not sure how being a customer of a strip club helps him keep his job."

"He probably raises a shitload of money. That'll keep you employed no matter what you do. It's a pretty damned smart strategy as long as you don't have any real demons or skeletons."

She laughed. *Everyone's got those.*

THOMAS TURNED RIGHT instead of the usual left out of the OU campus.

"Where are you going?" Rossi asked. "I thought we were done."

"I need a pick-me-up. There's a Starbucks close."

She didn't mind a bit. She loved an afternoon iced coffee.

"You're buying," he said.

Thomas waited in the unmarked car, engine running, while she picked up the drinks. Grande Colombian for him, a venti Colombian blend with a shot of caramel for her.

She paid for the coffees and moved out of the way for the next customer. She'd brought in her folder of notes and photographs to study while she waited. She took a seat at a table close to the coffee bar and flipped through the folder.

"I'm sorry." The girl who took her order stood next to the table. "Sorry, but we ran out of caramel up front. I can get you something else or else I can find more in the back. It'll take a couple minutes. Your choice. I'm sorry."

"It's okay. Hazelnut." She called Thomas outside to relay the news. He didn't mind waiting. They were done, and they were headed downtown from there, against the thick afternoon rush-hour traffic. She was deep into the folder when the coffee arrived.

"I put ten dollars on this since you had to wait," the girl said, setting down the drinks and extending a gift card to her. "We're not supposed to run low on things like that."

"Hey, thanks," she said.

The girl walked away, and behind her stood Alicia Arsenault.

"Hello," the video assistant said. "You remember me?"

"Sure. What can I do for you?"

Arsenault pointed to a color mug shot in the folder. "Is that . . . Tally?"

"You know him?"

"Yeah. What happened to him?"

Rossi straightened the folder and then closed it. "He died in a house fire."

Arsenault covered her mouth. "That's terrible. He came out here a lot."

"A lot?" She was interested now. "What's a lot?"

"At least once a week. Sometimes, three times a week. We have a lot of guys who used to play here that just show up. They're in town or have the day off. I think a few of them play hooky from work, you know? A lot of them want to talk to Coach. One guy showed up, he was starting out as an investment broker and wanted Coach to join a new group. Things like that. Guys hit up Coach Childress for insurance, cars, everything. The younger ones, they want job recommendations. The rest just come to relive the past."

"Was Tally selling a service or reliving the past?"

Arsenault shook her head. "I don't think he was selling, because Coach doesn't buy stuff. And Tally kept coming back."

Rossi walked Arsenault out of the Starbucks to the driver's side where Thomas sat, his window down, and reading email on his phone. Rossi handed him his coffee.

"You remember Alicia Arsenault? OU's video coordinator?"

Thomas nodded hello.

"She says Hance went to football practice once or twice a week and was pretty friendly with Coach Childress," Rossi said.

"More than once a week," Thomas said, and Rossi nodded. *The coach had hedged.*

Thomas looked at Arsenault. "Who else did he talk to regularly?"

"He talked to . . . players, assistant coaches, everyone who talks to him, I guess."

Arsenault named a handful of players Rossi had never heard of. At Rossi's and Thomas's request, Arsenault gave them a visual of a typical practice, Hance and the clan of boosters. After practice, Hance and the boosters regularly walked off the field together with Childress.

They walked her through it again, but nothing came up.

"Thanks for helping," Rossi said to her. "The same rules apply. We'll keep all this confidential and you should, too."

The video assistant walked back into Starbucks. Thomas threw the car into gear and said, "This is going to be a real shit storm."

19

KEANE DIALED ROSSI, and she picked up after two rings.

"I'm almost afraid to ask," she said.

"What? I'm just checking in," he said.

"Oh, I . . . never mind. What's up?"

"Who do you know at the local paper? I'm talking to reporters."

"No. Absolutely not. That is not a road you want to take."

He laughed a dismissal but was secretly happy that she was giving him advice and laying down an ultimatum. "Please. I love reporters. They're so . . . willing. The only thing they love more than writing is talking. They live to trade information."

"You don't have anything to trade," she said.

"I'll concede I don't have much. You know that. I know that. The paper doesn't know that."

"Again: no."

"This won't come back to anyone at OPD, I promise. It might not come back at all. It really depends how lucky I am. C'mon, who do you know?"

She sighed on the other end. "Know, as in talk to? Nobody. I have names, and I probably can connect a few names to faces because of a side-of-the-road press conference or two. And . . ."

"And what?"

"I went out with a guy in high school who later on was a reporter and then an editor at the Leesburg paper. A couple years ago, I heard he'd hooked on with the paper here. But I don't know what he does there. Haven't talked to him, wow, in maybe twenty years."

"Can you call him for me?"

"He might not even still be there. Even if he is, why? How would he help?"

He told her his idea. It took him a few minutes to convince her that she wouldn't have to make any promises or trades. "Besides, maybe you'll like talking to him again."

"Maybe you can go fuck yourself." When he didn't come back at her she said, "I'll call you back if I get anything."

She called back in fifteen minutes.

"That was fast," he said.

"No real news," she said. "He's still at the paper. He's a mid-level editor there now, but he works afternoons and nights. I left him a voicemail and asked him to call me back. If he's working today, he'll call me later."

"You sound confident."

"Back in the day, I was a fun girl to go out with."

ON A ROLL, Keane dialed the toll-free number for Blindside.com. He navigated through the answering prompts before he got a real person on the line. "I need to close an account," he said.

"You can do that online if you want, sir," said the man on the other end of the phone. "Do you have your login and password?"

"I do, but I'd rather do this over the phone." He was certain the man to whom he was talking was sitting in an office outside the United States, but he detected no accent.

"We can do that," the man said. "Can I ask you why you've decided to close your account with us?"

"You can ask."

After a pause, the man said, "Is there a reason you're terminating the account?"

"Because it's against the law in the United States to gamble and you didn't make me aware of that."

"Very good, sir, but that is in your terms of agreement, which were emailed to you. But we're more than happy to process your request at this time. Your account number, sir?"

He read off Sean's account number.

The Blindside call rep asked a routine series of security questions, all of which Keane had anticipated. He'd written down several sets of potential pieces of information just for this purpose. Sean's address and Social Security number. His cell number. Mother's maiden name. If the online company had an off-the-wall query— "What's your favorite color?"—he'd have to talk his way around it. That was one reason for doing this over the phone. There was always a chance to dodge security with a human being involved. Besides, he needed to do more than just close the account.

The questions were routine. Mailing address, home phone, mother's maiden name. He hoped Sean hadn't taken his account security to the point that he'd made up answers that weren't real – ones that only Sean might know.

"You want to close your account?" the man asked again.

"Actually, before I close it, I'd like to confirm my balance," he said.

"Let's see . . . we emailed a statement out . . . seven, eight, nine . . . nine days ago. And . . . no account activity since then. It's the same as your last statement."

"Eighty-six thousand and change."

"A little bit more, but yes."

He paused. In the background over the phone line, he heard others talking. He couldn't make out what was being said, but more than one person was there. *Call center. Not a small operation.* "How do I clear out my balance? Can you transfer that directly to my bank account, do you send me a check, or what?"

"We typically handle this one of two ways: we transfer the money for a hundred-dollar fee to a third-party account of your choosing and you can handle it from there, or we can send you a cashier's check for the balance minus one hundred dollars. If you want the check to be overnighted to you, there's another hundred-and-fifty-dollar charge. However you want to handle it."

"Third-party account?"

The operator said, "We can transfer it to your PayPal account or to a similar account but not to a bank account held in the United States. We can also transfer funds to a non-U.S. account. It's the customer's discretion what kind of account and where it resides. It's perfectly legal to send and receive money from that account. If we can accommodate a request, we will."

Keane cursed himself for not thinking this through. Not only could he not gamble, it was illegal for him as an FBI agent to profit from ill-gotten money. Even if it was from a family member. Or a former family member. He could skirt the law by cutting a third-party check, but checks were easy to trace. The flow of money on this one would be easy. But the problem with a check was the signature. Any check would be made out to Sean Riggins. It would be unusable.

"I think I'll do a third-party account, but I'm not ready to do that today. I'm going to have to call you back."

The call rep was more than happy to let him go, probably because he didn't have to sweat a conversation with his boss about how he failed to talk a good customer out of cashing out. Soon, though.

He opened one of the sliding mirrored doors of the hotel closet, exposing a small safe, and punched in a four-number combination. The safe beeped loudly as it unlocked, and the door popped open. There in one holster sat his Glock .45. In another was his Walther PPQ nine millimeter.

TEDDY PULLED FIVE steaks off the grill and piled them onto a platter. He closed a sliding glass door behind him and walked through his kitchen into a formal dining room. He placed the platter on a large mahogany table.

"Rare on the bottom, medium-rare in the middle, and medium on top. Cooked to order," he said.

Don grabbed the platter, speared a steak, put it onto his plate, and passed the platter to his left. Plates of au gratin potatoes, green beans, corn, and rolls made their way around the table.

Teddy took a seat at the head of the table and loaded his plate. As was his custom with a good steak—and when he cooked them, they were always good— he drew a long sip from a glass of cabernet, savored the first bite of steak, then took another drink. *Perfect is good enough*, he thought, satisfied with the marriage of red meat and wine. *At least I can enjoy this.* Once dinner ended, he expected an inquisition.

These were Teddy's recruits, his prized collection of men with a thirst for money and a passion for football. The other binding quality was that each believed at all times he was the smartest man in the room. There were six in all, but one was absent tonight, as he was every night. Usually they cackled at dirty jokes, debated the economy, and talked football. Tonight there were only two primary topics: Sean Riggins and Tally Hance.

"You know the best thing about eating here?" the real estate developer said to the group as he pulled a Cohiba from his shirt pocket. "You get to smoke your fucking cigar at the table. Christ, I don't think there's a restaurant south of Tallahassee where you can still do that. Fucking tree-huggers."

"Hear, hear," said Don, hoisting a glass of Scotch.

"Full service," Teddy said. "Technically, this is a state-owned house, so I guess you could make a case for this being a non-smoking building. Fuck 'em if they can't take a joke."

"Exactly," said the lawyer.

Don waited until the developer lit his cigar and blew his first full plume of smoke at the ceiling before clearing his throat and turning to the reason they were all there.

"So, Teddy," he said, turning to the president, "when does this business with Riggins get cleared up? Where do we stand?"

Softball question, but Teddy was all too aware of Henson's ability to direct a conversation. He'd never seen him sell a car, but he'd seen Henson conduct enough negotiations to know that he was a hard-charging, deal-driving son of a bitch who got his way more often than any man should.

"I think we're okay," Teddy said.

"Okay? How are we okay? The police aren't saying a goddamn thing to the media. The autopsy's still pending, and people are still asking questions. That doesn't sound okay to me."

"The police are fine. It's handled," Teddy said.

"That's not what my people are telling me," Don said.

"Your people?"

"Yeah, Teddy, my people."

Teddy drank more wine. Don liked to brag that he had moles scattered everywhere, including on Teddy's campus. It was possible, he conceded, those insiders didn't know what was really going on.

"What are your people saying?" the accountant asked.

"That the cops are still talking to our players about what happened that night to the dearly departed Sean Riggins."

A five-way conversation ensued. Teddy tuned out. He'd been down this road with Don already, the primary reason why this dinner party had been arranged. Henson wanted to get the "investment group," as he called the six, together for a collective exchange of ideas. *Exchange* meaning Don telling the others what they should think.

"You know, except for the last couple weeks, this has been a pretty damn good year," Teddy mused calmly to the group amid a lull in a diatribe by Henson. All eyes turned away from Don to Teddy at the other end of the table. Henson was too stunned to object.

"Well," the banker said, "my research shows that if we had bet every game that we had information on, we'd have all made a tidy profit. I didn't bet them all, but I've kept up with the numbers. It was about sixty-eight percent."

"Right at 67.7 percent," Teddy said. "Forty wins out of fifty-nine games. Our best year. Before this year, the best we'd ever done was 61.9 percent. So, everybody's making money, right?"

Teddy looked around the table and saw a few nods. Don glared back at him. "I'm correct in saying I didn't hear anybody complaining until Sean Riggins died."

"That's a goddamned big 'until,' don't you think?" Don said. "What happens if the police get too close?"

"I told you. It's handled. They're not getting close. They're not going to get close. We wanted the investigation to go away, and it's going away."

"You put a lot of faith in your mayor," Don said.

"For good reason," Teddy said. Getting Orlando Mayor Richard Williams elected had been one of the first projects of the group. The victory provided a confidence-building exercise that ultimately solidified the group and pushed it toward the current venture. The mayor had no idea of the group's existence, but he'd benefitted nonetheless. "That's what friends are for. Right, Don?"

The car dealer snorted and sucked the rest of his Scotch from a tumbler.

Although this was a close group and secrets were shared, there were many things the five other men did not know about Teddy. He was sure there were things about them he didn't know. In reality, they hadn't known one another that long. They ranged in ages from early forties to late fifties, which made the age span almost a generation. Their political views were mostly conservative. As university presidents went, Teddy was well right of center, a fact that his many critics within the student body loved to highlight in letters to the editor of the student newspaper.

Teddy had no idea how his friends hid their financial windfalls. They all shared a disdain of the IRS, and a couple of them worked hard to shield money from their wives and girlfriends, too.

Except for sharing tidbits, members of the group kept to themselves about their gambling finances. They were more than talkative about business, especially when business was good.

Teddy got up and withdrew a cigar from a humidor in the corner of the room behind him.

"Anyone else?" Teddy asked over his shoulder. Hearing three voices, he removed three Churchills from the humidor.

"You sure about this, Teddy?" the banker asked. "This is all just ending?"

"The kid's gone and the cops are done. They were chasing their tails before. Now they have their patsy and they're off on another errand."

"What about the family?" asked the banker.

"What family? There is no family. No brothers or sisters. His mother's dead. His father owns a little restaurant in South Florida. Coach Childress says he came up here to collect his son's belongings." He had no intention of letting Don know that the father's friend had picked a fight with the coach. He was sure Childress would keep that to himself, and there was no reason to raise the car dealer's concerns any higher.

"Hmmph," Don said as he labored to light his cigar. "We better hope it stays that way. I just don't think it will."

"Don," Teddy said, leaning forward, "how the hell did you get so good at selling cars when you're always the most negative guy in the room?"

Don blew out smoke. "Because I'm persistent. Don't ever forget that."

THE CELL PHONE lit up with an unknown number, and he answered quickly. "This is Keane."

"I have reporter names for you," Rossi said.

He smiled. "You masked your caller ID. Well played."

"You can never be too careful, can you?" she replied.

"Your old flame was happy to hear from you, huh? He remembered the good times."

She ignored the bait and gave him three names. "The first two work in the newsroom, the third one works in sports. They've all been there long enough to be considered veterans at the paper. My guy knows the news reporters better than the sports guy, but he says that guy has a solid reputation with everyone there."

"I appreciate this."

"Appreciate what? I never did anything. Remember that."

20

GATHERING INTEL WAS a deliberate exercise. Ten hours of off-and-on internet and FBI database searches left Keane weary with his investigative roadmap. Plotting the path was harder. The FBI trained him to approach every day the same way. It demanded every suspect he chased, and every case he built, be done with a mountain of evidence, all obtained legally so the suspect stayed caught.

Typically that meant working a tip from the bottom up, snaring informants—future court witnesses—and then climbing the organizational ladder.

Working with a staff directory of OU's football office and an online team roster, he made a list of possible informants. He started with everyone in the same class as Sean and then added all the players who shared Sean's position. He added his position coach, the defensive coordinator, and Duke Childress. Finally he added the little people, witnesses he loved the most. In his experience, volunteers, interns, and support staffers spun gold yarn.

No matter the organization, their status was always the same. No one cared what they thought, and few paid attention to them. But they knew a little bit about everything. Most loved to gossip about their bosses or anyone else with status. All they really cared about was being listened to.

He found his starting point: Jimmy Wyndham. The equipment manager was pleasant, accessible, approachable. As a bonus, he'd already met Wyndham. Maybe rapport could be established. Regardless, it was a calculated risk. Although Wyndham probably had dirt on every player, coach, and administrator, he might not talk. Worse, he might tip off the coach about a snooping outsider.

He'd pondered that as he dove into Florida's vast public-records database and compiled background on Wyndham. He liked what he found: unmarried, no kids, no house, terrible credit. A pair of DUIs on his record explained part of it.

It added up to a man with a troubled past who'd either sobered up, cleaned up, or both. Old media guides showed Wyndham as an OU employee for more than a decade. He'd been on the job before Duke Childress, and the coach had kept Wyndham on when he built his own staff.

That meant at least once, Wyndham owed the up-and-coming coach. There was no telling from the standard smile in his latest media guide photo if he was happy and loyal, or was unappreciated and angry. Keane would know soon.

THROUGH THE PREDAWN darkness, Keane watched Wyndham pull his car to the side of the OU football building and take his time getting out. A bright, single-bulb security light put off a glow that silhouetted the equipment manager and the white straw cowboy hat atop his head. It was tipped back. A relaxed look.

Wyndham held a tall, stainless-steel coffee cup in one hand, a plastic grocery store bag and a full key ring in the other. The manager was too busy scouring for the right key to see or hear him approach.

"Morning," he said.

Wyndham spun around and held up a key as a makeshift weapon. "Oh, it's you." He dropped the defensive pose. "You scared me. What can I do for you?"

"Need you to help me cut through the bullshit. The stuff your coach and the president are slinging around." He nodded at the door.

Wyndham unlocked it and held it open. "I wouldn't know anything about that." The manager flicked the lights on and led him past row after row of tall aluminum cubicles stocked with football clothes and equipment. Wyndham unlocked his office and dropped his keys on top of a pile of invoices on the end of the desk. Slid his lunch into a mini-fridge behind the desk and collapsed into an imitation-leather desk chair.

"Tell me about the cliques on this team," Keane said. "Who likes who. Who hates who."

"What does that have to do with anything?"

"It's just background information."

"I just don't see—"

"It's not that hard. These things are always the same. Guys who like to party together. Guys who like to hunt and fish. Guys who like to go clubbing. Guys who like to study. Guys with money. Guys with nothing. Just break it down."

"I don't think Coach would want me to do that."

"I'm sure you know what a conspiracy is."

"What does that have to do with anything?"

"I'll tell you what. Some real serious shit is about to go down around here. You know as well as I do that no university is pure. Once the cops dig in, once they find one or two things that interest them, cvcryone's going to get pulled in. Including everyone who might have known anything. Anybody who knows about unethical behavior, any wrongdoing, anything borderline criminal, all those people get rolled up and tossed out like yesterday's newspaper. You've probably seen something similar in your years."

Wyndham nodded. "There's nothing criminal going on around here."

"I'd call fixing games criminal."

"What? No one's doing that."

"If you believe that, you deserve to go. If you know in your heart that it might be true, you'd better help. You decide not to help, you can write your memoir from prison. Five to ten years ought to give you enough time to finish."

"Why do you care?"

He pulled out his credentials. "Because my day job is FBI."

Wyndham sighed and looked away. Then he reached into his desk and pulled out a media guide. Flipped to a page that listed all the players, started reading off names and analysis.

Keane took notes, stopping the equipment manager when a player sounded intriguing. There were eighty-four players on the team, but Wyndham didn't cover the first- or second-year players. He figured they were too young to have much of a connection with Sean.

After half an hour, he had the team divided into several different groupings according to likes and dislikes. Sean, Darrell, and Johnnie were in a group of clubbers. It was the largest faction on the team. There was no mention of gambling.

"Anything else?" Wyndham asked.

"Tell me about Tally Hance."

"He was basically Coach's guy. I wouldn't call him a spy, but he made sure to tell Coach anything that was going to hit the fan. If two guys were fighting over the same girl or if a player was going out and getting drunk too much. Stuff like that."

"How would he know more than you? You're around the players every day. You see them and talk to them. They talk to you. Why would anyone even trust him?"

Wyndham shrugged. "People liked him. He was a good guy. And, you know, I heard maybe he passed out money. Or let me put it this way: Word is he was generous."

He thought about how that might play out. "Was he close to Sean?"

"They were pretty tight. I don't know if Tally ever paid him, though."

Keane looked at the ceiling. Nobody living as a bouncer had enough money to pay off players. Hance had to be a middleman. "You pre-date Childress by a few years. You know him as well as anyone else here."

Wyndham adjusted his hat down and said nothing.

"You trust him," Keane said. "He trusts you. He tells you things he doesn't tell his wife. He probably tells you the best dirty jokes you hear."

"What's your point?"

"If you get called in to talk under oath, you'll have to tell the truth. We're not under oath here, and I'll just ask you: how many players is he paying?"

Wyndham shook his head. "You got the wrong idea. Coach don't cheat."

"Everybody cheats."

"I'm not saying there's nothing going on. I'm just saying Coach ain't part of it. If it goes on, he doesn't want to know."

Keane laughed. "It's called plausible deniability."

"All Coach cares about is that everybody be able to wear more than sweat pants and t-shirts to class and have money for food when they get hungry late at night."

"How does he communicate that philosophy?"

"Everybody just knows."

"He's got people doing his dirty work. Hance and others."

"Coach can't tell you anything about it, I'm telling you. He has no idea what happens. He just doesn't want to see any players walking around in rags. Some of our guys, they come from nothing. I mean nothing. You ever been to Pahokee? Overtown? The poor parts of Fort Lauderdale? Or Green Cove Springs or Lake Butler or Immokalee or Groveland? Places like that?"

Keane nodded. He'd played with two brothers from Miami who thought they won the lottery when they won scholarships to college. Three meals a day—all you can eat at the cafeteria, to boot—meant as much to them as playing on TV. He imagined how excited they would have been if they'd gotten hundred-dollar handshakes as a bonus.

"What do you know about the gambling?" he asked.

The manager frowned and shook his head. "If that was going on, I'd know about it, and I never saw any of that. Never heard about it. That'd be a big deal."

"There's a guy on this football team who was killed, and now another guy who was close to the football coach is dead. I don't know how much you know about police work, but those kinds of things don't just happen by chance. Things like this, they're connected."

"They're not connected to me." Wyndham held up his hands. "All I do is pass out jerseys."

"If Coach Childress isn't paying the players and doesn't know anything about the gambling, who's doing the dirty work? Who's paying players?"

"Same people that always do," Wyndham said.

"Boosters. What about Don Henson?"

Wyndham shrugged. "He's got big car dealerships all over. The athletic department leases cars from him."

"Yeah, but is he more than that? Does he come to football practice? Does he pal around with the coach? Or the president?"

"I see him at practice and at games but not much in the off-season. He talks to Coach. He talks to the president more."

Keane moved chess pieces in his head. Henson made sense. "Tell me more about the car dealer."

"He's the biggest auto dealer in town," Wyndham said. "New and used. He sells a shitload of cars and makes a shit-ton of money. I don't know the full story, because it was before my time, but I think he was the first car dealer around here to go against American models. He had the first Honda dealership here back in the day, then a Toyota dealership. Then he got a Nissan dealership. He does have a Cadillac place."

"He likes to expand and diversify, huh? Smart. A man like that doesn't tend to take no for an answer."

"You got that right."

Keane leaned forward. "Yeah? How?"

"It's hard to explain. It's like he's two people. I've seen him where he could charm the pants off Julia

Roberts. And then I've seen him just about cut someone's heart out. He's got a legendary temper."

Keane nodded. Car dealers were notoriously cold-blooded. "Where would you have seen either side of him like that?"

"Football games. Before and after. He's mostly a good guy, but I'd never want to be on his bad side. There's a guy who was one of his managers or general managers here a few years ago. He was a booster here. Gave good money and came to games but worked his ass off in one of Henson's dealerships. Everybody said he was the next Henson. Then one day he just disappeared. We never heard what happened. He just was gone."

"What do you mean *gone*?"

Wyndham rubbed his eyes with both hands and paused. "Henson fired him. Supposedly Henson owed him money for firing him, but I heard there was a big lawsuit and a lot of hell being raised. I don't know if he ever got his money or what, but I never saw the guy again. I don't know what happened to him."

"You remember the guy's name?"

"Ferragamo? Farrell?" Wyndham swiveled his chair, pulled an old game program from his bookcase, and flipped through it. "Here. Richie Ferraro. That's it."

He passed over the program, and Keane studied a five-year-old photo of Ferraro. It showed a man with an olive complexion, wavy dark hair, and no smile. A no-nonsense look. A man used to getting his way. Just like Henson.

Keane handed the program back.

Wyndham looked at the picture again, then put the book back on the shelf. "I'd forgotten all about him."

"And now?"

Wyndham shrugged. "I never saw him as a big money guy around here. Not like some others. If it was something he loved, well, like I said, Henson won. Ferraro's not around anymore."

"What else do you know about Henson?"

"He's got his own luxury box. They say he sits up there and spends as much time watching other games on TV and looking at his phone as he does watching our games."

Keane pictured that scene. He'd have to ask Henson about it when they met. But Henson wasn't the first visit.

21

IT TOOK KEANE less than fifteen minutes on Google and Lexis-Nexis to compile a passable dossier on Richard Ferraro.

He found a house in Georgia, a second property in North Carolina, and several cars registered in Ferraro's name. Four years before, though, the traces of Ferraro and Florida disappeared. It looked as if he'd gotten kicked to the Carolinas and worked his way back to a big city. Atlanta undoubtedly had more financial potential than Orlando.

Ferraro lived in Dunwoody, a fashionable and upper-middle-class Atlanta suburb. His 3,200-square-foot house, valued at more than $600,000. He also owned a house on Lake Lanier north of the city. Whatever had happened between Ferraro and Henson was now just a spot in Ferarro's rear-view mirror.

He dialed Rossi. "You ever heard of a guy named Richie Ferraro?"

"Do you ever say hello?" she asked.

"Hello." He waited a beat. "Have you?"

"Sounds like the name should be familiar, but I'm not sure why."

"He was an OU booster. Emphasis on *was*."

"Oh, him. Sure. Nice-looking, medium build, black hair. Dressed nice. There weren't that many big money donors back then. He was one of maybe ten or twelve that were always around."

"How old?"

"Now? Maybe early forties."

"You haven't seen him around lately, have you?"

"I haven't been around there as much as I used to."

"Yeah, but think. Have you seen him or heard from him? Or know anybody that has?"

She paused. "I don't know."

Keane kept reading the laptop screen in front of him, navigating more internet searches about Ferraro. "The answer is no. He got into a fight with his boss at the time, Don Henson, and nobody has seen or heard from him since. That's about four years ago. That seem strange to you?"

"Which part? The fight with Henson or the disappearing part?"

"The disappearing. Henson's a badass businessman. I've checked into him, and it probably won't surprise you to learn he takes no prisoners. And I mean none."

Rossi chuckled. "I know Henson. That's an accurate assessment. He's made a lot of money selling cars, and you don't do that without pushing people around. That's a cutthroat business."

"It's one thing to take no prisoners. It's another to make another person disappear."

"Richie Ferraro . . . he just vanished?"

"Just from around here. He's not dead."

She took her time replying. "That's something, at least."

KEANE MADE ANOTHER run at Sean's spreadsheets. Sean was almost certainly betting on football games, and these documents told him Sean was taking action from others. That was the trouble. There were *a lot* of others. The amount of money coming into his bank account from a mystery PayPal account wasn't regular, just on an as-needed basis. Either someone had transferred money on demand or else Sean moved the money to himself.

Forensic accounting was never his strength, but he forced himself to concentrate. One of the middle columns was an exact percentage of the wager. He realized while scanning the two columns, he was right: five percent. He compared the five percent to another column. Numbers in the other column varied, either five percent or zero.

That made sense. Losing bettors never pay a percentage. Winning bettors almost always do.

Sean made five percent off every winning wager. Keane did a few quick calculations: Three hundred bets every football weekend. Worst case for Sean, half were winners. That would mean he kept five percent of half his take from a hundred and fifty people. He'd make several hundred dollars a weekend, not enough to fill up his PayPal account. Then again, that all depended on how much he bet himself and whether he'd been winning.

He sifted through all the spreadsheets and confirmed the ratios. Why were all the spreadsheets separated? Why not keep everything together?

He pulled up Sean's contacts list and found the number he wanted. He called it and left a brief message. Tiffany called back two minutes later.

"If I were a football player and a friend of Sean's, and I were hungry, where would I go?" he asked.

FOR THE FIRST hour, Keane planted himself at the bar at Hardy's Wings & Things. "Things" apparently referred less to burgers and fries and more to waitresses with tight shorts and tighter tank tops. The assembled restaurant staff was a lineup of curvaceous girls-next-door. Throw in a menu loaded with cheap beer by the pitcher, and it wasn't hard to see why Tiffany said it was popular with males near campus.

He positioned himself to face the front door and nursed a bottle of beer before ordering food. Even if he guessed right, there was no telling how long he'd have to wait.

The answer was two hours. Johnnie Jones and Darrell Dubrow arrived with two friends—teammates, he presumed—and sat behind him. Three of the four were black and only one of the four could be classified as big.

Keane recognized Jones and Dubrow only because Q had told him they were friendly with Sean and because he'd studied their photos in the OU media guide.

"You ready to clear out?" asked his waitress, a petite brunette who leaned over his table to write on a napkin each time she stopped by. The cleavage show-off routine, he noticed, was a staple of every waitress there.

"Can I get an iced tea to go? Half sweet tea and half unsweet. Then the check," he said, sliding a credit card across the bar to her.

He pretended to watch a football game on one of the many overhead TVs while dialing into the conversation of the new foursome behind him. The waitress returned with his receipt and another lean.

"Thanks. I'm going to sit for a little bit and watch the game. If you need the table, tell me. Otherwise, I'll take my time."

She thanked him and fetched beers for her new table.

He waited them out and ordered more tea and wings to keep his waitress at bay. After two hours and six orders of their own wings, the foursome paid cash and walked out together and split into two groups. He followed Johnnie and Darrell.

They led him to a neighborhood mixed with townhouses, duplexes, and single-family homes behind the university, and pulled into a driveway in front of a house. He drove past them to the next street, made a right turn, and quickly parked against the curb. He gave the two players two minutes to get inside the house and get comfortable.

A streetlamp lit up Darrell's car and a small truck in the driveway. Keane noted one similarity as he walked past them. Both had rear decals for Henson Autos. He filed that away and knocked on the front door. Darrell answered, not quickly, and wore a curious look on his face.

"Yeah?" he asked.

"I'm a friend of Sean's dad."

It took four or five seconds for the news to dawn on Darrell. "Yeah, yeah," he said finally. "What can I do for you?"

"Can I come in?"

"Sure."

He walked into a great room defined by a big-screen television that seemed to be playing war games. Two backpacks lay on the floor against the wall by the front door. Except for the backpacks, the room was picked up. The apartment smelled . . . like flowers? The carpet showed tracks that it was freshly vacuumed. On the far side of the room in the adjacent kitchen, everything was put away. It was as if the kitchen were a model, not for use.

Johnnie sat on an overstuffed brown couch with a game controller in both hands. He paid no attention to his roommate or the visitor, kept his attention focused on the TV screen. Judging by the quality, it was high-def and high-end.

Darrell started, "Johnnie this is—"

"Conrad Keane." He stuck his hand out.

"Yeah, so?" Johnnie said, his eyes never leaving the TV.

"He's tight with Sean's dad," Darrell said.

"Sean's dad," Johnnie repeated with no emotion. And then it registered. "Oh, shit." He tossed the controller beside him and jumped to his feet. He looked at Keane, moved toward him as recognition crept in. Grabbed Keane's hand and shook it. "Yeah, yeah, yeah. How you doing?"

"I'm doing okay, considering," Keane said. "Up here taking care of Sean's things."

"Yeah, yeah. Hey, sit down."

Johnnie walked back to the spot where he had been playing his war game and sat again. Keane approached from the other side of the couch and sat halfway down. Close enough to Johnnie to read his face, far enough away that Darrell had to find another place to sit. He picked a brown recliner, one that matched the sofa, to the side of a walnut-colored coffee table.

The video game roared in the background. Whomever Johnnie was fighting before he walked in sounded like that person was now winning. Almost on cue, Johnnie reached over to the controller and hit a button. The game disappeared in favor of a black screen.

Johnnie's eyes narrowed as he took in Keane. Black shirt. Khaki pants. Short, neat hair.

"I've seen you," Johnnie said, leaning back and pointing at Keane. "You were at Wings & Things."

Keane nodded.

"You spying on us? Following us?" He straightened his posture.

"I need a few answers. I think you may have them."

"Man, only thing we know is football. That's it," Darrell said.

"Football and more football," Johnnie said.

Keane responded, "That's it, huh? Just football? I think you know more than that. What about what happened the night Sean died? I'm sure whatever you know, you've told the police." He paused. "I want to know what you didn't tell the police."

"Like what?" Darrell asked.

"Like what was going on," Keane said.

"Wasn't nothing going on."

"No offense, but I don't believe you."

"Why's that?"

"Because Sean's closest friends on the team were you two." He turned and looked at Darrell. "And I know he was into some shit."

The roommates looked at each other. Keane could tell what they were thinking: *Where the hell is this going?*

"What did Tally Hance want with Sean?" Keane asked.

Darrell said, "Who knows, man? Ain't nobody know that. Ain't nobody gonna know that."

"C'mon, now, you don't believe that."

"What's done is done, man. What's done is done."

Keane looked at Johnnie. "What about you? What do you say?"

Johnnie looked at Darrell for an answer, and Darrell shook his head.

"I have no idea," Johnnie said.

"You know what I think?" Keane said. "I think Tally was sending a message and it all went wrong.

And I think Sean was smart, but maybe not as smart as he figured, and got caught up with the wrong people."

"Sean wasn't caught up in nothing," Darrell said.

"Nothing," Johnnie repeated.

Keane laughed. "How the hell aren't you guys dead? You're like the Apple Dumpling Gang."

"Who?" Johnnie asked.

"What the hell are you talking about, old man?" Darrell spewed, and stepped forward.

Keane stepped quicker, three steps to Darrell's two and drove the heel of his hand under Darrell's chin. Hard enough to chatter his teeth and get his attention. Not quite hard enough to break his jaw.

Darrell collapsed backward and fell on his back.

"Hey!" Johnnie moved toward his roommate.

Keane pulled him forward and hooked the boy's right foot with his own. Johnnie's momentum carried him forward to the floor, where he landed next to Darrell.

"What the fuck?" Darrell said as he collected himself.

Keane said, "This isn't a game, son. What Sean was doing—what you were all doing—it wasn't for fun."

"We weren't doing shit," Darrell responded.

"In case you don't know it, you're in over your head. Pretty soon, a lot of shit is going to rain down. And it's not going to be pretty. Are you ready for that?"

"We haven't done anything wrong."

Keane glared at him for a moment and turned to Johnnie. "That your stance, too?"

Johnnie said nothing.

"Well," Keane said, "that's unfortunate. Because right now the police don't know about a big bank account and an online gambling habit. Not right now they don't. But they're going to know. I'd guess by tomorrow afternoon you'll be telling them everything you know. I don't think it'll be as cozy as this is right here. In fact, I think it'll be a little cold-blooded. I don't imagine you'll be playing football again anytime soon. Certainly not for good old Orlando U."

"That ain't right," Johnnie said. "That ain't right, man."

"There's a lot about this that ain't right," Keane said.

Darrell pulled himself to his feet and backed up. Kept his distance from Keane. "This is bullshit."

"What's bullshit is you guys thinking that throwing games is nothing. That's not nothing."

Darrell huffed. "We did what we were told."

DARRELL AND JOHNNIE wore down as they sobered up.

"Where'd all the money come from?" Keane asked. "All the money Sean spent on clothes, on the apartment? Where'd that come from? And he was driving an SUV? Where'd that come from?"

Darrell shrugged. "Sean never said. We all thought it might be his dad, but then, well, we met his dad. After that, we weren't sure."

"So what's your guess?"

"Somebody liked him. Don't know who."

"Do you know a booster by the name of Richie Ferraro?"

The two shook their heads.

"He might not be a booster now, but he used to be. Maybe when you first got here."

No reaction but no hesitation, either. They weren't lying. They didn't know the man.

"OK, then, who took care of you two?"

"You don't even want to go there," Darrell said

"Son, if I didn't want to go there, I wouldn't be here."

"It's different for everybody."

The room got silent.

"And?" Keane asked.

"There's a guy who takes care of a few of us, but there's more than one," Darrell said.

"Coaches or boosters?"

"Boosters."

"Who takes care of you?"

Darrell looked at Johnnie. It was Johnnie's turn to shrug.

"Tally's our guy," Darrell said. "Was our guy."

Johnnie added, "He always came around and took care of us."

"Where'd he get the money?" Keane asked.

"Don't know," Johnnie said. "He just always had it. It was always cash. I always thought he got it at the club."

He wanted to educate the players about the difference between strip-club money and real affluence. He'd considered the possibility that Tally had a job other than bouncer. That he was a possible drug dealer. Or that he ran errands or did favors for whoever did own the club. Cash favors. Either explanation was plausible. His instincts told him otherwise.

"You guys liked Tally, didn't you?"

Both players nodded. "Felt sorry for him, too," Johnnie said.

"Why?"

"He was one of those guys with a lot of big ideas but, you know, they never panned out. He never really did anything about them. He always said he wanted to open up a barbecue place, that he was saving up for that. But he had a lot of other ideas, too. He always talked about how a smart person could make a lot of money by organizing the best players in the country to sue the NCAA."

"Sue for what?"

"Royalties from jersey sales, posters, things with their number or picture on it."

"What, he was trying to pull together a class-action? Round these guys up?"

"It was all talk," Johnnie said. "It was just one of his ideas. He wasn't no attorney."

Keane pressed on. He looked Johnnie in the eye. "Tell me about throwing games."

22

KEANE ANSWERED ROSSI'S knock and caught the
scent of lilac as she walked into his hastily tidied
hotel room. He approved of her casual attire:
fashionable blue jeans, button-up cotton blouse,
short boots, and long earrings.

She said, "This is how you land all your women,
isn't it? Go on the road, work a case, call a meeting
in your room. I'm sure it's a winner."

"I don't travel that much," he said.

"So it's an unrefined strategy."

"That's fair."

She dropped into an overstuffed chair. He took
the couch and began sorting through a hundred-
page notepad that was a third filled. The pad
contained thoughts, projections, tidbits, and
factoids of evidence and possible evidence. Most of
it focused on Sean, the football program, and
money flow. His handwritten notes never saw a
court file. Intentionally, they were wildly
speculative, preventing him from locking onto one
crime theory too fast.

His investigative process wasn't the most
efficient, but it worked. By leaving all possibilities
on the table, he could find indisputable
connections.

"Everything that's going on is about gambling, about money," he said. "Sean was involved, Hance was involved, and other players are involved."

"You don't know that."

"I know part of it. They were betting on football games and who knows what else, and they were in way over their heads."

"How do you know?"

"Players talk. Sometimes they don't know when to shut up."

"You're interviewing players?

"I talked to Sean's friends." He told her about the sports bar and his intense discussion with Dubrow and Jones. He left out the visit to their house. "They were paid to make certain plays. Or possibly not make plays."

"Who paid them?" she asked.

"They wouldn't say. I reminded them they'd eventually have to talk about it, but they wouldn't budge. I think they're afraid."

"How many other players?"

"A handful. They weren't sure how many of the others knew about them, but they were sure they didn't know about everybody. It sounds like all the players who were picked were given their assignments individually."

"How did they make sure?"

He shrugged. "A fumbled handoff here, a missed tackle there. A penalty in a crucial situation."

Her eyes grew wide and she shook her head. "This isn't a frat-house parlay-card scheme. You're describing a scandal that could ruin the university. People get fired over stuff like this. Important people."

"Not my problem."

"If this is all true, I can't believe Duke Childress knew about it. He'd never go along with a scheme like this."

He smiled at her. "Never underestimate the will of a coach to win at any cost. Even the pure ones can't help themselves."

"You don't know him."

He studied her face. "Fine. Educate me."

"He's been the coach here for a long time. My first couple years on the force—when I was a beat cop in Leesburg—I worked security at the stadium. The first year, I worked the stands, handled the drunks. You're assigned to keep your eyes open and make sure people behave. The other years, I was on the field. When you're there, your primary responsibility is the safety of the players, coaches, support staff, and referees. Most of the time all you have to worry about is crowd control after a game, especially if there's a last-second play or if there's a big upset and OU wins."

He nodded. "Fans try to rush the field."

"Yup. And that can get hairy. But at a typical game, you spend most of the day enjoying the game and keeping your eyes open for any sort of weirdness. For some reasons I was always on the OU sideline, so I just paid attention to the players and coaches. I watched Childress a lot."

"Why would you do that?"

Rossi shrugged. "Everybody said he was a good coach. His teams were good. They won a lot of games. I guess I . . . wondered how he managed it all. I watched what he did, how he related to his players, his coaches. Fans."

"How did he handle it?"

"He was pretty controlled," she said. "He'd lose his temper, but he'd never rant. He never let a bad call or a dumb mistake ruin the day. I never heard any of the players complain about him. A few of them seemed to fear him, but they all respected him. That was actually impressive."

Keane nodded. He'd been around enough football coaches to know the type. He thought back to his half hour in Childress's office. The best coaches were no different from the best teachers or the best CEOs: they led by demanding the best of everyone and by ensuring that success got rewarded. He didn't know if Childress was a leader or just a guy who knew how the game of big-time football was really played. He could be both.

"I think he's probably like every other coach: a control freak," Keane said. "Besides, I don't think he's the main guy here. Don't get me wrong. I wouldn't be shocked if coaches were paying players. I would be shocked if they had anything to do with gambling."

She nodded but betrayed no thoughts to one side or the other.

"There is one thing. This is going to be harder without Hance," he said.

She broke her blank expression with a furrow. "Hance was tight with the school president."

"You're kidding. How?"

She broad-brushed through their interview with Simpson, including the details that the president liked gentlemen's clubs and admitted that Hance steered him out of a potentially damning news story.

"Jesus. He didn't confess to lighting the fire, did he? Or the shooting?"

He added notes about Simpson to his pad, drawing arrows from his name to Hance and from Hance to players.

Rossi said, "We didn't tell him about the shooting. We stuck with 'suspicious circumstances.' All he knows is that there was a fire."

He absorbed that information and went through his notes. His profile of the president was more scant than it should be. There was no criminal background and no finely detailed personal background. He culled basic biographical information from OU's website. There were enough newspaper references to Simpson as a former state-wide lobbyist to give Keane an idea of who this man was.

The nagging question to him was: Why? Why would a lobbyist, by all accounts successful and rich, want to trade down for a university president's job? As much of a grind as legislative lobbying could be, the red tape and politics of university life were unending and mind-numbing. The salary for a major university president was solid, seven figures for people who knew how to cozy up to donors, get capital projects off the ground, and grow the school. But somebody like Simpson could make tens of millions by investing in a shady deal or two. And the Florida Legislature churned out shady deals as consistently as the tides moved in and out.

Rossi's interview with the president cast new light. Simpson was smart. Clearly confident. Detectives showed up at his office and accused him of hiding pertinent details to their case and of being close to a murderer. Not only did he say yes, he further tightened up the relationship. As if he didn't care. Or as if he knew the police couldn't prove anything substantial. Or, quite possibly, as if he knew he did nothing wrong.

He opened two beers and set one in front of her. Another whiff of lilac.

"Thanks." She took a sip and looked at her own notes.

He sat back and stared at the ceiling. Three black football players and a white one hanging out together all the time. Not the strangest collection, for sure, especially on any athletic team. Was there a second puzzle here beyond teammates that made this foursome a bond?

"What?" Rossi asked, interrupting his thoughts.

"I think it's possible there are multiple things going on here."

"Yeah, multiple dead people."

"Maybe more than multiple crimes. Maybe multiple conspiracies."

Again she gave him a poker face.

He said, "Wonder what the chances are Coach Childress is running one game and the president is running another." He let that hang out there. It didn't sound so dumb after all. "Is it possible the coach and the president don't know what the other is doing? I guess what I'm asking is, are these guys close? Would they be in bed together? You've been around this program. You know these guys. Possible?"

"I don't think I'd go that far. In fact, it's almost a miracle Childress is still coaching here. Three years ago, the team was losing, and there didn't seem to be any hope he could turn things around. Simpson was fairly new, a couple years into the job, but he stood up to the boosters who wanted the coach fired. The next year, the team got better. Now this is one of the best seasons in the school's history."

"But are the president and coach tight? Do they finish each other's sentences? Do they argue? Do they argue in public? Or do they agree to disagree? Does the president defend the coach? The politics are important."

Rossi mulled that over. "They're close because they have to be close. I don't think they're drinking buddies."

"Two agendas?"

She shrugged. "With Teddy Simpson, there's always an agenda. These guys are from different walks of life. One guy's a coach through and through. The other guy's a big-time politician. Well, former lobbyist." She paused again. "Where's this coming from?"

"We're missing some pieces. We've got a bunch of small ones, and they don't seem to go together."

"Some don't fit and others don't belong. Once we know what the full picture looks like, they'll all make sense. You know how this works."

He gave her a sarcastic grimace. "I've done it once or twice. Which is how I know we have the right pieces and they don't add up to the full picture as we see it. That means the picture's different."

"Philosophy question: How do you know what you don't know?"

"Obviously I can't. But I can acknowledge what I don't know. And for sure I don't know the full picture. And you don't, either." He stared at her as she measured his reasoning. She reached for her beer and tipped it back.

He said, "Do you know the single biggest reason why judges and juries and defense attorneys kick cases to the curb? The biggest reason why the Orlando Police Department and the FBI both fail to convict people when we have a good case?"

"Proof," she said.

He shook his head. "Not proof. Suspects. We don't collect enough of them. We don't eliminate enough of them."

"I do."

"You know how every time there's a high-profile case, guys like my boss and your boss go crazy because the media convicts the primary suspect right after the arrest? You get that here, right, from the talking heads?" He was sure Orlando's TV anchors and reporters were the same as everywhere else, full of crap and not facts.

"We're guilty of the same thing they are. I mean, we don't convict these people in the public eye, but we damn sure help. The media feeds the beast, and we feed the media. It's gotten to the point that every law-enforcement agency in the country, even the FBI, focuses too much on the guy we've got and not nearly enough on the ones we don't. We arrest, we lock in, and we build around that one person or group. And when we build the case, we wall ourselves in with it. And we can't see out. Most of the time, there's a good reason not to see out. Because we've got the right guy."

Rossi arched her eyebrows and let him continue.

"But you know what? Sometimes we have the right guy, and sometimes we don't. When we don't we lose. Every now and then, we arrest the right guy and we still lose. Why? Because we didn't spend enough time trying to prove ourselves wrong. After 9/11, that changed because we all got our budgets juiced up. But before that, and again now, we're dealing with cuts. You try to make every investigation efficient, and to do that, you make sacrifices. You don't spend a lot of time clearing people you don't think you need to clear in the first place. Because you've already got an A-1 suspect."

She drank from her beer and shook her head. "You're arguing against the way everybody in law enforcement builds a case. The driving motivation is always, 'Go find who did it.' Not 'Go find who didn't do it and see who's left.'"

"Defense attorneys always tell a jury that someone else could have committed the crime," he said. "They're not always wrong. Our process is flawed because we don't always know all the facts, but there's also a human flaw. We come to a decision, we come to a belief, and we think we're right. And guess what? We're not always right."

"We're right a lot," she said. "The ones we lose, we lose because we don't have enough evidence. We have the dope but not the dealer. Or maybe not enough of the dealer's connections. Or we have a dead body but not a gun. And without a gun, you can't trace the ownership, the bullets, any DNA. We've all had cases where nobody talks. Gang-related cases, good luck. Witnesses show up in court and so do all the gang members. All of a sudden, witnesses can't remember anything. That's not a TV drama. That's reality."

"I'm not saying they should all be airtight. Just tighter. The Patriot Act gives us a lot of latitude, but we can't make it a crutch." He flipped through his notes, re-reading things he'd written over the past ten days. Most of the facts were committed to memory. He flipped back to the beginning and refocused only on notes next to which he'd added a larger question mark. He stopped flipping and studied one question-marked item in particular. He read it. Read it again.

"The players told me Tally gave them money, hundreds every month," he said. "Where'd it come from? You say the coach wouldn't be involved. So who?"

"Maybe he was the one paying for them to throw games and winning money off them."

"I don't see a strip-club bouncer as the brains of this operation. There's another hand here."

"A booster?"

"Probably plural. These guys are like fraternity brothers. They can't do anything alone."

He wrote "booster" in the pad and then a large question mark.

The sudden progression silenced both of them. He pondered what a multiple-person scenario would mean. Systemic corruption. Rogue boosters. Plus either an uncaring or in-the-dark president and football coach. It was almost unfathomable. Almost.

"There could be a lot of moving parts here," he said. "One or two or more boosters throwing money around. Maybe the coach. We're not sure where the president fits in. Plus Hance and whoever killed him. God knows who else out there."

"Big leap."

"The money's bigger than it should be. I assume you've seen Sean's bank account?"

She nodded. "A couple of big deposits. We assumed from the father, but now you say no."

"Pull the deposit slips. It wasn't Q. Guaranteed."

"How can you be so sure?"

"I have his computer."

Her eyes narrowed. "We have his computer. Last time I checked."

"You have one of his computers. Turns out he had two of them."

"Where the hell did you . . ."

"One of Sean's friends had it."

"We talked to his friends."

Keane shrugged. "What can I say?"

Rossi slammed her beer back on the table and stood up. "I want it. Right fucking now."

"C'mon. You said it yourself. You're done with the case. You're working on Hance."

She jabbed a finger at him. "Right. Now."

He'd already evaluated the hard drive and copied its contents. He had what he needed. And he realized he had no choice. He disappeared around the corner and returned with the MacBook.

She grabbed the laptop, threw the power cord in her purse, and headed for the door. He followed her.

"I was going to tell you—"

"When, after the body count went up again?"

"Hey, that's not—"

She dropped her purse at the door, spun on her left foot, and drove a hard, straight right directly below his ribcage. It knocked the air out of him. His knees buckled slightly and he doubled over in both pain and breathlessness. He fell to the floor and felt the hotel door hit the back of his head.

"Stop interfering in this case, right now," she said. "No more interviews, no more investigating. Stay out of it. Or you won't like our next visit."

He closed his eyes and heard a car start and make its tires squeal as it sped away.

23

KEANE FLEW TO San José, Costa Rica, and took a cab to Banco Publica. An assistant manager named Frederico escorted him to a non-descript side office and punctuated a pleasant look with clasped hands in front of him. "How can I help you today, sir?"

He told Frederico his needs.

"Very well, sir. Please wait." Frederico bowed and left him alone. He returned with the most well-dressed man Keane had ever met. Jose-Filipe de Jesus wore a tan suit with a pressed white shirt and gold cuff links, and a royal blue tie with a matching pocket square. When Jose-Filipe sat and crossed his legs, Keane noted that the man's socks were a close match to his tie, and his darker caramel shoes complemented everything else. The ensemble mixed perfectly with his light brown skin tone and dark brown hair that was closely cropped and loosely parted to one side.

"Frederico has explained you have a special request," Jose-Filipe said.

"I didn't realize it was that special, but I suppose it is," Keane said, and he explained the details.

"I think we can help you today. Let me get paperwork started."

Rossi WORKED THROUGH the computer and realized Keane had gotten it right. His brother was a college student, football player, boyfriend, a gambler, and probably a bookie.

The laptop was evidence he had bet on college and NFL football games. That he played poker online for money. That he won. A lot.

He could have financed most of his leisurely college-boy lifestyle, but she doubted he could have funded all of it. Not all the clothes, all the video games, the laptops, the furniture and almost certainly not the car. She'd seen all the paperwork on Sean's SUV—Henson Chevrolet had been more than happy to comply with a subpoena—and already knew that it'd been paid for up front and not financed. There was no discussion of how a college student with little family support had the cash up front to pay for such a car. The detectives were still waiting on Riggins's bank records, but if they were like those of most college students, financing a few nights of pizza a week was a stretch. Then again, very little they dug up about Riggins fit into the college-student stereotype.

Rossi had never investigated bingo, dice, lottery fraud, or sports betting. Her two years in vice were spent mostly on drugs and prostitution, staples of communities everywhere. No one cared about gambling. She'd heard the stories of violence and Vegas, and she'd seen the movie *Casino*. Were Riggins and Hance caught up in circumstances that crazy?

The number of spreadsheets and their cryptic nature bothered her. There were nineteen of them, all formatted similarly, but there were only numbers, with one column of two letters. *Initials,* she thought. *A lot of them.* Beyond the formatting, not one of the sheets looked like another. Except for the fact they were made up of long columns of numbers and that they made little sense to her.

Using a landscape setting, she printed all of them. She taped the pages together, top to bottom, so she could examine each document in its entirety. She then taped each of the longer sheets, side by side, to the far office wall.

Each spreadsheet had an almost identical pattern of numbers in the first column. The numbers started at eight and were two or three digits. Then they started with nine, and they were again only two or three digits long. Then they started with one. *Or was that ten? Yes, a one and a zero: ten.* Following that came a series of numbers beginning with eleven, and then a series starting with twelve. *Dates.* From August, the eighth month of the year, to December, the twelfth month of the year. She looked at a desk calendar and realized the numbers that made up months and days mostly matched up to the dates of fall Saturdays and Sundays, prime betting days for college and pro football. There were a smattering of other dates mixed in, which made sense. Schools played games on Tuesdays, Wednesdays, Thursdays, and Fridays to obtain prime-time TV coverage.

Got you.

She needed more. Eventually she'd crack all of the sophisticated coding, but without a key and without the author of the spreadsheets alive, she'd never be able to authenticate them. A prosecutor could introduce them as evidence, but after that, it was all supposition. The person who created them—Riggins, she assumed—was careful not to name people or teams. Hell, there wasn't even a dollar sign. A good defense attorney could argue this was nothing but intricate data accumulated for a research paper.

178 | David Ryan

The only money she had was the unusually large amount in Riggins's bank account. And it didn't match the numbers on the spreadsheets. Either Riggins had lost almost as much as he'd won or else he hadn't been much of a bookie and wagered away too much of his profit. Or else he had another bank account or multiple accounts. They'd done a search for any accounts and had come up empty.

She racked her brain and then cursed at herself. Where was the money?

On her laptop she pulled up two form letters and pecked away until she had subpoena requests for Google and PayPal. She went back to the sheets on the wall and again marveled at the number of entries and the complexity of them. *There had to be a mentor. Or a boss.*

She wrote the word *leverage.* They had it now with Duke Childress and Teddy Simpson. OU would never want the spreadsheets to get out. And she and Thomas could facilitate that secrecy. Or else they could stick a fork into the university by making sure this story led the evening news.

A line from a Harrison Ford movie hit her: "You've got a chip in the big game." They had a chip, all right. Not a bad day.

24

FOR THE SECOND time in two weeks, Rossi beat Thomas to work. "You do want to get promoted," he said when he walked in, never breaking stride en route to the coffee machine.

She looked up from her spiral notepad. "Couldn't sleep. Got something."

Thomas waited until he'd cream-and-sugared his coffee to answer. "What's new?"

She filled him in on the laptop but lied and said Keane had called her to turn it in as soon as he'd gotten it from one of Riggins's friends.

"You've looked through it? Is Hance's name anywhere in there?" He tilted his head at the laptop.

"Just by initials. I think."

"I don't have anything that has Hance making book out of the club," he said. "Unless you do."

"Not Hance. It was Riggins. I don't know how deep he was in, but he was in deep. And not a lot of debt. He was winning. Football, basketball, poker, blackjack. He was his own bookie. He did everything on the internet."

Thomas sat down and looked surprised. "Football and basketball? He won on those?"

"Not as much on basketball as football."

"Even with the point spreads? Did you compare the spreads to the results?"

She nodded. "He won. He won more on college football than anything."

"Don't tell me."

"Yeah, he did."

"For or against?"

"Both."

"Wow." He sipped his coffee. "Who knew about it?"

"That's the question. And who else was doing it? If anyone at the school knew, they didn't volunteer the information. I doubt they're doing any kind of investigation."

"Hell no," he said. "That'd be the end of the world for them. They'd launch a gambling investigation, especially one that's got teeth. . . . Hell, everybody loses their job."

"Yeah, well . . ."

"Look, if Riggins was betting against his own team—"

"Which he was . . ."

"Then somebody else was doing the same thing. There's never just one."

"I think it's a lot bigger than just players."

"Who else? The coaches?"

"Maybe. Or another person connected to the team."

"Huh. What kind of records do you have? You have a sense for how long this was going on?"

"Looks like two years. This year and last year."

"And no names?"

"Just initials."

"You match any of them up?"

She nodded.

"Well?" he asked.

"I'm thinking the president."

Thomas absorbed that theory. She already had. A university president betting on games. It would be a national scandal, one that would leave scars for a generation. A dirty football program would be the least of the school's worries. OU could face challenges to its academic accreditation, its core. It would at least face a barrage of unflattering media.

"What, the kid was throwing games for the president?" Thomas asked. "And Hance was the enforcer for the president? And that's the connection? Hance to Sean Riggins?"

"That's most of it. It wasn't just the president. I think it was more like a club. Like one of those old-lady investment clubs. I think the president and his pals were all betting on games. And I think some of the players were helping them. Including Sean Riggins."

Thomas shook his head and took it in. "You got information on Simpson and his boys in there? Because if you do, that's the motherlode."

"I don't know." She laid out what she had. Spreadsheets of Sean Riggins's action. Statements from accounts they hadn't seen, accounts with an offshore company called Blindside.com. It was an international gaming site for sports, blackjack, poker, and more. All the games Sean Riggins liked.

A few minutes later, she dug up notes from the bottom of a nondescript file that intrigued her. They were just a few lines of text that included the initials "TS" and "DH" and sat under a heading of GAMERS.

TS. Teddy Simpson. DH. Don Henson. Or David Hance. TH. Tally Hance. Not concrete. She had to admit the initials could stand for a lot of people. But not bad guesses.

"Speculation. A bunch of maybes," Thomas said.

A second set came under the heading POSSIBLES? and had five sets of initials. The third set, with the heading of ??, was the longest. There were ten sets of initials, but none stood out to her. The heading told her Riggins might have known what he was involved in but not who.

She studied the lists again but nothing in her brain broke loose. She picked up her desk phone. This time, she wanted the department's caller ID to show up on the other end. She offered a warm hello to the woman's voice on the other end. The two of them rarely talked to each other these days, but during her time participating in game-day security detail, she'd gotten to know several other sideline dwellers. One was a female academic tutor for the football program. "I'm wondering if you would have any game-day football programs from one of the recent home games."

She wrote down another phone number as she listened. "I owe you one. Thanks."

She hung up and dialed again. She introduced herself to an unfamiliar voice, also a woman's, and name-dropped her acquaintance. Then she repeated her query for the programs. "I just need copies of a few pages," she said, and she gave out her email address.

The results hit her inbox fifteen minutes later. She printed out an attachment and stapled together five pages. The official list of OU's boosters was extensive but official, names the school had printed in every football game program that season. Every major university kept similar lists, and every school proudly published it as often as possible. Undoubtedly there were a few names missing, for not every donor wishes his friends and family to know where personal money has gone. But among the well-heeled, broadcasting one's charitable giving is routine. Part of the pedigree.

She guessed the list held at least five thousand names.

The list was categorized by money with quaint names such as Lightning Level, Thunder Level and Coach's Level. Donor tiers were segregated by how much money each person or company gave to the OU football program the year before. Rossi counted eight levels of giving, from students who donated $25 all the way to foundations and corporate sponsors who delivered upward of $100,000.

At the top was the Presidential Level, reserved for the $100,000 donors. Including corporations, several of which she recognized as being owned by prominent OU alums, she counted forty-two names in the first group. At least $4.2 million to the program right there. Lot of money flowing in. If these were people who could buy football players, they had big bucks.

She allowed herself a fleeting thought about what Teddy Simpson, Duke Childress, and others at OU might have had to promise donors in exchange for their money. Above and beyond the usual perks, that is. She found Simpson's name and circled it. *He donated to his own club. How nice.* Don Henson's name wasn't there. Henson Automotive Group was. She circled it. Two down.

Using the initials from the spreadsheets, she worked her way through about half of the large list. She opted on her first search to disregard the four lowest categories of givers. That eliminated anyone who gave less than $5,000 to the football program. There was one exception. David Hance. He was there, a Storm Level giver. Which meant he donated between $250 and $500. Not exactly a rainmaker, but here Hance was a black-and-white connection.

When she was done, she had nearly three dozen names or companies circled. Too many. If that many people were involved, whatever was going on never would have stayed a secret.

Rossi called the OU alumni office and asked for Sara. She had taken care of a recent speeding ticket in exchange for a small amount of surreptitious assistance. Gradually they narrowed the list to a dozen and then to nine because three businesses were owned by people already on the list.

All nine had made tax-deductible contributions to OU athletics. Four she considered household names. The other five included two local bankers, an heir to a pharmacy fortune, a well-known insurance agent, and a lottery winner who used to be a high-school science teacher. The ex-teacher was the only woman of the group.

She discounted the ex-teacher immediately. The only women of influence she saw around the football team during her years working security were members of the school's athletic board, its board of trustees, and wives or girlfriends of coaches and donors. The teacher, though a major benefactor since hitting her six numbers, fit into none of those categories. They'd look at her, but she doubted it would amount to anything.

She picked up the phone and redialed the alumni office.

"Something else?" her friend answered.

"One more thing. I need addresses," she said, and read off the names.

25

THE FLIGHT FROM San José to Atlanta was uneventful, and Keane was grateful for four hours to nap and think. He worked through the known facts, but they didn't tell a full story. Sean's gambling still made no sense. He made a note to track down Johnnie and Darrell again. But first things first.

Once through Customs, he picked up an airport rental car and drove northeast through the damp, gray chill. GPS took him to Dunwoody, and then to a gleaming, three-story, mirrored-glass building, site of Southern Estates Development Corporation.

Within two minutes of getting off the elevator on the third floor and identifying himself to an executive secretary as an FBI agent, he sat in an overstuffed chair in Richie Ferraro's office. The former OU donor looked like he had been pulled from a J. Crew catalogue, although the wavy, dark hair from the photo in the game program the equipment manager found for him was less accurate. Gray hair had started in at his temples, framing deep-set brown eyes and strong brow line. A prominent nose completed a fit, angular appearance that presented an aura of gravitas.

Ferraro didn't look like a man who could get run out of town by anyone. And then he spoke, revealing a soft, almost squeaky voice that belied his presence. "I hope I haven't done anything wrong. And if I have, I promise you I have no idea what it is."

"I'm not aware of anything," Keane said. "I'm here about Don Henson."

"It's too bad you didn't call ahead. That's not a subject I talk about."

"Mr. Ferraro, you're aware of the OU football player who died recently?"

Ferraro frowned. "The news said it was a bar fight. What's Henson got to do with that?"

"We don't know if he does. Which is why I'm here. I can assure you that anything you can tell us won't go any further. We're hammering out a few details and that's about it. You're not central to our investigation."

"And yet you are here."

He stared at the man across from him. A large oil painting hung behind Ferraro, telling visitors about expensive tastes. Despite ample wall and desk space, he displayed no personal mementos or photos. "What were the circumstances of you leaving Orlando?"

"I needed a job. When I found one, I left."

"You needed a job because you were removed from your job, isn't that right? And you didn't have the option of even staying in Orlando. You were told your job was done and you were not only out but gone."

"That's a misrepresentation of the truth."

Always a dance. "What did you do to get yourself into so much hot water?" he asked. "What could you have done that touched such a nerve with Henson?"

Ferraro looked to his left and stared out of a glass window three stories up. After a moment, he looked back at the FBI agent. "If you must know, I stole his thunder." He paused again. "Do you know Don? Have you met him, talked to him? You know what he's about?"

"I haven't had the pleasure," Keane said. "Soon."

Ferraro flashed a knowing grin. "You're in for a treat. You'll see first thing that Don likes being the center of attention. Things happen because of him, if you know what I mean. He's the straw that stirs the drink. Even if he's not, he is. He can't stand the thought of not getting the credit for a great idea or a successful venture. You know the type. These are guys that always have to win. It's like he never learned how to lose."

"Such as?"

"Such as you name it. If he wants to buy new jerseys for the football team and somebody else somehow beats him to the punch, well, let's just say he'll make sure his donation is credited for the jerseys and the other donation goes to something else, whatever Don doesn't care about. If he wants to be the guy, he's the guy. That's the way it works in his world."

"What did you do to get fired?"

"I crossed his line."

"How'd you do that?"

"He found out I gave more money than he did one year."

"Come again?"

"You heard me. We were both pretty big donors, and the way it works is, every year you give at least the same amount you gave the year before. That's part of the deal. One year the deadline for contributions is coming and I made mine. Paid for my tickets, my skybox, a couple other commitments. And I realized I'd had a pretty good past couple years and had a lot more money floating around. I asked around about what little bit extra I could do, and I heard about how they needed a few improvements to the weight room. I kicked in some money for that, and the next thing I knew, they were talking about naming the weight room after me. I had no idea."

"And Henson didn't like it."

"He went apeshit. I mean, throwing-stuff-around-the-office crazy. Saying, 'No one under me is going to give more than me,' and, 'No one's going to embarrass me like that.' It was unbelievable."

"Just like that?"

"Just like that. I told him I didn't ask for any naming rights and frankly didn't care. In his mind, I'd gone behind his back and been disloyal. Like I said, it's all about him. But that's not what really drove that whole situation."

"What was?"

"I had more disposable money than he did. I mean, he was worth more—a lot more, I think—but he wasn't liquid. I assume you understand."

"Makes sense," he said.

"It turns out he'd been bled to death by two bad investments and his, um, way of life. He needed money for other things. He had some other dealerships he wanted. There was a rumor he'd gotten a cheerleader or dancer pregnant and had to take care of that. Anyway, he had a lot going on, didn't have the cash, and here I was, about to have my name on a plaque."

"Bad investments? Like what?"

"No idea. Don didn't share his money tips. Thank God."

"You have an idea."

"I really don't." Ferraro offered nothing more and betrayed no emotional attachment one way or the other.

"You gave money he didn't want you to give, and then you're gone," he said. "How did that happen?"

"It took about a week, maybe less. There was that scene in his office. The next week, he called me to go to lunch, asked me to come pick him up. I walked in, he told me he couldn't tolerate what I'd done, and then he fired me. Handed me a fat check to cover my bonuses and severance and told me I'd be getting a refund on my skybox and tickets."

"He could do that? Pull those strings?"

Ferraro laughed and scratched at a blemish on his desk. "Whenever he wanted. I told him I planned on staying in Orlando, even though I had no idea where I was going to work. And he said no. Said I could move back to where I came from but that I wasn't an OU guy any more. We argued for about an hour, but he had his mind made up, the check already cut. A week later, I got a check from OU covering all my annual giving. I heard later that Don liquidated one of his stocks and wrote the school a big check to cover what they had to send back to me."

"You got all your money back?"

"All of it from that year."

"So just like that, in a week, you were gone."

Ferraro nodded. "I was told in no uncertain terms not to come to the campus, not to go to games."

"And you stayed away."

"I had some . . . incentive to stay away," Ferraro said.

"More money," he said.

"More like more health."

"He threatened you?"

"He did," Ferraro said. "Imagine that."

"What are we talking about here?"

"We're talking about him telling me that if I didn't leave town and surrender every professional association I had with anyone in Orlando, he'd make sure I wasn't able to spend any of my severance. I'd seen him talk to people that way before, but that day he was . . . possessed. I believed him. He meant what he said."

"You don't strike me as a guy who takes being threatened well."

"I'm not."

"What'd you tell him?"

"Not a thing. I broke his fucking nose."

"You what?"

"He delivered his ultimatum and I took the check and then I punched him. Hit him square in the nose and broke it. There was blood everywhere. But it was just one punch, the only one I threw."

"Naturally, he sued."

"He didn't. In a way, I think Don respected what I did. I mean, he had to have surgery to fix his face—it was a hell of a punch, I gotta say—but he knew I wasn't going to fight him on what he wanted after the punch. Partly because when I hit him I gave him the leverage to get me out. But even if he hadn't had that, I'd have left."

"Why? You said you'd just told him you weren't leaving."

"That was a bluff. It wasn't worth staying if I was going to have to fight Don at every turn. And believe me, it would have been a fight. He would have cut me off everywhere he could, and that guy has a lot of friends in high places. Besides, if I could make money in Orlando, which, believe me, isn't that much of a money market compared to a lot of others, I could make money anywhere."

"What does that make Henson? The most powerful guy in Orlando?"

Ferraro gazed outside again. "I don't know about that. But he probably thinks he is."

He detected a slight change in Ferraro's expression, a narrowing of his eyes. As if he were replaying a past meeting with Henson. Or maybe just remembering the circumstances of how he got here. Working for Henson had cost the man a good deal of his livelihood and more. Probably a large chunk of his self-esteem.

But Ferraro had rebounded well. Real estate had replaced cars in his sales pitches, and maps of three current or future residential developments hung on display on the wall to Ferraro's right. Every lot had a colored dot attached to it. Red signified sold with a house under construction or built. Green meant sold, yellow was for pending sales, and blue was for lots still available for purchase. The maps contained little blue. Life was undoubtedly good at Southern Estates.

"What can you tell me about Henson's relationships with the OU football program and the president?" Keane asked.

"I don't really know the president," Ferraro said. "Met him a couple times but talked to him long enough to say hello. I know Don had a hand in bringing him in. I remember Don liked the guy. I assume that's still true, but I don't know. As for Coach Childress, he always got along with Don. Hell, Don gave so much damn money, you had to get along with him or else, you know, you'd be gone."

"You think Henson buys players?"

Ferraro laughed. "Only a few back then. Probably more now."

"It wasn't a secret?"

"Secret? God, no. It was almost a game. Everybody did it. I did it. Most of us had one or two guys we handled. Don and the rest, they had four or five or more they dealt with."

He asked, "How many others when you were there?"

"It was a small group back then, maybe half a dozen. There weren't that many guys who made enough money that they felt like they could just give it away like that."

He stared at Ferraro. Without hesitation, the man had just admitted to being the poster child for corruption in college athletics, a businessman buying athletes and universities. He knew if such shenanigans were going on at a school like OU, they were certainly going on in the country's more established programs, the ones whose teams played on national television every weekend.

Keane had always suspected a level of money flowing to players under the table, but he'd played football at a much smaller school and had never witnessed it personally. All he or any of his teammates ever got was an occasional free barbecue lunch. But what Ferraro had described was systemic abuse. This was like a Wall Street banker acknowledging that insider stock trading was not only happening but was considered standard operating procedure.

"You're surprised?" Ferraro said. "Surely you're not a Boy Scout."

"No. It's just pretty brazen. You weren't nervous about getting caught? The NCAA?" Had the college football's governing body learned of a systematic paying of players, OU's program would find itself in deep trouble.

"Those clowns couldn't find their ass with either hand. Just to be safe, we told the coach not to turn in any school about recruiting violations or cheating. We told him we didn't want that kind of war."

"He couldn't have liked that."

Ferraro shrugged. "It goes both ways. Duke knew that. But let me ask you something. With all the things I'm sure you've seen in your job, you're worried about this?"

He arched his eyebrows. Gave an answer without answering.

"Don is what, a suspect here?" Ferraro asked.

Keane ignored the question and offered his own. "Does Henson gamble?"

"You mean, does he go to Vegas?"

"More like underground stuff. With a bookie. Or online. Does he bet on games?"

Ferraro's brow crinkled. "I don't remember anything like that. With his personality, it wouldn't surprise me to hear that he does, but if that were going on when I was there, I'd have known about it. And I don't remember anything about that."

"You've been gone how long?"

"Six years."

"To be clear, he was helping out players six, seven years ago, but as far as you know he wasn't betting on games."

"That's fair."

He put the pieces together. Seven years ago, the scam hadn't been cooked up. And internet gambling wasn't yet prevalent.

"What the hell is going on down there?" Ferraro asked.

Again Keane ignored Ferraro's question. "What about any of the other people in your group of boosters? Did any of them gamble?"

"On sports? I really don't know. I'd hear talk about point spreads from time to time. Everybody that follows sports talks about that, right? But I never heard about anybody putting money down. I mean, it may have happened, but I never saw it."

He nodded and veered to another subject. "Beyond your professional life, what's your story? Successful guy, single I assume?"

"You've done your homework."

"Where do you call home? You don't sound like you're from the South."

"Hardly," Ferraro said. "New York. Upstate. I guess it's true what they say. Everyone from New York ends up in Florida eventually."

"You didn't stay."

Ferraro laughed. "That's a fair point."

Keane nodded and thanked Ferraro for his time.

"I'll walk you down. I'm on my way out," Ferraro said.

They shook hands in the parking lot, and Keane started to his rental car, then called back to Ferraro.

"I almost forgot. Do you remember a football player named David Hance? Tally Hance?"

Ferraro looked at him, then up at the pale sky in thought. "Name doesn't ring a bell. Who is he?"

"Like I said, just a guy who played at OU."

"And he's wrapped up in whatever's going on."

"He was."

"Well, next time you see him, give him a little free advice."

"What's that?"

"Tell him not to cross Don Henson. And do me a favor, too, will you? Don't tell anyone down there you talked to me. I could probably take on Don now, but I don't want to have to. I don't feel like rebuilding my life again."

He watched Ferraro climb into a car across the lot. He intentionally fumbled with his keys as he watched the man drive away in a black Lincoln Navigator.

FERRARO ALWAYS DELIGHTED in telling Henson something new. "I just had a visit from an FBI agent who wants to know if you're a scumbag gambler."

"What'd you tell him?" Henson asked.

"I told him you were. I told him there wasn't a team, horse, or dog you wouldn't bet on."

"Jesus Christ. That's fucking wonderful. That's just—"

"Relax. I told him you're competitive but that I'd never seen you bet or heard about you betting. You're covered."

"I'm covered? Bullshit. Who was the agent?"

He froze. He realized he hadn't gotten the agent's card. Come to think of it, the agent hadn't offered one. He hadn't asked for one of his, either. "His name was . . . Keane."

"What, exactly, did he tell you? Did he tell you he was working on a case involving the university?"

"Well if he isn't, then he asked a lot of questions that shouldn't matter to him."

"That's just great. That fucking Teddy. He can't keep control of anything."

"You need to make this shit go away. And go back to remembering I don't exist."

He hung up and thought more about Keane. He'd given him enough information to chew on for a while. And they'd meet again, he was sure.

26

ROSSI STROLLED INTO the Maitland Community Bank prepared to ruin David Ramer's day. Although her research showed that the bank president had probably experienced a slew of shitty days recently. Years of record profits fueled by commercial development were gone. SEC filings showed three quarters of too many bad loans and a balance sheet still overloaded with too many risky ones. She doubted Ramer, who had assumed control of the bank when his father retired a decade before, had ever seen such a downturn.

She followed Ramer's assistant into his office and smiled when she heard the assistant tell Ramer, "She said it was important."

She brushed past the assistant and formally introduced herself. Ramer motioned for her to take a seat and shoved a stack of papers into a brown accordion folder. "What's so urgent?"

"It's about your gambling," she said.

"My what? How could . . . what the hell are you saying?"

"We have evidence that you and your friends are betting on football games. And that you're paying football players at OU. And who knows what else? Maybe we'll eventually discover you're fixing football games."

"That's preposterous. All of it."

"We don't care much about paying players. The gambling, that has our attention."

Ramer stammered before finding his voice. "This is all nonsense. Utter nonsense."

"We don't think so. Also, I'm here to ask you to cooperate. In the end, that will look favorably for you when others are going to prison."

"Are you insane? I'm not going to prison. I haven't done anything. Nothing." He lifted out of his chair and thrust a finger at her. "Who the hell do you think you are?"

She raised her palms and lowered them, hoping to calm him. "Please sit down. I'm not here to arrest you. I didn't come here to play games. I'm here to ask your help. I thought you of all people would appreciate the facts as we know them."

"I appreciate good customers and loyalty and a great many other things, but I don't approve of misguided allegations being thrust into my face."

She stood and pulled her handcuffs. "Unless you want a perp walk in front of your staff, you'll kindly sit your ass down. If you want to trade insults, that's fine. I'll give you mine in a subpoena that lets my forensic accountant go through your books transaction by transaction. And then we'll get to your personal books, see how those match up. You understand?"

Ramer sat, his eyes telling of his disbelief. "Detective, I don't appreciate your accusations. In fact, I resent them. And I won't answer them. Certainly not here."

"Can you tell me about your time with the OU football team?"

"What time? I go to games."

"And practices?"

"Hardly ever. Maybe twice a year, and that includes the spring game."

"You fly on the team plane."

"A couple times a year, yes. Some of the places they play are so damned remote you'd be a fool to fly commercial if you had any alternative. So, I pay the money and get on the team plane. Trust me, it's not as glorious as it sounds."

"Try me."

"Look, I admit there are perks. You fly with people you know. Security isn't non-existent, but it's not invasive. No taking off your belt or shoes or any of that. They scan your bags, but that's not a big deal, either. The boosters that make the trip, we can bring our own liquor as long as nobody gets drunk or out of hand."

"Sounds nice."

"Then there's the trip home. You leave right after the game. Win or lose, day or night, rain, fog, or snow. Your bring your luggage to the game or you pack your luggage up on one of the buses when you leave the hotel to go to the game. That's not really what I'd call ideal for travel. You're also traveling with coaches and staffers who get pretty pissed off when they lose. It's pretty much all or nothing in that regard. Although what sticks with me is the smell."

"The smell?" she asked.

"You're on a plane with seventy football players. Not all of them smell very nice, even after a shower."

She chuckled. Her football security days had familiarized her with the odor—a sweaty, dirty sock masked by ten competing colognes. "Tell me: What do you know about a man named David Hance?"

Ramer frowned. "Who?"

"See, that's the wrong answer."

"I've never heard of this person."

"You might know him as Tally, but no matter. He's a friend of Teddy Simpson and several prominent contributors to the university. Or was, I should say. Mr. Hance is dead."

"If you say so."

"He died in a house fire. It was recent."

"That was him in that fire on TV? That's a shame."

She fought the urge to go after him. The banker was lying. He wasn't bad at it, but he probably wasn't as good at it as he thought he was. Regardless, today's visit had accomplished her goal. She'd stirred the pot. She stood and nodded. "Sorry to interrupt your day, but just so you know, this isn't going away."

"Next time, I'll want my attorney," he said.

"Next time, you might need one."

KEANE CALLED ROSSI for the third time in an hour. For the third time in an hour, the call went to voicemail. He'd left a message the first time, a peace offering, but nothing the second time and nothing now. He got it. She was pissed.

He finally dialed the main OPD number and asked for her. As he expected, her work phone went to voicemail. He punched out and waited for the rollover call to be answered.

Finally, it was: "Detective Diaz. How can I help you?"

"I'm trying to reach Detective Rossi," he said.

"Hold on," Diaz said, and the line went silent. Then Diaz was back. "She's not here. I can transfer you to her voicemail. Hang on."

"It's not urgent. But if you leave a note on her desk that I called, do you think she'd be able to call back tonight or in the morning?"

"Probably the morning."

"Then you can send me to her voicemail."

Diaz transferred the call, and Keane hung up. "In the morning" meant Rossi was either out of the office or off until tomorrow. He needed to call Blindside.com and finish what he'd started.

FERRARO DECIDED THE best thing about old Orlando money was familiarity. People who had it loved living near longtime friends in vintage houses and in old neighborhoods. No people guarded them, no gates protected them.

Thanks to Henson, he'd learned a pertinent fact that applied to tonight. Just before Labor Day, David Ramer had put his wife on a monthly budget, which she'd protested loudly and often. He'd finally lost his patience and responded by asking her how she'd like being on a monthly allowance the rest of her life—with no chance of ever increasing it. He backed up his threat by announcing he could find more than a couple of attorneys who owed him to fight for his money over her rights to half of it.

She responded by shepherding their kids to her mother's in Jacksonville for the long Christmas break. Ramer was alone at home, he'd confided to the group last week.

Ferraro twice drove through a tree-lined neighborhood in Winter Park, being sure to follow the posted speed limit. He wanted to make sure the holiday decorations on Ramer's home weren't going to light him up. But Ramer's holiday lights were understated, just like their owner. Ferraro drove away and glanced at the clock on his dashboard: 9:17.

On the third pass, he pulled into Ramer's long driveway. Just an old acquaintance paying a festive visit during the holidays. He walked up the front sidewalk and rang the bell. After a few seconds, he heard shuffling behind the stained oak door. He was sure Ramer was assessing him through the peephole. He'd be a ghost from another time. No worries. His gun was safely tucked away.

"What do you want?" Ramer asked upon opening the door.

Ferraro shoved the door hard with a shoulder, knocking the banker back deep into the foyer.

"What the hell?" Ramer yelled.

Ferraro stepped in quickly and closed the door. He pushed Ramer through the kitchen and into the den. Finally he dumped the banker on the couch and towered over him.

"I hear you're not holding it together very well, Dave," he said. "That's not a good sign."

"Tough year," Ramer said.

"Your life is coming apart and there's no telling what you're going to say. What do I have to do to make sure your life ends the way it should?"

He waited for the banker to answer. There was no reason to rush this, and he had time. He took it.

An hour later, he walked out of Ramer's home satisfied. The process had gone smoother than he expected. The banker had barely fought him. Not that it mattered. What mattered was that he now was certain the banker would never tell the police or anyone else about him or about OU.

27

KEANE STEERED THROUGH downtown and west to Winter Garden, an old town that seemed reinvented to capture foodies and antiquities lovers. He found the light-green, stucco-covered ranch house he'd seen on Google. A black, distinctly nondescript sedan parked out front told him he had the right address.

Rossi walked out the front door as Keane pulled two bags of groceries from the trunk. He took her in: blue jeans, a white v-neck blouse, hair tumbled onto her shoulders, which gave her a wilder look. A good look.

"You need to leave," she said.

"Peace offering," he said.

"I don't need one. I need you to be on your way and to stay out of my case. Otherwise, you'll be talking to the state attorney about an obstruction charge and to your boss about your job security."

He closed the trunk and put on a small smile. "I don't know where you get obstruction from the fact I gave you information. Good stuff, too."

"You held back. You obstructed right up until you didn't."

"Everybody holds back. Do you tell your partner everything? I mean, *everything*?"

She gave him an expressionless stare.

"Of course not. You probably haven't told him things about me. Do you and Thomas tell your chief everything you think he should know? No. Husbands and wives, do they tell each other everything? Hell no. See? Happens all the time."

He closed the gap between them and stopped at three paces when she put her hand on her hip.

"That doesn't make what you did any better," she said.

"You know what would be worse? If I hadn't told you anything. What if I'd just vanished, gone back to work, and poked around from afar? Would you have felt okay about that?"

"I—"

"You'd never even know about it. Tell me, were you even looking for another laptop? Did you even know one existed?"

"That's beside the point."

"That's exactly the point. You don't like my tactics, yet you use the same ones and you know it. It's just that this one time, you didn't commit the sin of omission: someone else did. Are you hungry?"

She narrowed her eyes and cocked her head back a notch. "C'mon in."

He dumped the groceries in the kitchen and looked around. The great room was modernly decorated, with yellow and green walls, paintings and prints of flowers, Venice and a beach scene. Area rugs accented polished maple-wood floors.

"Nice place," he said.

"Bought it after I made detective. The market was in the toilet and I got a great deal."

She gave him a quick tour of the three-two, a split plan with one bedroom converted to an office with a futon. The guest bedroom was done in a beach theme, with a mini surfboard on one wall and on another a wooden sign that said: IT'S 5 O'CLOCK SOMEWHERE. The taupe-colored master bedroom featured a large walk-in closet.

"It's doesn't have as much room as it could, but I like the layout," she said. "And the backyard."

She opened a sliding glass door that separated the dining area from a covered patio that housed a hot tub. A bamboo privacy fence stood around it.

"Your own little piece of paradise right outside your back door," he said.

"Got that right."

"Just remember: no drinking and hot-tubbing. That's bad for you."

"I know," she said. "I do it all the time."

Back in the kitchen, he unloaded the groceries and asked for pots, knives, and a cutting board. "I hope you like Italian."

She said, "I did tell you my family owns an Italian restaurant, right?"

"You just said restaurant."

"They make pizza, pasta, antipasto, soup, salad, and bread. All fresh. And if you ask my dad for a special dish, he'd make it for you."

"Homemade bread? Like garlic knots?"

"Exactly like garlic knots."

"Huh. I should have let you get the bread." He set aside a baguette and package of butter.

Rossi pulled two Bud Lights from the refrigerator and traded him a bottle for two packages of fresh mozzarella.

They drank and talked shop as he made a red sauce, chopping onions and garlic, sautéing them in olive oil and adding tomatoes and tomato sauce and a variety of herbs he found in her pantry. He tasted the sauce, decided it was too acidic, and stirred in a palm full of sugar. Tasted it again. Not bad. He covered the pot and turned the heat to low.

He drained the last of his beer and dug out a corkscrew from her silverware tray. He found two wine glasses, then popped open the Chianti he had brought. "Wine?"

"Not yet," Rossi said.

"Suit yourself." He poured himself a glass to accompany the last of the dinner prep. "What about Caesar salad?"

"I'll take that."

Keane rinsed and dried the romaine and whisked together a faux dressing out of olive oil, garlic, pepper, and Parmesan. He threw the dressing and salad into the refrigerator and collected his thoughts. "Pot?" he asked.

"What?" Her eyes were wide.

"I need a large pot for the pasta."

"Oh. That. Right."

"What did you think—"

"Nothing." She pulled a stock pot from a lower cabinet and handed it to him.

He added water and dropped in a handful of salt. He set the burner on high. He washed and dried the cutting board and held up a bulb of garlic. "I hope you're okay with this."

She grinned. "You could have asked before you put that handful of them in your sauce."

He caught the hint of a smirk on her face, confirmation she was enjoying her own hard-ass routine. He peeled skin off of five cloves, minced them, and covered them with kosher salt. Then he worked the garlic and salt into a paste. He threw a stick of butter into a cereal bowl and microwaved it until it started to melt.

The water pot reached a full boil, and he added the dry spaghetti and lowered the burner to simmer.

He focused back on the bread and added the garlic paste to the bowl, then mixed the seasoned butter. He sliced the baguettes in half, long ways, spread the butter mixture along the insides. He closed up the bread and set it aside and then cleaned up his considerable mess in the kitchen.

When the pasta was al dente, he ladled red sauce in the pan, tossed it, and plated the meal. He brought the pasta and a basket of garlic bread to the table. Start to finish the process took just over an hour. Not a personal record but damned good for being in unfamiliar surroundings.

She pulled the salad from the fridge, dished it out and poured herself a glass of wine.

"Cheers," he said, and they clinked glasses.

"Geez, you're a foodie," she said after her first mouthful of pasta. "This is really good."

Keane dipped his head, accepting the compliment. "Thanks. I like to think I handle a kitchen knife as well as I do a gun. I never wanted to be a stereotypical agent."

"Meaning single and living on fast food? Or an asshole with an attitude?"

He shrugged. "Maybe both. I like attitude better than fast food."

"Obviously. What about the single part?" she asked.

"I don't mind it."

"Never married?"

"Close once," he said. "Didn't work out. One day it will. What about you? You're single, and clearly a skilled decorator. I'm sure you could have thrown together everything I just made in less time than it took me. You probably even repair hot tubs."

"I have my moments."

He noted her dodge. She might have an ongoing relationship, but if she did, it wasn't serious. The house showed no signs of accommodations for a significant other. Virtually every photo featured her or another person with dark hair.

His phone vibrated in his pocket. The screen said "Q," and he declined the call. Q was a night owl. He'd return the call later.

They took their time with the food. He liked that she liked to eat. And that she liked what he made. Anything with tomato sauce was a go-to recipe for him. Every woman he dated had loved his Italian.

They traded stories about work, family, and growing up. She was a Central Florida native, and she seemed pleasantly surprised when he divulged that he'd grown up in the state.

"How did you end up in Tennessee?" she asked.

"Work. I finished college, went to law school, and moved to Atlanta, only to figure out that being a corporate lawyer was long hours of boring work. I missed the outdoors."

"Yeah, everybody says that about the FBI, all the glorious outdoor assignments." She laughed. "That's not a reason at all."

"Using your mind and your skills to find people and to build a case, that sure beats sitting in a back room evaluating contracts and negotiating changes to them. To be good at this, you have to get away from the computer and get in the field. The best agents meet people in their homes and neighborhoods and get them to talk. Although a fair number of times we have sources who walk into the office and drop a case in our laps."

Rossi shook her head. "I never get that. It's all chase, all the time. How much do you miss Florida?"

"I miss the weather in the winter. Summers are hot everywhere, so that's a wash. But I've been gone long enough that I appreciate the change of seasons."

"That's it? You don't have any family pulling you back?"

He stared at her, shocked. She covered her mouth when she realized what she'd said.

"I'm sorry. I didn't mean—"

"It's okay. My dad had a brother, and he visited us some when I was a kid, but he's gone. My mom was an only child. My grandparents on both sides, they're passed."

"I'm sorry. That's . . . sad. Were you and Sean close?"

Keane shook his head and composed his thoughts. He'd thought about this answer many times over the years and had only talked about the subject once, to his former fiancé. "We should have been a lot closer. You'd think that brothers, even two decades apart in age, would be tight, especially with us both being football junkies at a young age and with no other family to speak of. But we weren't. My career was taking shape when Sean was in grade school, and when he was in high school I was cutting my teeth in the FBI. I was too . . . self-involved. And my mother—our mom—liked having Sean to herself. When I'd come back to see them, she enforced the fish rule for visitors."

Rossi nodded. She knew it well: seafood and house guests both start to stink after three days. "Your mom was single? Never remarried?"

"She loved her job as a waitress, loved her son, and loved controlling her world. I didn't understand her for a lot of years, but one day it clicked. That's when I stopped fighting all her rules." He paused, and his mind flashed back to one of the final arguments he'd had with her. "That's a long way of saying that Sean and I were friendly, but we weren't close."

She watched him as she took a sip of wine, but let the comment hang.

"I'll have to try this sauce with your dad's garlic knots," he said.

"He'd probably want to try it, too."

"What does he think of his daughter fighting crime? Catching killers?"

"He's proud of me. He brags about me. But he worries. Mom too."

"Understandable."

"Maybe. I don't think they worry about me getting shot. I think they worry I won't find a husband and give them a grandchild. Or grandchildren."

"Ah." He raised his glass. "Parental guilt. Where would we be without it?"

She toasted and sipped and stared, lost in thought.

He decided she had a very pleasant face.

"Question," Rossi said finally. "What was the happiest time of your life?"

"That's some ask. But . . . I've never really quantified that."

"Really. Ever?"

He looked at the ceiling. "Not really."

"What are some of your favorite memories?"

"I had a lot of fun playing ball in college. And going to school."

"What else? What about high school? During law school? In the FBI?"

Keane dug back into his memory bank. Not everything was ready for withdrawal. He said, "I had a dog when I was a kid. Hell of a dog."

"What kind of dog?"

"A mutt, a mixed terrier. Sparky. Barked like hell every time somebody walked by the house, but he slept with me every night."

"And now?"

"Now? Sparky's long gone."

"I meant, who sleeps with you now?"

"Oh. That's more of a solo operation."

Rossi raised her glass. "Here's to flying solo."

He thought: *Now or never.* He said, "Did you like what you found on the Mac?"

"I'd have liked it a lot better a week ago." She paused. "Your brother was in the middle of a lot of bad shit going on over there."

"You have a motive?"

"I think it's all there. Motive, suspects. It's just not apparent. I'm sure you saw that."

He nodded. "What was on his other laptop?"

"Schoolwork and social networking," she said. "A bunch of music. Videos. Facebook pages, email, class notes, papers he'd written for school. Pretty basic stuff for a college kid. But here's the thing. There's nothing on either one that ties back to Hance. Not that it matters now."

"You'll find it," he said, but she was right. It wouldn't matter. Whoever ended up prosecuting the case could paint Hance in whatever light was needed. Statements from players and coaches would be enough. He was certain there was a text-message log that would help. He didn't have access to them and wouldn't for months, long after they could help him. "Tell me: Who benefits?"

"Too early to tell. But this is getting very complicated, and I don't need it to be."

"Every case can't be an easy open-and-shut."

"No, it's not that."

He took in her frown and made a guess. "You're getting pressure to close this before you're ready to."

She gave him a fake smile but said nothing. She twirled another fork full of spaghetti.

"Well, from what I see . . . if you think Hance was the guy . . . if you really think he was the guy who killed Sean, then he was a middle man. He was doing favors for Sean—or doing something for Sean—on behalf of a third party. And they were both getting paid."

"For what?"

"For Sean, possibly to play football. Maybe for information about the team. Maybe for playing football badly. Or for another reason we don't know yet. For Hance, maybe to make sure Sean played. Or that Sean was . . . comfortable."

"The problem is, without your brother and without Hance we have to get somebody to flip, or it's all circumstantial."

He waved off the idea. "Ah, it's easy to sew that up."

"Easy for you to say. I'm used to dealing with dumbass drug dealers who shoot before they think, not gamblers and money launderers. I'm not a white-collar kind of girl. Those cases take way too much time to build and close. Blue-collar cases, the down-and-dirties, they practically close themselves."

"No they don't. Don't sell yourself short. Every case has to be built. Some are just naturally easier to build. Dead body, weapon, motive, altercation, witnesses, they all come together in one time and place. But you're right. Cases like these, you have to follow a process. It'll take time but if you follow the steps you'll get there. The hard part is going to be matching the data on the computer with live people who were breaking the law. You're going to have to crack Sean's code, put names to the initials and match the names to actions. You're going to have to find help from the inside. Probably more than one person, because with that many names there's a good chance there are different groups of people, groups that probably don't associate with one another. But once you break the dam, things will fall into place pretty fast."

"Jocks and fraternity brothers," she said.

"Exactly. And boosters."

"And coaches."

"And presidents."

She shook her head.

He said, "It won't take as long as you think. But soon enough you'll flip two or three key people and hit a tipping point. The momentum will swing your way. Then it's a matter of pulling all their bank and credit card records and matching them up to the win-loss column on Sean's spreadsheets. You're actually pretty lucky in one regard."

"What's that?"

"Tell me, in all you've done so far, have you seen or heard of any cash changing hands? Real money?"

"Only the night this started."

"Exactly. Gambling is traditionally a cash business. That's what makes it so attractive."

"Besides the fact it's addicting?" she asked.

"That's a big part of it, too. But from an operations standpoint, when you deal in cash you can choose not to have any records. Usually there's an account book that lists the winnings and losings, but these guys don't go around using QuickBooks. Once they go that route, they're creating documents that'll send them to jail."

"If they get caught."

He nodded. "But this is different. All this was done online. From start to finish. We don't have any paper yet, but these transactions are sitting on a server waiting to be printed out."

He walked her through his theory, that Sean started taking bets and laying them off on an online bookie. He ran them all through his online account and shuffled money to and from his PayPal account to pay the winners and collect from the losers. And to keep his digital bookie happy.

"You make it sound like he was a kingpin," Rossi said.

"I think he was. From the records I saw, this was well-planned. Maybe not at first, but at some point it became quite sophisticated."

"You sound surprised."

"Only a little bit. Q told me Sean saved his business a couple years ago, that Sean came home from school over the summer and took a hard look at what he was doing with the bar and made him change things. Made him buy updated registers and put in quality control systems. They worked. And Sean, a couple days before he was killed, told me he suspected someone was stealing from the restaurant. He said the receipts didn't match the books. He was pissed his dad hadn't picked up on it."

"Maybe the dad did know. Maybe somebody was stealing and he didn't want to deal with the conflict." She paused. "Or maybe the dad was coming up short on purpose. That would fit a pattern. Specializing in white-collar crimes, you've probably seen that a lot."

Keane nodded. He'd seen it dozens of times. "The only reason to steal from yourself is to hide money from the state sales tax commission or the IRS. Q's bar does well but not that well."

Rossi portioned out the rest of the wine. "You know we got Sean's bank records."

"I figured. Routine."

"Turns out Sean had more money in his accounts than you'd expect for a college kid who comes from a pretty modest background."

"'Pretty modest.' That's good."

"I'm guessing."

"You don't know the half of it."

"Less than modest?"

"Not destitute. Not on food stamps. But let's just say his upbringing was decidedly difficult. Didn't get much support at home."

"No?"

"Q did about all Mary allowed him to do. But she was a piece of work. She raised Sean by herself and did her best to keep everyone else away. Never wanted a thing from anybody. Sean getting a football scholarship was probably the first bit of sanity of his life."

Rossi's phone vibrated on the kitchen counter. She checked the caller ID and answered.

"What's up?" she asked. Then: "What? When?"

She hung up and gave him a hard look. "We've got another body."

28

THE CRIME SCENE was an unwelcome festival of lights in a staid, upper-class neighborhood. Rossi counted seven Winter Park police cars running their blue-and-reds while neighbors, two of them in pajamas, stood in a nearby yard snapping pictures with smart phones.

She flashed her badge to get past the Winter Park officer at the perimeter and then got clearance from a detective who said, "Your partner's already here."

"Stay here and mind your manners," she told Keane and hustled up the front steps of a two-story red-brick home that said old money.

Thomas met her at the front door. "Upstairs bathroom. Bled out in a bathtub. He's cut from ear to ear across the throat and cut on both wrists."

"How long?" she asked.

"Maybe an hour. We may have just missed him."

She considered how they'd barely missed Hance. Now this. "Bad losing streak, partner."

"Yeah."

"Is there anything that he told you that makes more sense now?"

She closed her eyes and thought back to her interview with Ramer, defiant. He'd all but promised to go down fighting. "He wasn't scared of me or anything else. I don't think he ever saw this coming."

Thomas nodded.

Rossi drew in a deep breath and exhaled. "But I have something else to tell you."

KEANE CALCULATED THE politics of Orlando detectives walking into a Winter Park death house when Rossi emerged, wearing booties on her shoes and gloves on her hands, from inside. She showed no signs of distress after whatever she had witnessed inside.

"We're going to let you in, okay?" she said, and handed him a pair of clear gloves and fabric shoe covers. "Don't touch anything, don't offer any comments, don't say anything unless you're asked. Thomas isn't happy about this, but he's going along. For now."

"How about the boys from Winter Park?"

"They're not happy, period. They're hoping this is related to Hance and that they can lay most of the case in our laps. Look around. A crime spree around here is when the neighbors are all missing their morning paper from the driveway."

He put on the hand and foot covers and followed her inside a two-story home that had a decorative blend of 1940s Florida and modern taste. Dark oak wood floors showed pock marks. The front sitting room featured a large and ornate red Oriental rug. A light gold eggshell paint on the walls running up to elaborate crown molding, all white. He spotted small white speakers perched in two corners and figured there were probably more he couldn't see.

The master bedroom had another darkly stained wood floor, also oak, also dating back at least seventy years. A king-sized mahogany sleigh bed sat in the center of the room. Over the headboard hung an oil painting of a man and woman in repose. On the opposite wall hung a flat screen TV. Keane guessed it to be fifty-two inches, overkill for a bedroom.

Thomas stood next to Rossi at the bathroom door on the far left side of the room. He extended his hand toward the opening: *Come on in and take a look.* Crime-scene technicians processed the scene, documenting it with photographs and dusting for fingerprints.

David Ramer lay fully clothed in an oversized, stand-alone white tub, surrounded by burgundy water. The color starkly offset his pale face. Ramer's eyes were open, his hair wet. His chin was tucked into his chest because of the shape of the tub, but on both sides of a 5 o'clock stubble Keane could see slice marks and remnants of blood.

Keane tracked the cut on Ramer's throat and two on his right wrist. *Defensive wounds*, he thought.

Keane surveyed the bathroom. On a normal day, it was probably pristine. White vanity, white tub and a white toilet surrounded by four-by-four-inch, black-and-white tiles on the floor and walls. Brushed nickel hardware was lit up by a matching overhead light.

Pinkish puddles of water gathered on the tile floor next to the tub. Smeared red handprints were on both sides of the tub. Arterial spray dotted the wall behind the tub.

He craned his neck and looked at the wall to his left. He saw no blood. "Who called it in?"

"Next-door neighbor heard a noise," Thomas said from the doorway. "Said he thought his neighbor's house was being robbed, but said he didn't see anything."

"Thoughts?" Rossi asked.

"Not much blood for a stabbing," Keane said.

"It's all in the tub," Thomas said. "It's deceiving."

"He didn't fight much. There's not a lot of water on the floor."

"Possible he was killed before and the bathtub was filled after," Thomas said.

Rossi said, "The killer found a way to get Ramer upstairs with no fight. There are no signs of forced entry, so Ramer probably answered the door. He was convinced to come upstairs. I wouldn't think a knife would do that, so that means a gun."

He said nothing.

"You call yourself an FBI agent? I'm disappointed," Thomas said. The detective paused a beat and pointed at the far wall. "The killer's right-handed. Whoever cut his throat did so from left to right." Thomas made a slashing motion across his own neck and then did it again as he explained. "He started here and finished here. He pulled harder as he finished. Make sure he got it right. He dug in at the end and hit an artery and probably the jugular. He didn't hit an artery on the left side. Otherwise, we'd have more blood over here."

"That's pretty good," he said. "Did you find the knife?"

Thomas shook his head.

"Anything to make you think you have DNA hanging around?"

"Not unless Ramer scratched the killer. Or unless there's blood on the side of the tub that isn't Ramer's."

"Any scrapings might be useless because of the water. The blood . . . good luck."

"We're not hopeful."

"One possible problem with your theory," Keane said.

Rossi's eyebrows moved up in a question.

"The front door could have been unlocked. The killer could have walked right in."

"This is a nice neighborhood, but it's an older neighborhood. No security guards. Not a gated community. People lock their doors."

"I'm just saying."

The three of them gave the bathroom a once-over and left.

Keane turned to Rossi. "What makes Ramer special? Why him?"

"This could be an isolated incident. We don't know if this is connected at all to David Hance or your brother."

"Bullshit. You know it is."

Thomas said, "Hard case to make. You can find threads to link the victims, but we've already closed one case and put that on Hance. Then Hance dies, killed by gunshot, then burned. Ramer looks like he was stabbed or slashed to death. No gunshot. You know enough about this to know killers have patterns. There's no pattern."

"You said you think he had a gun. To get Ramer up to the bathroom."

"He didn't use it. If he put a bullet into the back of Ramer's head, that would fit the pattern."

"There is another pattern that fits both killings," Keane said.

"What's that?" Thomas asked.

"The killer found a way to get close without attracting attention."

Rossi and Thomas looked at each other. He saw her shrug.

"That's not all, is it?" Keane asked.

"Hance knew Ramer," she said. "They had mutual friends. It's also possible they were friends. Or friendly."

"A runner," Keane said. "He did favors and ran errands. It probably involved money. And football players."

"Pretty thin," she said, and turned to Thomas. "We need to talk to Teddy Simpson again."

They walked out of the house and into the glare of lights. Two local TV trucks were parked across the street, satellite booms raised. Keane saw two cameramen positioned at the end of the driveway, collecting far-away video for the next newscast. They'd wait to talk to the on-duty public information officer, who would be on her way as soon as word got around that there were TV trucks in a decidedly high-class part of Winter Park. They'd stay until the money shot: David Ramer's body being taken out of the house.

The three of them stepped to the front of Rossi's car and away from the focus of the front door, a good thirty yards from the street. Keane angled his body so that he faced the house and his back was to the cameras.

"Do you think you can control yourself if we allow you to come with us back to the campus?" Thomas asked him.

"Since you're so kind to ask," Keane said, "of course."

"Hopefully, that's good enough."

"I'll say our goodbyes and catch up," Rossi said, and she peeled off to shake hands with the officer in charge. She was back in three minutes.

"A caller to 911 reported seeing a big black SUV circling around about a couple hours ago. He didn't think anything of it until we showed up with all the lights and crime tape."

"Big black SUV?" Keane asked.

She nodded.

He thought: *Lincoln Navigator.*

29

IT WAS NEARLY one a.m. when Keane, Rossi, and Thomas arrived in two cars on the OU campus. They buzzed Teddy Simpson from his front gate. Thomas pushed the call button while Keane and Rossi watched from her idling car.

Nothing.

Thomas buzzed again. Waited, buzzed a third time.

"I'm coming! I'm coming," a voice sounded through call box. A drunken Simpson asked, "Who is it? What do you want?"

"Orlando police," Thomas said. "We'd like to speak with you."

"Goddammit . . ."

The iron gate creaked open. Rossi drove onto the property first, followed by Thomas.

Simpson opened the door before anyone rang the bell. He wore black slacks and a white, open-collared Cuban shirt. He reeked of expensive cologne, and in his hand was a glass half-filled with an amber liquid.

"Orlando's finest. Please, come in," Simpson said, stepping aside. He looked at Keane, "And you, too."

The president raised his glass. "As long as you're here, can I get you anything?"

They declined but accepted an offer to sit. Keane sank into a side chair of an upscale man-cave of a living room. ESPN flashed highlights on a sixty-inch flat screen, the network crawl delivering sports news and scores. He'd expected nothing less. Teddy fell back into an oversized leather chair facing the TV.

"We're sorry for the late hour, Mr. Simpson," Thomas began. "We have news."

"And here I thought today couldn't get any more intriguing."

"What's that?"

"Nothing," Teddy said. "Long day."

"We're sorry, but David Ramer was killed tonight."

"What?" Simpson blurted. His glass suddenly tipped, and a splash of Scotch hit the floor. "What? Where? How? . . . Jesus."

"He was at home," Thomas said.

"Christ, what the hell happened?" Simpson rose and began pacing and rubbing his temples. "What the hell is going on?"

"We were hoping you could tell us," Rossi said.

"I have no idea. Jesus. Who'd want to kill Dave? Jesus, this is awful."

"We think Mr. Ramer was involved in a business or personal deal with you that got him killed," Thomas said.

"With me? That's not possible. Dave's a banker. Who kills bankers? Christ, even Bernie Madoff's still alive."

"It's over," Keane said. Rossi shot him a look that said *not now*, but he wasn't done. "This is the third body. These two detectives, they're not going to leave any stone unturned now. Not that they would have before, but there's going to be a race to tell the best story. Either way, your days running this school are over."

Simpson dropped back into his chair and cradled his head in his hands. When he raised his head again, Keane saw red around his eyes. And then the president started to talk.

They listened for nearly an hour as Simpson, aided by another two glasses of Scotch on the rocks, outlined how an inner circle of boosters and friends conspired to gamble on college football, cheating an overseas online betting company in the process. Most of the facts lined up with what Keane had surmised, but the scope and intricacy stunned him. The group started out with a pool of $500,000 and ran it through multiple accounts overseas. Simpson also operated several separate personal accounts.

The president served as a de facto group leader because of his network of "informants"—other presidents and chancellors at other universities, people who liked to show off their first-hand knowledge about their football teams. Simpson logged extensive notes about players and teams. He and others in the group then evaluated how to use their inside information to make the smartest bets on certain teams.

"What about records of the bets?" Rossi asked.

"If we needed them, we could get them," Teddy said. "I'm sure the offshore company has them."

"You'll never get them," Keane said. "This is not a U.S. company. You'd have to bring a lot of pressure to bear. We're not talking about terrorism here. Besides, if this story ever got out, football here would be over. And at a big school like this in the middle of a football-crazy state, that's suicide."

It had happened before. Tulane had shut down its basketball program after players were caught fixing games. And this scandal, with tentacles that reached the university president, dwarfed that one. OU would be at the epicenter of the sports world for all the wrong reasons. This might even jeopardize the university.

Simpson kept talking. "There are a lot of places where this is all perfectly legal."

"How do you figure?" Keane asked.

"There's not a single account in this country, not a credit card or anything else, where I'm connected to this. The trick is keeping all the money over there, not bringing it back."

"Tell that to the IRS," Keane said.

"No, thank you."

"I'll give you credit. Everybody seems to have kept their mouths shut until now."

"Of course. Why would anyone want to kill the golden goose?"

"Or a twenty-two-year-old kid?"

Simpson's voice lowered. "That never should have happened."

"A lot of things never should have happened. And now other people are dead too. Why don't you tell the detectives about all the things you and your friends were up to?"

The president stared back at him. And then he unfurled the past five years of his life. OU's football players did not gamble, were not privy to the conversation of his group. They were rewarded for information, for cooperation. The more they helped, or maybe the better they played, the more payoffs they got. Cash. Rent payments. Car payments.

Simpson insisted Coach Childress had no clue about the gambling, though he admitted the coach often saw only what he wanted to. He didn't know if Childress was aware that multiple players on his team were on the take.

The president raised a new possibility. He'd witnessed players who weren't involved with his boosters wearing nicer clothes than usual, showing off new cell phones and electronics. "I've wondered if maybe Duke had his own game going."

Keane couldn't tell if the statement made an impact with Rossi and Thomas. He considered it plausible but not likely. He reminded himself that they were hearing the confession of a man who used to manipulate politicians for a living, a master at deflection and deception. The best defense was a good offense.

"We need names," Rossi said finally.

"HOLD ON," KEANE said. "Richie Ferraro?"

Simpson looked surprised that any of his guests picked that name as a stopping point.

"The guy in Atlanta? He's in your group?"

The president nodded.

"I thought Henson ran him out of town?"

Now Simpson looked confused. "Why would you think that?"

"That's the story he told me."

"You talked to him?"

Keane caught all three of them staring at him. "In person. Seemed like a nice guy. Though he wasn't very complimentary about your friends. Mr. Henson chiefly."

"Jesus," Simpson said. "How'd you know about him? Nobody knows about him. We never talk about him. That's the rule."

"Whose rule?" Thomas asked.

"Ferraro's," Simpson said.

"Why?"

"He prefers being a silent partner. A very silent partner."

"What does that mean?"

"You'll have to ask him. I have nothing to say about Richie Ferraro. I don't ever talk to him, and I don't know that much about him. Others know him better than I do. You'd have to ask them."

"Would one of them be David Ramer?"

"Yeah."

"Who else would one of them be?"

"Any of them."

"Henson?" Keane asked.

He shook his head. "I doubt he's on Don's Christmas list."

The three of them took turns trying to convince the president to unveil details of Ferraro's role in the group. Teddy answered questions with questions and diverted to other subjects.

Keane realized they were witnessing a rare sight. Ferraro scared Simpson.

"You realize eventually we're going to compel you to talk to us," Thomas said.

Simpson didn't budge. "You do what you have to do. I haven't asked for an attorney. I think you'd agree throughout this whole thing, I've been cooperative. But if we're going to talk about certain things, including Richie Ferraro, then I'll want to exercise my right to counsel."

WALKING BACK TO their cars, Keane urged Rossi and Thomas to arrest Simpson, but the politics belonged to them, not him. "This is going to get really messy."

"No shit," Rossi said.

"Once we get the sign-off, we'll be back," Thomas said. "It won't take long."

"You hope," Keane said. "Ferraro must have leverage on Simpson. He completely shut down."

Rossi said, "We'll see."

Thomas eventually made the decision about how big tonight was going to get. And how messy. Except for the banker's next of kin, nobody would receive a surprise visit or call. Nobody. Nobody would get arrested.

In the morning, Thomas would go to a judge for a subpoena for cell records. They wouldn't have them for a few more hours, maybe by noon at the earliest. Eventually, the records would connect members of the president's inner circle. And they would show patterns that a prosecutor could eat for lunch.

Keane didn't care about records or subpoenas. He rubbed his eyes with his hands, covering his face, and shook his head. "We need to knock on doors."

KEANE EXPECTED ROSSI to come at him. She didn't hesitate. "You didn't tell us about finding Ferraro," she said.

"I was getting to it." And he did: He told her about Ferraro's life-changing run-in with Henson and how Ferraro described his former employer. He conveyed Ferraro's notion that Henson was an egomaniacal prick.

"From what I remember, he plays to win at everything he does," Rossi said. "He owns a slew of car dealerships. He makes money even when the whole industry struggles. Like he's got a Midas touch. He sells Hondas in one place, Toyotas in another. Sells Kias. He makes money like a pure American capitalist, but he likes his foreign brands."

The longer they talked, the more they both agreed the issue was less Ferraro and more Henson. And that Henson warranted a closer look.

"You said you remembered that Ferraro had a fight with Henson. You didn't say anything about a broken nose," Keane said.

"Ferraro broke his nose?"

He relayed the anecdote from Ferraro of his punch to the face that necessitated Henson getting surgery. "That would be pretty memorable."

She pondered that for a couple seconds. "I don't remember that, but that doesn't mean it didn't happen. Did Henson sue?"

He shook his head. "Ferraro said Henson actually respected what he did."

Rossi chewed at her lip and shook her head. "That's not the Henson I know. He doesn't turn away from anything."

He tucked it away for later review. His memory was nagging him. There was a fact lingering from his interview in Atlanta, and he was struggling to connect it.

"So, we know Henson and Ferraro had a bad falling-out. Before that, though, how were they? Were they ever close?"

"I think they were thick as thieves. Like I told you, this is still a pretty small place, and just because OU has so many students doesn't mean it's this giant conglomeration. It's still a fairly small community. Everybody knows everybody. And everybody knows everybody's business. That goes double for any major boosters."

"Ferraro told me Henson was influential in getting Teddy Simpson here as president."

Rossi nodded. "That's probably true. He probably has more than half the board of trustees listening to him on anything he wants to talk about."

That made sense. "Ferraro was kind of fuzzy on details about the president. Couldn't really remember his name, wasn't sure what he did before he got here. He said he was in the midst of his fight with Henson when the president got picked to work here, and they never got close."

"So?"

"If your circle of friends is involved in picking the new president of a university, don't you think you'd remember a few details?"

Rossi nodded. "Yeah. I do."

"Plus, he's tight with Henson. That's enough for me."

30

KEANE AWOKE IN his hotel bed at eight, and his eyelids fought off moving. Four hours of sleep felt like fifteen minutes. He rolled over into light penetrating the window blinds and smiled. December in Florida means another sunny day.

He replayed last night. He'd counseled Thomas that not interrupting the sleep of a handful of prominent local businessmen to answer questions about their dead friend David Ramer was a mistake. Most people don't know how to lie well or react in their own best interest when confronted in the middle of the night. Thomas had acknowledged that, but they were also right. Keane didn't have to concern himself with politics. At least not there. They were up to their eyes in it.

He showered and was making coffee when his iPhone rattled. Caller ID read: Q.

"How are you doing? You okay?" he answered.

"I'm hanging in there. Mostly, I'm thinking about what you're doing," Q said.

"You have no idea."

"I have an idea. Saw you on TV this morning."

"How the—" And then he remembered the camera lights outside Ramer's home. The cameraman must have gotten a shot of him talking to Thomas and Rossi. He supposed the killing of a prominent Orlando banker would make for statewide morning news on a slow day.

"Looked like you were at a crime scene," Q said. "What happened?"

"This is a little bit bigger than we thought. But the man who killed Sean, that is over with. That happened just like they said. And that man's dead."

"What? Jesus, Keane, you should have called me."

Keane paused, felt his hair tingle. "You're right. I should have."

"Who was it?"

"A guy named David Hance, but everybody called him Tally. He played for OU a few years ago but was still involved with the football team—and he was probably involved in the gambling. Maybe Sean owed him money, but I think he might have been a messenger for a third party. I think he was supposed to scare Sean that night. Whatever it was, he went too far."

"What about the banker?"

"He's a pretty high-level football donor and fan. That's the only link so far."

"How do you know all this?"

Keane thought for a second. "The detectives aren't telling me much."

"But they are sharing. What is it?"

"They know about Sean and the gambling. I gave them the laptop. I don't know if they're going to push, but they're sold on it."

"Can you get them to keep Sean's name out of it? He can't defend himself, and everybody else will put everything on him. Like it's all his fault."

"Chips fall where they fall. If Sean was dirty, it'll come out. We'll have to live with it. Sean made his own bed."

"Man, that's bullshit," Q said. "If he was in deep, somebody pulled him in. Don't let them do this."

"Look, I'm still trying to figure this out. I thought the football coach was pulling all the strings. But it turns out the school president is no choirboy. He has a group of friends who like to pay football players and gamble on the side. At least a couple of these guys are worth a lot of money. They were betting on games, and Sean was involved. It's possible there was point-shaving going on. If that's the case, you'll be seeing things on network TV."

Keane waited for Q to say something but heard only background road noise from the cell phone. "You there?" he asked after several seconds of silence.

"I'm here," Q said finally. "If the players were fixing games, that'd cost Vegas some money."

"I thought about that, but it wouldn't. Remember this was all done on the internet. The guys in Vegas wouldn't care about an offshore internet company getting scammed. In fact, they'd probably like to see more of it to drive the offshore guys out of business." Keane then realized he had no idea how an internet gambling ring would seek retribution for being crossed.

"What about the police in Costa Rica?" Q asked.

"Who knows? They don't work with the FBI."

"What if the internet company gets taken down for so much money that they go out of business? They'd want to pin that on somebody."

"If the company died, there'd be another one lined up right behind them," Keane said. "You also have to understand how much money these companies are probably making. They'd have to lose tens of millions—maybe hundreds of millions— to go down."

"So . . . what are you still doing there?"

".Just helping the locals. We have . . . an understanding."

"You're involved now? Officially? Because I don't see the Orlando Police Department being able to investigate this much better than the Costa Ricans."

He considered how much to say. "They'll need enough for a motive for who killed Hance. But the whole thing here, it's crumbling. It's just about over."

He left out details of how he knew but told Q about the OU boosters arguing with one another. And that the disagreement probably led to the killing of the banker.

"Just like that and you're out? The coach, the school president, all that shit Sean was involved with . . . Is anybody going to get punished?"

Keane let that hang out there before he answered. "Look, people are going to lose their jobs. A couple of them may even be innocent, but the school trustees will make a clean sweep. The boosters . . . they'll get embarrassed in the media and they'll be done dabbling in college football. They'll get good lawyers, but they'll go to prison."

The line went silent again before Q finally asked, "Who do the cops want to arrest?"

"They're not exactly sure. They'll probably arrest them all and worry about it later. It's a tough PR move, but . . ."

"Who would you arrest?"

"I'd start with Henson and Ferraro."

Q paused. "Who the hell is Ferraro?"

Keane explained his trip to Atlanta and how Henson and Ferraro met, how they once were close and now were not.

"How's he involved?"

"I don't know yet, but he is." Keane thought back to his trip to Atlanta, remembering Ferraro as calm and unconcerned about his surprise visit. Maybe it hadn't been a surprise after all.

"When are they going after Henson?" Q asked.

"I don't know. They're being careful with him. They're scared of the backlash." When Q didn't respond he said, "Don't worry. I'll call you as soon as it's done."

KEANE WAS READY to roll, except for his shoes, and decided he had time to play his long shot. With the last of the coffee next to him, he set up on the hotel couch and propped up his stocking feet on the coffee table. He pulled his laptop into place and began his daily research update through Google searches and the *Orlando Sentinel* website.

He downloaded every local article he found related to Sean's death. He read all of them once, then toggled among them and compared bylines, hoping for one match. He noted that none of the writers quoted Thomas or Rossi. Instead, they used information from the same public information officer who had stood before the TV lights last night. Three bylines stood out: a police reporter, an OU education reporter and a sportswriter. Their specialties didn't matter. He felt sure he could manipulate any of them.

Typically he had more facts about a case than the reporter, and he needed the reporter to help him flush out a suspect. Not this time. Now he needed help with recent background about Sean and about the university.

One article about the football team's reaction to Sean's killing carried a single byline. And it was the right one, the sports reporter's name Rossi's ex-boyfriend gave her. He pulled out his phone and dialed the number listed at the end of the story for writer Charles Bone.

"This is Charlie," said a young, impatient voice on the other end. "Who's this?"

"I'd like to have an off-the-record conversation about Sean Riggins," Keane said.

Bone didn't miss a beat. "It's not off the record until I know why."

"Because I have information that you should know. And I'm not sure the police will tell you."

Keane heard a rustling of papers and envisioned the reporter reaching for a notepad. Then Bone came back on. "We can start there, but I'm not promising anything. How do you know Sean Riggins?"

"Off the record, I've known the family a long time," Keane said. "I knew Sean the day he was born. Is that good enough for you?"

"That doesn't explain how you'd know much more than what the police are telling the public or telling us."

Keane drummed his fingers. "Look, I'd like to find some common ground here. I can provide you details of the Riggins investigation that your colleagues don't have and won't have. It's probably not information that'll make the sports page, but I think it'll boost your stock with your editors. And your colleagues who cover the police will be jealous. You'll have a Deep Throat that they won't."

"They have pretty good sources."

Keane chuckled. "Not that good. I've been reading what they've been writing."

"Why are you calling?"

"I need to find a source who can help me understand Coach Childress, the football program, and the university. Somebody that knows the players, too. I assume you know most of them."

Now Bone laughed. "As much as the school lets you know them. Media access isn't that good, but the players spend time on Twitter. I see what they post. And I hear things." Bone changed the subject. "Who are you? I assume you're with OPD?"

"You can write that I have knowledge of the investigation."

"How high up?" Bone asked.

"That will come later."

"Fair enough. I'll talk to you on background but not off the record. I assume you know the difference?"

Keane knew writer-speak. Whatever Bone learned from an off-the-record conversation he couldn't print, but he could use the information to squeeze new facts and details from another source. If he talked to Bone on background, the reporter could print the conversation with anonymous attribution. Background carried risks, but he *had* initiated the call.

"Let's make this easy," Keane said. "We'll talk on background, and if you want to use any of what I say, I'll give you enough to check me out. You do what you want, use what you want."

"Deal," Bone said.

"Ask me three questions. I'll tell you exactly what I know, with the understanding that you can print it. You can identify me as 'a source close to the investigation.' But I won't disclose how I know something. After that, I ask you three questions and you answer."

"I'll have to get that cleared. I'll have to know your full name and title and have a way to verify it."

Keane shifted the phone to the other ear. "What do you have for me?"

The phone connection filled with the sound of Bone pecking on a keyboard. "Do the police think that somcone inside the athletic department was responsible for Sean Riggins's death?"

"No." Keane paused, then added, "I know you're smart enough not to ask closed-end questions."

Bone groaned. "Let me think." The line went silent for several seconds. "How about this? What is it about your situation that has you so interested in the mugging death of a football player?"

"That's better," Keane said. "I told you: the family. When you Google me, if you know what you're doing, you'll find that although I don't live in Florida anymore, I was raised here. Last question."

"Fine. This one has two parts," Bone said. "How much of a shit storm is still to come, and is the Riggins case the only thing going on here?"

Keane mulled his answer. What he said next probably would make it onto the paper's website within minutes, but he had to give the reporter a story worth printing. "The investigation is going in the right direction, and it shouldn't take much longer to wrap up. Everyone involved so far is being cooperative and helpful. Sean Riggins touched a lot of lives, so the time factor is making sure we touch all the bases about his life as a football player and as a student."

"That doesn't really answer the shit-storm part of the question," Bone replied.

"Yes it does. But I'll agree it does depend on your definition of shit storm. Now it's my turn."

"Hang on."

Keane heard more typing. When it stopped, he said, "Who is David Hance? Everyone called him Tally."

"What's he got to do with this? Jesus, was he involved with Riggins?"

"You knew him." Keane pictured the reporter scrambling to multi-task and ask Google about any known connections between Sean and Hance.

"I didn't cover the team when Tally was a player, but he was always around," Bone said. "You know, ex-player who can't let go. Supposedly he was a volunteer in the football office, but I don't know how much work he really did. . . . He was always hanging out with the players. He may have been Childress's source for what goes on among the players behind the coaches' backs. You know, who's fighting, who's partying and all that. I don't think Tally hurt for money, but I never knew what he did."

"You must not frequent strip clubs."

Bone chuckled. "You haven't been around many sportswriters. Why do you say that?"

"Hance was a bouncer at The Jaguar. If it's like all the other gentlemen's clubs I know, that place is swimming in cash."

"Among other things."

Keane thought about his next question. "I've read all the nice things everyone said about Sean in your stories. What was his reputation among the players and coaches?"

"Not that much different from what we've written, but he had a stubborn streak that drove the coaches crazy. He was a good student and a good player, and he knew it. He could think for himself. Coaches, they just want people to do as they're told. Sean tended to freelance on the field, and I'd hear coaches talk after a game about how a defense broke down because he was out of position. There'd be times that he'd make a great play, so it was hard for the coaches to bitch about the freelancing all the time, but you could tell they didn't like it."

Kcane understood. Every great football team had that player. Risk-takers who occasionally hurt the team but often elevated it. He'd never figured Sean was that guy.

"My last question is, how tight a ship does Coach Childress run?"

"He used to be more of a hard ass, but now he's more of a player's coach than people think," Bone said. "He had a couple years where they didn't win much, so his job was on the line. And he knew he had to recruit better and get more buy-in from the players. Somewhere along the way he relaxed a bit."

"The inmates run the asylum."

"Not really. But Childress doesn't suspend guys like he used to. There were times he'd sit a guy out for a whole game. Now he'll just park the guy on the bench for the first quarter, a symbolic suspension."

"What about NCAA rules? Is he a stickler?"

"He's a black-and-white guy, believes in the rulebook, but he knows there's a lot of gray out there and that he has to believe in that, too, if you get my drift. All these schools cheat. I mean everybody. Childress follows the rules more than most, but he's been known to bend a few."

"Which ones?"

Bone paused. "The NCAA has regulations about how many hours a week players can spend on their sport. Practice time, game time, travel time, weights, all that. The school has to document all that. But I've heard about study-hall periods that turned into chalkboard sessions."

Keane figured that was an easy rule to break. And a minor one. "That all?"

"I've heard recruiting visits get kind of wild. Bars, strip clubs. I never got enough good information to write it, but I know it's happened."

"You think players took recruits to The Jaguar?"

"You know . . . maybe," Bone said. "The Tally connection would make more sense."

Keane jotted down notes and hoped Bone kept talking, but the reporter caught on.

"Do the cops think the same person who killed Riggins killed Tally, too?" Bone asked. "Do they think someone else might be next? Jesus, I'd have to get that confirmed—"

"That's a fourth question."

"C'mon, you opened the door. You can't leave me hanging. Not after what I gave you."

"Let's see how you handle your new information. Maybe we'll talk again soon."

Keane hung up and sighed at his stupidity. It hadn't occurred to him to look up player posts on Twitter.

31

KEANE WAGERED THAT a man who owned half a dozen successful car dealerships spent time at each of them to motivate sales managers and general managers. His hope this morning was that Henson liked to count his money as much as he liked to motivate.

He drove up to a tan, unremarkable, one-story cinder block building south of downtown. A maroon Cadillac sedan and a white Toyota Camry sat parked beneath a sign that read: HENSON AUTOMOTIVE, INC. Inside, a small waiting area held a desk, two chairs, and a water cooler. Refinished wood floors creaked as he walked in and greeted a secretary who sported stylish silver hair pulled back by a decorative clip and lips colored perfectly with dark red lipstick.

She clicked away on her laptop and gave him a prim look. "May I help you?"

"Big car company like this, I expected something special." Her expression didn't change, and he stuck out his credentials. "I'm here to see Mr. Henson."

She looked at his badge as if she were reading the day's obits. "I don't recall an appointment. Did you make one?"

"I didn't. I was hoping you could squeeze me in."
He smiled.

She got up and pointed to two armchairs next to
a small rectangular glass coffee table covered by car
magazines. "Have a seat. I won't bother you with
coffee."

He stood instead. She disappeared through a
door and came back in two minutes. "Right this
way." She led him through the interior door, down a
carpeted hallway, and to a corner office.

Don Henson, tall and tan, was on his feet. His
smile flashed a bank of white teeth, but Keane
studied the man's nose. It was perfectly sized and
looked as if it had never seen another man's fist.
Keane took in the rest of him as they shook hands:
tan slacks, a white golf polo, and stylish light-brown
loafers.

"To what do I owe the honor of an FBI visit?"
Henson asked. "Tell me the bureau needs a new
fleet of cars in Florida."

"Sorry about that. I just came down to tell you
it's over. I know about what happened to Sean
Riggins. And I know what Sean was doing, what
you and your buddies are doing. It's over. I'm
putting an end to it."

"Agent Keane, I have no idea what you're—"

"I'm not here officially. I'm here on personal
business. And that's your fault. You guys made it
personal when you decided to fuck with Sean. But
you had no idea Sean kept extensive records. Lists
of games and teammates and dates and amounts.
And a list of people who were running things. Guess
what? You're on the list."

"I highly doubt that." Henson's smile was gone.

"Oh, I wouldn't make that up."

"I don't know what you're talking about. If you think I broke the law or did something you consider improper . . ."

"You know what? I'm not the least bit interested in your bullshit. I came here to tell you two things: It's over, and when you get locked up, you'll know who did it."

"You're making a mistake."

"I've made my share of them, for sure, but this won't be one of them."

Keane closed the door behind him and nodded at the secretary on his way out. "Thanks for the help. By the way, I'd start looking for another job."

TEDDY'S FINGERS WORKED an oversized calculator on the same set of numbers. Twice. Three times. Again. And again.

Over and over, he finished with the same news. All his accounts around the country and world and his total value was barely two million. All the donations from Big Sugar, Big Tobacco, and Big Republicans. Where had it all gone?

The stock crash, a housing bubble, his resulting panic, and a depressed economy took care of almost half. Another sliver he'd simply pissed away on women, gambling and, well, good times. Multiple trips to the Caymans. Trips to Europe. He was single, and he had money. Why not experience the women of the world?

And, of course, he'd invested in his legacy at OU. Contributions to building funds, anonymous and not.

But now? A mere two million? Four years before, it had been more than four times that. At this rate, he was going to have to go back to politics. Make back his money. The idea of manipulating politicians again depressed him. It was so easy there was no sport in it.

He emptied half a travel bottle of Bailey's into a cup of coffee and started to drink it when his cell phone went off.

"I just got a visit from an FBI agent," Henson hissed.

"Did he have a lady cop with him?" Teddy replied.

"What? You're not surprised by this?"

"I've met him." He filled in Henson with last night's visit, leaving out all the salient details of his confession.

Henson said, "And the fact the FBI is looking around your campus isn't something you cared to share? With me or with the board?"

"It wasn't an official inquiry. He's a tag-along with OPD."

"Well, he didn't tag along for me. The asshole just showed up and threatened me."

"Relax, Don."

"Jesus, Teddy, this isn't getting caught with a hooker giving you a blow job in a bar. You can't buy your way out. This is the FBI."

"It's under control," he said.

"And he's asking questions about players getting money and people around here betting on games. And the son of a bitch sounds vindictive."

"This is all under control."

"It's a long way from under control, Teddy. You were going to take care of this. This was going to be all over. What happened to that?"

"It's just appearances. This thing is over. We're fine. OPD is just going through the motions."

"I don't think so."

"Did this guy mention anything else? Anything specific?"

"Yeah, he said he knew what had happened to Sean Riggins and that he was going to take care of it. That he aimed to see us in jail."

Teddy pictured Don in jail and smiled.

"Did you hear me?" Henson demanded. "Goddammit, you said you had this handled, Teddy."

32

ROSSI CLOSED THE door to the interview room, while Thomas paced to the other side and back. He looked her in the eye and poked an accusing finger.

"I don't mind getting my ass chewed for something I did. But I don't like it much when it happens because of someone else," he said.

"Me?" she asked.

"Your FBI friend. He went to Henson's office and threatened him, and Henson called the OU president, who called the chief, who called Beale, who wants to know what the hell is going on."

Beale, she thought. They didn't need the chief of detectives any unhappier than he already was. "What'd you tell him?" she asked.

"I told him the truth, that Sean Riggins has a brother who is FBI. Beale turned more shades of red than I thought possible. But don't worry. I took the bullet."

Rossi smacked the side of her leg. "Shit, shit, shit. I'm sorry."

"We have to keep Keane under wraps. Where is he?"

"I'll find him," she said.

"Tell him his stunt probably will cost him his job. Hell, if he were just trying to get a speeding ticket fixed, it'd get him fired. But tell him it's over. I'll deal with Beale."

SHE CALLED KEANE. "When you pushed Henson's buttons, you started a chain reaction. My boss wants to know why the FBI's involved in our case, and if they're not, why an FBI agent is accusing potential witnesses of crimes they may not have committed."

"You could make something up," he said.

"Yeah, my boss tends not to like that. You probably hate your job, but I like mine."

"What'd you tell him?"

"I didn't. Thomas did. He told the truth. And my boss is pissed. So am I, by the way. I turn my back and you go all Mel Gibson."

"He's pissed because he thinks you knew."

"Maybe, but he's made you the enemy."

Keane laughed. "You're calling to officially tell me to cease and desist."

"It's not funny. But yes, and to tell you odds are my chief will make a call or two up the line. You're probably in danger, professionally speaking."

Keane filled the other end with silence.

"You don't have much time before there's going to be blowback for you. Just wanted you to know," she said.

"Thanks," he said. "I had to be back at work in a couple days anyway. Guess we'll have to push a little harder."

She huffed. "You need to stop pushing. I mean it. This ends now, or I'll arrest you myself."

"Run the links here. Who got to who? Is this really coming from Simpson? He's really trying to protect a car dealer?"

"I've been telling you, he's much more than just a car dealer. He's a big part of the OU community. He gives a lot of money."

Keane paused. "Okay. . . . What'd Childress say about the president?"

"He wouldn't say anything about the president. Those two have too much history. The president loves football and the football coach loves the president. He says he's not aware of any improprieties there. For all he knew, Teddy Simpson was a straight shooter and a good boss."

"Wait, something doesn't fit. I got a guy in Atlanta who's scared of riling up Henson years after they've already cut ties, and this football coach is more loyal to Simpson than he is to a guy who could crush him. That doesn't fit."

"Simpson could fire him on the spot," she said.

"C'mon, you know how this goes. If Henson wanted Childress fired, he could get it done in a day. He'd probably need Simpson's help, but he'd get it however he needed to. This doesn't make sense."

"You're surprised a coach is more loyal to someone at the school than somebody outside the school?"

"Look, they're all gone, no matter what. Once this hits, everybody's smeared. The coach, the president, the boosters. It's just a matter of degree. But nobody close to this at the school is going to have a job. And that's the nice scenario. I think you already know this."

She thought about that. "What are we missing?"

"Maybe there are people in the group we haven't identified yet."

"I'm working on that." Her anger at him had subsided. *He changed the subject*, she thought.

"Look, regardless, you need to stay put. Let me do my job."

She heard a momentary fade-out and realized Keane was getting another call. He ignored it.

"Did you hear what I said?" she asked.

"I'm sorry, what?" Keane said.

"I said you need to let us handle this. In other words, don't do anything. If Thomas wants you arrested, he's going to ask if I know where you are, and I'm going to tell him. You don't want him coming out there."

"Don't worry about me. Just push. This is what we wanted. Somebody's scared because we're getting too close. Keep pushing. I'll call you later."

"Don't hang up—"

But he was already gone.

33

KEANE SCANNED A mid-evening crowd at the Wing Shack and spotted Darrell Dubrow and Johnnie Jones in the rear corner where no one could approach them from behind. "Thanks for coming," he said as he sat.

"Didn't have much choice," Dubrow said. "One of those 'or-else' situations, sounded like."

"Not at all. I'm just in a better position to help you than I was before, and I'm willing to do that for a bit more information."

"We told you everything already. We didn't hold nothing back."

"Let's be clear. You held plenty back. There's still a lot that people don't know about what you two, Sean, and a few others were up to. But you know what? That's okay. Secrets are going to hold, and people might even slide on those."

Johnnie shifted on his barstool. "What don't they know?"

"For starters, they may never prove you guys were throwing games."

"Man, that'd be nice. But I don't know." The football players looked at each other, then back at him.

He looked at the teammates. "Who's going to tell them? They have all the records Sean kept, but they're going to need more than spreadsheets. They're going to need someone to explain them, someone who understands everything on them. Is that going to be you? Or one of the boosters who has money and a good attorney?"

They stared at him, waiting for the hook. He had them.

Keane pressed on. "That person's gone, and they're not getting him back. The only person who could lay it all out, explain every little detail, was Sean. They may have Sean's records, but they don't have him. He's not coming back to testify. Without him . . ."

"All they got are guesses," Johnnie said. "And guesses don't count."

"They have more than that, but it's all circumstantial. It'll be hard unless at least one person cracks and talks. It's basically on you guys."

"Us?" Darrell asked.

"You two and whoever else was in on this. The cops are still investigating, so they'll find more records. But in the end for you guys, it's all about who's going to talk and testify. You'd do well to keep the circle closed. If I were you, I'd spread the word."

Johnnie shook his head and smiled at Darrell. "Damn. That's something."

Darrell nodded at him. "Is that what you came to tell us? Because that's good news. That doesn't sound like an 'or-else' to me. No offense."

Keane shook his head and reached for a menu in a rack holding ketchup, buffalo sauce, salt and pepper. He scanned the list of fried foods and salad and put the menu away. Then he looked around for a waitress. He caught the eye of one, smiled and mouthed *water*. He turned back to the players. "I came to trade," he said. "You guys know what DFS is? Daily Fantasy Sports?"

Puzzled looks crept over both the players' faces.

"You've never heard of this? You set up an online account and make a deposit. Then you pick the sport and pick your fantasy team for that sport for that day. That's the appeal. If your team sucks one day, you get to pick a new team another day. And you compete against other teams every day. They say you can win significant money. And for now, in most states, it's all legal."

Darrell and Johnnie looked at each other again. Johnnie shrugged.

"I don't understand where you're going with this?" Darrell said.

"Mostly I want to satisfy my curiosity. There's one thing that doesn't make sense in all of these."

"What's that?"

"I've seen Sean's records. He documented everything. Or at least it seems like he did. But I didn't see anything about gambling on fantasy sports. That's hard to believe. I mean, that's learning the ABCs of gambling. Online, easy, inexpensive. Hell, people tell me it's exciting as hell. But you guys didn't get into it."

Darrell looked at Johnnie again, but neither spoke up.

"Well?"

"I don't know what you want us to say," Darrell said.

"Tell me why. Or tell me why not."

`"Who says we didn't do fantasy?" Johnnie asked. "Where'd you get that?"

"From the way Sean documented everything—"

"He got out," Johnnie said. "He started out doing fantasy, but he got out."

"What do you mean, 'started out'?"

"Couple years ago, that's what we started doing. I don't know who was the first to do it, but a bunch of us got into it. Sean, too. We played football and basketball mainly, so it slowed down in the summer, but we played it. I don't know why Sean didn't keep anything on it, because he sure played. But after a while, he didn't like it, so he quit."

"He quit because he didn't win, because he lost money?"

"You could say that," Johnnie said. "That was one reason. He said it was rigged so you couldn't win. So he quit."

"He was mad about it, too," Darrell said. "He only lost a few hundred, but he was telling everyone not to play, said we weren't going to win unless we were really lucky."

"Because he was competing against professionals," Keane said. "And probably against computers."

The players nodded.

"That's what Sean said," Darrell said. "A lot of the same people won over and over. A couple of them would have ten or twenty teams, and maybe half of them would win money. Sean said they were computer guys who ran the players through software to find out which guys to pick. And it worked."

"Algorithm," Keane said. "They run players through one and it gives them a desired draft order. Although most algos are sophisticated enough to pick a team or multiple teams. I don't know how fair it is, but it's smart."

"Sean said it went against the way they advertised the game. They make it sound like you're playing against a hundred guys just like you. Makes it seem . . . real. Or legit."

The waitress delivered Keane's water and asked about food. He declined but pulled a twenty-dollar bill from his wallet and put the salt shaker on top of it.

"I'm not hungry, but you guys stay and eat." The teammates gave him a look of approval and he asked, "Are you still playing?"

"Not really," Johnnie said. "Sometimes, but not regularly."

"Sounds like you're moving in the right direction at least. Sean was smart to get out."

Darrell swore and drank his tea. "Man, I should have gotten out when I first thought about it."

"When was that?" Keane asked.

"Last year. It never felt on the up-and-up, but Sean pushed me to stay in. Last month we had a fight about it in the locker room."

"A fight?"

"Yeah, after practice one day Sean was giving me shit about not following through in a game, not selling things hard enough to make it look like we were busting our ass. I kind of snapped and went after him. Told him to shut his mouth about it."

"You guys came to blows?"

Dubrow shrugged. "More him than me. He clocked me."

"Sean wouldn't let you out. I guess I believe that." He got up to leave and studied the two friends. "Yeah, I believe that."

BUOYED BY HIS chat with Darrell and Johnnie, Keane worked out a plan as he drove back to his hotel. Ferraro described Henson as a savvy businessman who oozed charm. He saw an emotional madman. He wanted his gun close, just in case.

He parked outside his room and turned the car off. He fished out his hotel key and heard a familiar *crack* as he got to his door. As his brain registered the sound, stronger than a handgun, he heard another *crack* and flinched as a chunk of the brick façade next to the door front ricocheted off his cheekbone. His face stinging, he quickly swiped his key card. The door rejected it.

At the same time he heard a third *crack*, he was driven into the door and then the ground by a blow from behind. His upper right arm exploded in pain. Blood and tissue spattered on the door and brick. He fell to his left side, his head knocking against the sidewalk. Another bullet landed in the brick and sent chips flying.

Adrenaline took hold. His one arm useless, he rolled into the short hedgerow that framed the sidewalk. The bushes gave him cover from gunfire and, he hoped, provided an angle from which the gunman couldn't get to him.

He looked up and saw he was fifty feet from a stairwell. *Better to be a moving target.* He tried a snake crawl, but again his right arm failed him. He scraped his left hand and elbow and dragged his right shoulder along the sidewalk. Another shot ricocheted off the walkway and into the door of another room, also behind him.

By the time he made it to the stairwell, two more bullets had missed their target. He lay down for three seconds and fished for his cell with his good arm and punched up Rossi.

"I've got a shooter at my hotel," he screamed. "It's going on now. Get people here."

He clicked off and tried examining under his arm. Blood saturated the cotton and washed through a hole in the front. His hand quivered as he tried to lift his arm. He felt hot and clammy at the

256 | David Ryan

same time. His breathing quickened. *I'm going into shock*. He needed to stay awake.

The shooting stopped, and it was as if it never happened. He heard a guest leave a room twenty feet away, get into a car, and drive off, oblivious.

A kid with long hair and a skateboard eased past the stairwell and stopped. "Holy shit, man, you're bleeding."

"Can you go to the front desk and find a towel? I've got to get this under control."

The kid returned with two white towels. For the first time, the kid noticed a red trail down the walkway to his resting place. "Holy shit."

"Kid, there's about to be a fleet of cars coming screaming into this place. Can you go up front and show them where to go? Go on."

Alone again, he unbuttoned his shirt and peeked as his wound. Red muscle and pinkish fat lined the edges of a missing chunk of flesh. A high-velocity bullet had done its job, and judging by the pain in his back. It probably went through bone on its way through him.

He balled up one towel and jammed it under his arm. With the second towel he fashioned a makeshift tourniquet, using his teeth to pull it taut. He lay against the staircase wall, closed his eyes, and said a quiet thanks for the distant wail of a siren.

KEANE DIDN'T MOVE until a half-dozen sheriff's deputies rolled hard into the parking lot. That came after a SWAT unit surrounded the hotel and cleared the scene.

A deputy found him sitting upright in a stairwell, still conscious, still bleeding.

"Missed the artery. Lucky man," the deputy said.

Rossi arrived before fire rescue and skipped the formalities. "How bad?"

He said, "Through-and-through under my arm. I won't be going to the gym anytime soon."

She nodded. "Who, you think?"

"Somebody who can't shoot."

"Maybe not, but he hit you."

"Barely. Somebody got lucky."

"Yeah, you."

"No idea. Henson? Ferraro? It's not a hired gun He had a chance to take me out with his first couple shots and didn't touch me. He didn't use a hollow point. He's not a shooter."

"Or maybe he is and he didn't want you dead."

He pointed down the hallway. "He bounced three or four more shots off the wall and sidewalk and finally put one through me. I dove near the bushes. Lucky."

"Nobody yelled at you, called out, did anything that indicated why you?"

"In my experience, shooters shoot first and call out later."

"Yeah? How much experience do you have at this?"

"Counting tonight? One time."

He lay back against the steps and closed his eyes. He dialed his mind back thirty minutes. What did he see? What did he hear?

The answers were: nothing suspicious and nothing out of the ordinary.

Rossi said, "We'll chase this down as best we can, but unless we get a serious break, this is going to end up with your guys."

He knew she was right and that one unfortunate FBI agent in Central Florida would get his time wasted. Unless the shooter had dropped a driver's license or left a business card, the number of potential suspects was untold. They included anyone he'd had contact with while he was in Orlando and anyone he'd investigated in Tennessee who might want him permanently removed from the FBI. And before he left home, he'd been poking around a white-collar marijuana ring.

He was out of luck and he knew it. He'd have to report the fact that he got shot. "You realize this probably would have gone differently if I'd been carrying my gun," he said.

"I thought you Feebs always had to carry your gun," she said.

"C'mon."

"Seriously. Don't you have it with you at all times?"

"Having it with you and having it on you are two different things."

"You're saying if you'd been on the job, you'd have had your gun on you and, what? Our gunman wouldn't have gotten away?"

"Not necessarily. But if I'd had my gun, you damn sure better believe I'd have returned fire."

She shook her head in disbelief as paramedics arrived. One of them moved her out of the way, seized Keane's right arm, and began a medical interrogation. "Does this hurt? What about now? Or now? Do you feel this? Are you feeling lightheaded?"

And on and on. Keane said, "Just bandage it up. I'm not going to the hospital."

"You're going. Gunshot victims get a trip to the ER and a police report. Double winner."

ROSSI WALKED INTO the ER as a small team finished prepping Keane for surgery. She noted the morphine cocktail dripping into him from an IV.

"They've already given you painkillers, so whatever you tell me now is useless," she said. "Unless you remember anything good."

Keane shook his head. "You'll have to find this guy on your own. Think you can do that?"

She turned to a nurse. "Can you ask the doctor to sew up his mouth while you're in there? It would save him a lot of trouble."

ROSSI SET UP shop in the cafeteria and began writing notes. Keane would be in surgery at least an hour, longer if doctors found major damage. It looked to her that he'd probably keep the motor skills in his right shoulder, arm, and hand, but she'd seen the results of other bullets to shoulders. There was a chance Keane would have pain the rest of his life. There was also a chance he'd be forced out of the FBI. And even if he were forced to a desk job, he'd have to prove he could shoot with his right hand.

She tapped out what was already known: No witnesses, no hard suspects. And too many potential suspects. The crime-scene guys found a spent nine-millimeter shell across the street from the hotel, which was good news and bad news. The casing proved the shooter was not a professional. The nine millimeter was the most popular handgun in America, the mom and pop of personal weapons.

She figured there were no less than thirty thousand of them in Florida alone, and those were the ones that were registered. Not exactly narrowing the pool of suspects.

She then typed out the names of every booster and school official she'd talked to or considered in the past two weeks. Then she added a note to herself: *Check on gun ownership.*

KEANE WOKE UP to a snort. Not bad, just a slight nasal grunt. There sat Rossi, her head tilted to the back and side of a vinyl-upholstered, standard-issue hospital recliner.

He said, "Who's supposed to be resting here?"

"What? Huh?" Rossi jerked awake, wiped her mouth and dialed in. "How are you feeling?"

"I feel like I've got a long needle in one arm and a hole in the other." This, in fact, was his exact situation. The newly installed IV felt like someone had inserted a screwdriver into the underside of his forearm.

He faintly remembered an appearance by the surgeon in recovery but now recalled nothing about what the man told him. Maybe a mention of bone fragments.

He flexed his right hand and felt no pain in his shoulder. He raised his elbow to a dull ache under his arm. The sensation crept into his upper back and lower shoulder. All of his shoulder was encased in bandages.

"You're up!" A tall, dark-skinned nurse rushed in, felt for his pulse and looked at her watch. Her ID badge read DANIQUE, and her scrubs were as unique as her name: purple pants and a wildly patterned top, also primarily purple. "Are you in any pain?"

"Pain is such a relative concept," Keane said.

"Hmm, yes it is, which is why I asked. We don't have you on the PCA yet. We'll get you on that in a little while."

"PCA?"

"Patient Controlled Analgesic. PCA. A pain button. Any time the pain gets too bad, just push it."

"Where has *that* been all my life?"

Danique laughed. "Did you see the doctor?"

"Not that I remember. What do you know?"

Looking at his chart she said, "Looks good. You lost a little muscle, and it looks like the bullet hit the lower part of your scapula. We removed a few bone fragments, and others came out with the bullet. But the integrity of the scapula wasn't compromised."

She flipped back and forth in the notes.

"He doesn't think you have any nerve damage. That's very good. You were lucky."

He nodded. He couldn't deny that, but he hardly felt lucky. He felt helpless. A crease in the curtains showed darkness and the reflection from a nearby set of street lights. It was late night or early morning, depending on how long his operation took.

"When can I leave?"

"A couple days maybe. You probably won't need any more surgery, but we're watching to make sure there's no infection. That's the big thing."

She checked his IV and made notes in his chart. When she was done, she promised to bring him ice chips.

Rossi said, "What do you remember?"

He walked her through it again and she said, "One hit out of eight or ten? This guy can't shoot. You're not exactly a small target."

"That's what I'm thinking," Keane said.

"Think harder. I'll come back tomorrow. Get some rest."

She yawned on her way out, and he took inventory of the shit storm that was about to arrive. He had gotten shot while not on the job, which made the situation worse than if it had happened while he was working. FBI agents tend to get wounded from time to time but always in the line of duty. This was entirely different.

He'd get a visit from another agent, and he'd likely face an official inquiry into his actions while taking time off in Florida. Politics would get played, and his best interests wouldn't be the bottom line. His future might depend solely on how much of an asshole he wanted to be when the time came.

He closed his eyes and pondered a life outside the FBI. A strange concept.

34

KEANE ENDURED THE longest eighteen hours of his life. The ER surgeon used fifteen stitches to close the gunshot wound but refused to make him an outpatient, insisting on monitoring for an infection before letting him leave.

Nurses added a new IV bag every two hours and twice brought him food. His three treks to the bathroom weren't pain-free, but he was getting used to moving around without putting his arm into positions that felt like daggers in his shoulder.

On one of his trips to the bathroom, he used a hand-held mirror a nurse gave him to study a reflected image of the bullet's entry point. The whole area was deep purple.

Thanks to pain pills, his arm hurt less than the afternoon visit from two of the FBI's finest, Agents Dombrowski and Cramer, both from Tampa. The shooting of a fellow agent, especially one away from duty, raised concerns, they said. And suspicions. They needed to know if he was targeted and why.

Dombrowski was slim-wasted, tall, tan, and bald. He gave off an air that he could compete in a triathlon at a moment's notice. His obligatory navy sport coat hung off him as if he'd recently lost weight. That contrasted with Cramer, who looked like a corporate shark. A full head of black hair was slicked straight back, and his red power tie offset a gray pinstripe suit.

One agent stood at the foot of the hospital bed. The other took a spot at Keane's side. It wasn't the ideal interrogation room, but with no roommate it offered a modicum of privacy. Dombrowski and Cramer displayed a temperament that told Keane they'd probably been sent here against their wishes. All they wanted to do was get their interview and go home.

Keane talked them through his past ten days, starting with the last days Sean was alive in Boynton Beach and ending with his surgery. He left out the parts about his family relationship with Sean and his speculation about the gambling. If either agent were any good, they'd figure it out soon enough.

"You've basically been participating in an investigation with Orlando police while you've been down here," Dombrowski said. "That about right?"

Keene looked him in the eye. "Not at all. I promised the kid's dad I'd help him understand what happened to his son and why. That's all I've done."

Cramer pointed his notepad at him. "Looks like you pissed somebody off."

"You're quite the detective."

"Who would that be?"

"You'd have to ask OPD. I assume they're looking into it. Are you?"

"Not yet," Cramer said. "Don't worry. We'll talk to OPD."

He was certain they already had and probably would again. He wondered how badly Rossi had chopped him up.

The agents pivoted their questions to Tennessee and the open cases he'd left behind. Keane told them about an accountant who was skimming money from a high-level marijuana dealer and had gotten fingered by the secretary he was sleeping with on the side.

"Not exactly Scarface," he said.

"But the dealer, he could have sent a gunman to Florida after you," Dombrowski said.

Keane pointed at his shoulder. "Some hitman. All he got was this. That's amateur hour."

Cramer tucked his notebook away. They were done. "How did you rate a private room?"

"It's Orlando. I guess it really is tourist-friendly." He waited for a reaction but got none. "I'm going home as soon as my temperature comes back to normal. Should be any time now."

The agents promised a follow-up and left, but their body language suggested they had no zeal to investigate a fellow agent or get involved in crimes that were local. The first, second, and third priorities of the FBI these days were all terrorism.

Rossi, looking as tired as he felt, popped in as soon as the agents left.

"You look like you could use a beer," she said.

"And you didn't bring me one. . . . You met Frick and Frack, the friendly agents from Tampa?"

"They introduced themselves this afternoon. I didn't get the impression they wanted your balls. They sounded like this was a major inconvenience. Which, by the way, it is for all of us."

"Yeah, a big distraction."

"Do you have any more clarity? Did you remember anything?"

He didn't, and that surprised him. Something nagged at him, but he couldn't pull it out of his brain. "But I have been thinking. I don't think Ferraro's responsible for this."

Rossi cocked her head and gave him a surprised look. "What makes you say that?"

"Ferraro strikes me as the kind of guy who, if he wanted you dead, you'd end up dead."

She nodded. "You could still be in danger."

"I did strike a nerve."

"You do that a lot."

SPORTING A NEW sling for his shoulder and arm, Keane needed half an hour to convince the hotel manager he wasn't the reason his room still had crime tape around it and why the maintenance staff would be replacing the door and patching bullet holes in the surrounding brick façade.

Short, white, twenty pounds overweight and in his mid-forties, the manager sported a starched, regulation short-sleeve shirt, and a perfectly knotted tie. He reeked of self-importance and made clear his preference that Keane find other accommodations. "I think it would be best for all concerned," he said.

Keane chuckled. "Why would it be best for me?"

"The room rate is going up, I'm afraid," the manager said, punctuating his news with an intentional smile. "You'll save money elsewhere, I'm sure."

"The rate was pre-negotiated. I had an open reservation, which was clear when I checked in."

"Ah, there must have been a miscommunication. Rates are always subject to change. It says so on our website. And on the reservation confirmation you were given when you arrived."

Keane nodded, but he had more desire to sleep than to fight over money. He'd used his federal-employee status to secure a government discount on the room rate. Now it was essentially being removed. "Put me in a new room at the new rate."

The new rate turned out to be fifty percent higher than the old rate, but his second-story room smelled fresh, and the air conditioner worked. After he put out the DO NOT DISTURB sign and plugged in his phone to charge, he swallowed a pain pill and tapped the thermostat to seventy-two. He took off his clothes, then gingerly slid under the sheets. It took him a couple of adjustments to position a pillow under his elbow and get his shoulder into a comfortable position. He closed his eyes and waited for the meds to kick in. For the first time in a long time, he thought about nothing. And faded away.

EXCEPT FOR TWO trips to the bathroom and two more rounds of pain pills, Keane slept for seventeen hours. The back of his upper arm felt like he'd gotten hit with a baseball bat, and it looked it too. A bandage covered up his stitches and deep purple skin, a bruise that figured to linger for a couple of weeks. Even after his prescription ran out, he'd keep Advil in business for a while.

He lay in bed and took stock. He had to admit he was lucky to be alive. *But somebody was a pretty damn poor shot*. The shooter had been no more than forty yards from him. Not on top of him but close, all things considered. With his back to the shooter, he'd have made a wide enough target. Sure, he'd gotten hit. But after that one bullet, nothing else was close. Several shots were well right of him, and others were short. *Who the hell was trying to warn him off?*

His shower and clean-up routine took almost an hour with bandages, and free breakfast was long gone when he arrived downstairs late morning, and the residual coffee was lukewarm. He downed two cups and took two more to his room. It was time to get back to work.

"HELLO?" CHARLIE BONE sounded as if he'd just woken up.

"Are you one of those sportswriters who stays up late and wakes up late? How cliché," Keane said.

"And you're one of those federal employees who wake up at the crack of dawn and assume the rest of the world does too. Back at you."

He didn't assume this, of course, and this was the exact reason he'd called Bone, banking on the fact he'd be asleep or, at the very least, unprepared for a source to call. "What are you hearing?"

"Are you kidding?" Bone replied. "The university is in a panic. Everyone's in lock-down mode, radio silence. What the hell's going on?"

"Are we playing the question game again?"

Bone groaned. "I'd rather not."

"You heard about the hotel shooting?"

"I did. One wounded, nobody killed. What's that have to do with OU?"

"I was the wounded."

"What?" Keane heard bedsprings creak, and he pictured Bone sitting up in bed. "Nobody said anything about a law-enforcement officer being shot. . . . They didn't catch the guy. . . . How does this tie in?"

"I never said I was law enforcement," Keane said. "But I'll let you use that. Is anyone talking about Hance?"

"The people who are saying anything, that's the only person they're talking about, and it's all on background. Most of it is piling on, people saying they knew he was a bad guy from the beginning."

Keane nodded to himself. Post-mortem smear campaigns were a popular diversionary tactic. It's always easiest to blame the one person who can't defend himself. "In this case, don't believe what you hear. This isn't about Hance."

"Then who is it about? And who shot you?" Bone asked.

"Off the record, nobody knows. For sure people are trying to keep things quiet. We've touched a nerve."

"Well, shit. Give me something I can use."

"You can write that the police are expanding their investigation and are questioning people who are closely tied to OU. How's that?"

"OU athletics? Or the school?"

"After this, everyone's fair game. Off the record."

FOR THE SECOND time, Keane patiently worked through the automated phone system in place at Blindside.com. He endured the same questioning and answered the same way. Yes, he, Sean Riggins, wanted to close his account.

He transferred the $85,000 balance to a recently created account at Banco Publica, set up under the name Mid-Florida Realty Co. With a friendly handshake that included five hundred-dollar bills and the promise of a ten-percent "establishment fee," Frederico, the friendly assistant bank manager in Costa Rica, had carried out a promise to help Keane during his visit to San José.

A paper trail existed because Keane hadn't had the money or time to navigate the Costa Rican way of conducting clandestine business. If an American investigator wanted to fly to Costa Rica and dig through business filings, Keane's name would surface. It would simply take someone determined enough to do it. He was betting no one would care that much.

Frederico would take his $8,500 cut shortly after the Blindside transfer arrived.

Keane's next call went directly to Frederico. "Hello, my friend. Do you remember me? You helped me with some paperwork a few days ago."

"Of course, sir," Frederico said. "Is everything satisfactory?"

"The transactions that we spoke about are happening now. You will see the first one in a few minutes, maybe even now."

Keane waited as the man tapped on computer keys.

"Ah! Yes, sir, it has arrived." Frederico confirmed the balance and reminded him of the money split. "Shall I proceed?"

Frederico had agreed to transfer the remaining $76,500 to a series of bank accounts in a daisy chain that he had access to. The last transfer would be to PayPal. It wouldn't accept money from companies with reputations of Blindside.com, but Costa Rican banks were in the clear. Next year, Keane would have to declare the money as income and pay federal taxes on it. He'd do it, gladly.

But before any of that, right now, Keane had to make a decision that would impact his career and possibly the rest of his life. In nearly two decades as an attorney and a law-enforcement officer he'd seen businessmen commit crimes both minuscule and grandiose and walk away unpunished. He'd also known of colleagues who cut corners, got sloppy, and got caught. They'd paid a steep price. Now he walked that line.

"Let's do it."

35

KEANE DROVE THE perimeter of the university three times, taking care with each speed bump to spare his sore arm more pain. On each loop, he cruised past the on-campus home of Teddy Simpson. He searched for places to hide, but there were no good options. It was a neighborhood of one.

Simpson's house sat more than a hundred yards from the nearest building. Across the street was a four-lane, two-way road divided by a grassy median. On the far side was a row of pine and maple trees. There was no good place to park in plain sight and watch anonymously.

He made a U-turn and circled behind the house. The fence went all the way around, but a large podocarpus hedge grew on three sides. *Too close*.

He steered back into the heart of campus, parked in a metered lot, and thanked modern medicine. There were few things in life worse than being sick or wounded away from home, but oxycodone definitely helped. The doctor had agreed to write one non-refillable prescription to last him three days. And day one was all right. A little Oxy for the pain, Tylenol for swelling, presto. His right arm felt ten pounds heavier than it should, but it didn't ache. His stitches even held. For now.

He walked back to the house and nestled behind the tall shrubs. Once he parted a few branches for a sightline, he could see the road, the driveway, and part of Simpson's back pool area. His phone vibrated and he fished it out of his pocket with his left hand.

Rossi. He tucked the phone away.

Henson arrived first, followed quickly by two others. All white, all at least forty, all with serious expressions. Teddy Simpson greeted them all, then went back to his back patio to finish steaks on his grill.

Through a pair of binoculars, Keane saw the group congregate around the outside bar by the pool. The arguing started immediately.

TEDDY FINISHED THE steaks and directed his friends back inside. He was deep into his second Scotch. The last meeting was disagreeable. This one promised to be a disaster.

Henson gulped down two fingers of bourbon and decided not to wait for the rest of the group. "You swore you had this under control, Teddy, and I'd have to say this is about the most not-under-control situation I've ever seen. We need to start thinking about options and alternatives."

"Alternatives? We have three dead people, and they all have ties to us," he said to Henson. "By the way, you were pretty damned vocal about all of them. And now we have a shot-up Fed."

Henson glowered. "You're an idiot. I had nothing to do with any of this."

"No? You called to gloat about Hance. Hell, you were delighted."

"Me? He was your boy."

"That's right, he was. And you burned him, didn't you?"

"I didn't do anything to him."

"What about Dave?"

"What about him?"

"Somebody killed him. And once again, you were pretty angry about him."

"Fuck you. You're insane."

"You're saying you're just as much in the crosshairs here and did nothing to deserve it?"

Henson said, "I'm saying we're getting hunted down, and you think I'm to blame. I'm saying you're full of shit."

Simpson laughed. "You're more full of shit than I am, and that's saying something."

KEANE SQUEEZED THROUGH the hedge and didn't hurt at all. Pulling himself up and over the aluminum security fence was the killer. His shoulder talked back and he felt a tug. Blood started to stain his shirt.

He hustled to the side of the house, away from the pool, and made his way to the front of the house when he noticed the front gate opening. A silver Mercedes convertible drove in, and a moment later, a tall, slender man in a dark suit walked to the front door.

Keane squatted behind a bush and watched the man, who had a wave of silver hair to match his car, knock on the door and enter without being asked. He listened carefully for the ping of an alarm, a sign to tell the homeowner that his front door had been opened and closed. He didn't hear an alarm. He heard shouting.

He maneuvered along the front of the home to the corner of a large window. There in front of him was a formal living room but no people. The arguing was coming from the back of the house.

Staying close to the stucco exterior and hidden from street view by shrubs, Keane worked his way to the side of the house near the screened-in pool. There were two screen doors, one on each side of the pool. One was next to him and a cluster of phone and electrical lines. The other, fifty feet away and on the other end of the patio, opened to a walkway that led to the side of the garage. In between were a large glass patio table and chairs, an outdoor bar, and an outdoor kitchen. And separating the patio area from the house were four panels of sliding glass. They were closed, but they couldn't contain all of the yelling coming from inside Teddy Simpson's home.

He hunched close to the porch screen. He recognized Simpson's voice and then Henson's, but no conversation. The yelling made him smile. He leaned his head against the house, closed his eyes, and focused on the voices inside. And wondered how best to play this.

TEDDY TUNED HIS flat screen to ESPN and collapsed in a chair away from the group. A litany of NFL injury updates scrolled by on the bottom of the screen, unbearably teasing bits of news for anyone who gambled on pro football. He barely noticed.

The four men haggled about their predicament. They let Henson bellow and accuse everyone else of deeds done and ones left undone. They'd heard it all before.

"What the fuck is your problem?" Henson finally grumbled at Teddy, his anger already spewed at the others.

"I'm just taking in the moment," Teddy said.

"Jesus Christ, what moment?"

"The one when you finally realize it's dead and gone."

"You're drunk."

"Maybe. But it's over. We did what we did, we played a grand game and had our fun, but now it's over. We might as well alert the attorneys and brace for impact."

"We're fine. We just need to lay low and control the damage."

He stared at Henson, who was glaring back at him. "Three people are dead, and the cops are going to roll some heads, you moron. What part of *murder investigation* don't you get?"

"Teddy, the fact is, most murder investigations take less than a week for the cops to make an arrest. It takes them a few more weeks, even months, to make the case the prosecutor wants. Sean Riggins? Please. It's simple: they'll pin that on Tally. And Tally? It's all circumstantial. Him doing favors for us, for you, those weren't criminal. We'll be fine. On the other hand, you probably want to start thinking about what's going to leak out and if that's going to put the football team on probation. Get them knocked out of bowl games for a while."

"If our little game ever leaks out, we won't have to worry about games because we won't have a program to worry about. We'll get shut down. We'll be lucky to get one more season in. We'll all be looking for new careers."

"Maybe," Henson said. "I'm sure your friends in Tallahassee will take you back. You're too good."

"Wonderful," Simpson said, and sipped his Scotch. "Just wonderful."

36

KEANE HEARD THE goodbyes. He stretched his legs. Under the cover of darkness, he moved along the side of the house, from the back to the front.

The front door opened and the foursome filed out. Simpson closed the door behind them without saying a word. The driveway gate creaked open, and one by one, SUVs and luxury sedans pulled out.

The last car, a dark red Cadillac, rolled past the gate and hesitated. *Henson.* The gate closed, but Henson didn't move.

Keane looked up and cursed. He was lucky not to have set off the motion detector on the flood-light directly above him. He was stuck.

The Cadillac finally moved. It went right out of the driveway and rolled slowly past the brick mailbox and in front of the house.

He pulled out his phone and got the camera ready. *Maybe one clear shot.* The car looked clearer to his eyes than it did on the phone screen. He made certain the flash was off, focused, and snapped the car's picture.

The Cadillac stopped.

He crouched down behind a small hedge, daring not to touch anything that might move. The phone lit up and vibrated with an incoming call. He looked: Rossi. He declined the call and put the screen against his leg to minimize any light.

The Cadillac hadn't moved.

And then it did, accelerating quickly away.

He looked at his new photo, a grainy image of a too-dark car. Worthless.

HENSON WAITED AT the edge of the driveway and scrolled through his phone contacts. He found the number he wanted and called. He pulled out of the driveway as he talked.

"What's going on?" the voice on the other end asked.

"Teddy's coming unglued. He looks like he's sinking."

"Suicidal?"

"No, not like that. Just morose. He's ready to move on."

"He's lost money before," the man said. "He'll be fine. Teddy Simpson can find money under any rock he turns over. That's his gift. What was he doing when you left?"

"What he always does, drink and watch ESPN. I swear, I need to get him a woman."

A sudden bit of light near the left corner of the house caught his eye. *What was that?*

"Hang on," he said into the phone. He stopped and looked at the left side of the stucco home but saw nothing but grass and shrubs all the way to the row of hedges. Nothing.

"What's going on?" the man asked.

After five seconds, he said, "I thought I saw something, but I guess it was nothing. Maybe a possum."

"Is Teddy a problem?"

"Teddy's a wild card. You know how he is. I don't know what he's going to do."

"Call me when you do."

FERRARO HUNG UP and thought about Don and Teddy. They'd been friends a long time, certainly longer than he and Don had. *And to think that FBI agent bought that story about us hating each other. Then again, you never know.*

37

KEANE SAT ON the mulch, leaned against the house, relieved. He called Rossi.

"Where the hell are you?" she demanded.

"I'm around," he said evenly.

"You're not around. If you were around, I'd know about it. Our guys showed up at your hotel earlier and you weren't around. Where are you? And why are you whispering?"

"You sure you want to know?" he asked, and didn't wait for an answer. "I've been listening to the OU president talk to his partners about all the shit they've been stirring up around here. An interesting mix of people. And you know what?"

"What?" she asked.

"The football coach was nowhere to be seen."

"Fine. I'll be at your hotel in fifteen minutes, and you damn well better be there."

"Skip the hotel. Meet me at Simpson's house."

"Why?"

"Because I'm hanging out with the president."

"Keane, we agreed there'd be no bullshit, and now here we are. Don't do anything. I'll be there in fifteen minutes."

LIGHTS FLASHING, ROSSI pushed hard across the East-West Expressway. From the station, Thomas had talked three times to patrolmen sent to watch and contain Keane, and in between he'd called her to vent. The patrolmen never found Keane. Which told her Keane was back to running his own game. Maybe even a spy mission.

She mashed the accelerator a little harder.

TO HIS SURPRISE, Keane found an unlocked door and let himself in. No chime, no alarm. He closed the door softly and headed for the TV he heard in the back of the house.

When he got through the long foyer, he stopped and stuck his head into a great room. A large, granite-filled kitchen on the left, a spacious living room on the right. Beyond them he saw the large sliding-glass doors, the back patio, and pool. No wonder he'd been able to hear everyone. He'd just been beyond those doors. Had any one of them bothered to come outside to smoke . . .

"You forget something?" Simpson's voice, slightly slurred, rose above the din of a college football game on the TV. His back to the kitchen, Simpson sat in an oversized leather chair studying the flat screen.

Keane walked into the viewing area and said, "I don't know, did I?"

"Christ almighty, how the hell did you get in?" Simpson bellowed. "Who the hell are you?" He rocked out of his chair and studied his visitor. "It's you. You're FBI."

"I am."

"Then you know you can't just come in here. This is illegal as hell."

Keane moved in front of Simpson. "I was in the neighborhood and thought you might be in danger. Besides, I'm not worried about it having to stand up in court. We're not going to get that far."

Simpson tipped his glass at Keane's bloodstained shirt. "Shouldn't you be in a hospital? I heard you got shot."

"What do you know about that?"

"Only what I saw on the news. Looks like it hurt."

"Flesh wound," he said. "You have any ideas on who might have done it?"

Simpson shook his head. "Believe it or not, I'm a pacifist. Is that what you came to ask? Who shot you?"

"Who were all your friends? The ones who just left?"

Simpson sat back in his chair, drink in hand. "The names I gave you and your police friends? That's them. Gracious supporters of the university."

"One of them was missing. You guys figuring out how to carry on now that Ramer's dead?"

"Not everyone is. I don't think that's the wisest course of action."

"You're bailing?"

"Time seems right. I'll cut my losses."

"You didn't lose much. At least, not financially."

Simpson looked at him. "Point taken."

"There will be the little matter of the Hance murder."

"Tally? What, you think I burned his house down? I don't handle disputes that way."

"So there was a dispute."

"Of course. But I won't go into it. And I didn't hurt him—or kill him."

"I'm sure the detectives will talk to you about it. I just have a question about the money you made. How'd you hide it?"

Simpson laughed. "It's easy when it's all overseas. Starts there and stays there. I don't use any credit cards to move it. Gambling in England is completely legal, so I just leave the money there. That's one of the things Riggins screwed up. He told me he was using a credit card as a go-between. It was just a matter of time before he got caught. He needed to stop that."

"You don't declare any of that income."

"Sure I do. That's what makes it all legit. To the IRS, it looks like investment income."

"I know all about you. You built a life on telling people exactly what they want to hear and making money off it. You're a master. You didn't get to the big leagues of national politics, but you've been the man in Florida, which means you're good. No offense, but I don't believe you. I don't think the police will either."

Simpson shook in disbelief and collapsed onto the sofa, spilling his drink in his lap. "All the things I've done. All the things I've gotten away with. And you're going try to put me away for a crime I didn't commit? Jesus Christ."

"Yoda, Mr. President."

"What are you talking about?"

"Yoda. You know, from *Star Wars*? 'Do or do not. There is no try.' I'm not going to try to put you away. I *will* put you away. Count on it."

Simpson took a deep drink, laid his head back and then turned to stare at Keane. "All this because of Riggins? Jesus, this seems personal to you."

"Sean was my brother—half-brother."

"You don't think I know that already? No offense, but you don't look anything like him."

Keane ignored the president's bait. "Sean lived and died with the consequences of his decisions, but you and Childress and your other buddies, I think they helped those decisions along. For what? For money? What kind of school is this?"

"Son, universities are nothing without money. It makes everything go 'round. You've been around. Surely you know that."

He nodded. "That's the prevailing theory."

Simpson said, "Tell me, how well did you know your brother?"

"Not well enough."

"Well, he was a damned smart kid. He'd have been a millionaire one day, I'm sure of it. He had a businessman's mind. He knew what he wanted. Hell, he used us as much as we used him."

"Who's *us*?"

"Everyone. The coaches. The boosters. Me. The school. Everyone."

"Yeah, well, he got nice clothes. A nice apartment. A fat bank account. You sons of bitches taught him how to gamble, so eventually he'd have lost all that he got. He—"

"Taught him how to gamble? He was gambling?"

"Of course he was gambling. He was doing the same thing you and your pals were doing. Betting on games. Including betting on his own team. And betting against them, too."

"He was winning?"

"Of course. Just like you. How could you not know this?"

"How much?"

"Enough."

"Seriously. More than a few hundred?"

"Just a little."

Simpson paced his living room, talking to himself and nodding as he went. He looked up at Keane. "What else?"

"You had no idea Sean was probably the biggest bookie on campus?"

Simpson shook his head. "How would anyone know that? All this stuff, it's online. You pick games in the comfort of your own home. All the . . . transactions . . . are between you and a company that will never have to talk to a prosecutor in this country. It's quite a remarkable setup."

"Okay, but why would David Hance want to hurt Sean? You had a good thing going and then the lynchpin dies."

"You'd have to ask Hance."

"How convenient for you that I can't."

Simpson shrugged.

Keane took a step closer and jabbed a finger at the president. "You want to know what I think? I think Sean found out how much money you and your friends were banking and decided whatever you were paying him wasn't enough And he held out for more. Or else."

"Unfortunately, we'll never know. But like I said, he was smart."

Now Keane shook his head. "There is one thing I don't understand. Why would you risk your career, the university, everything, for money that was hardly life-changing? Unless you were making millions from this, it can't have been worth what it's going to cost you."

"Jesus, son, don't you know how to have fun?"

Rossi opened the door with one hand and kept contact with her service gun with the other. She heard voices and sensed the flickering light of a TV from the rear of the house.

"President Simpson? You here? Orlando Police," she called.

"Back here," Simpson said.

She walked into the great room. Keane stood near the back wall and across from Simpson, who was seated. She moved to the right to see both of their faces.

"What's going on? Are you okay?" she asked Simpson.

Simpson said, "Mr. FBI and I were just having a chat. Of course, he broke in."

"Not true," Keane said. "The door was open."

"Mr. Simpson, did you invite Agent Keane into your house?"

"I did not."

"Keane, do you have your gun?"

"Why would I need a gun?" Keane said. "I have a bullet hole in my arm. I think my stitches broke, and I'm bleeding. I couldn't shoot if I had one."

"Answer me: Do you have your gun?"

"Of course not."

Rossi took her hand off her gun and faced Keane. "Let's go. If you're lucky, the president won't press charges."

"Relax. The president and I just had a nice conversation about his group of high-class gamblers. And how he says Sean got everything he wanted."

"Keane, seriously. I don't want to arrest you for being an asshole."

"I just have one more question," Keane said.

"No, you're done. Let's go," Rossi said.

He held one finger up at her and looked back at Simpson. "What's your AOL address? Your email?"

Simpson frowned. "My personal account? What's it matter?"

"It is you. BigStick1955. You walk softly and carry that big stick." Keane smiled. "You're so done."

Rossi stepped between them. "That's it. We're done."

Keane started toward the front door but stopped at the threshold and looked back at the president. "Sean didn't get everything he wanted."

"No?" Simpson asked.

"No. He wanted to live."

ROSSI LAUNCHED INTO him as soon as they closed the front door. "Have you lost your mind? Because what you just did, you're going lose your fucking job. I can bury it in the paperwork, but it's going to come out. You're probably going to get charged, because these people you're fucking with have friends. Politically connected friends. Really rich friends. Hell, *they're* all rich."

"It had to be done."

"Not by you. It's not your job."

He said, "You didn't ask him who all his friends were. All the ones who just left."

"I know who they are," she said. "I talked to half of them today."

"Who are they?"

"A banker. A lawyer. A car dealer. For starters."

"Of course, they're connected around town."

"Of course."

"Which explains why you've arrested none of them," he said.

"Gee, you sound like a disgruntled family member of a victim who thinks the police can't do their job right."

At the end of the driveway, she pushed a button on the back of the gate control box. The gate swung open. They walked to her car outside the gate.

"How'd you get in?" he asked. "The gate was locked shut."

She said, "Probably the same way you did."

"I have my car. I don't need a ride."

"We're going to my office while I decide if I need to arrest you."

He stopped and squared up to her and looked her in the eyes. "Tina, this is the tipping point. These guys are rattled. You've got to bring all these guys in tonight."

"It's a murder investigation, Keane. You know the drill. You don't just round everybody up."

"You're a good cop. You're going to be a great cop. It's easy to see you've got wonderful instincts. You don't have much empathy for a wounded FBI agent, but hey, you see things. You pay attention to details, and you let them take you to the right places. You have to do your duty, but trust your instincts. And this is it. You know these guys. You know how this town works. If you sit back and let this play out without nudging people along, these guys are all going to lawyer up. You'll end up with a lot of paperwork and nobody with an incentive to talk about what happened."

"Keane—"

"Tina, trust me. Do this."

38

FERRARO HAD RACKED his brain about evidence he might have left at Ramer's. He was certain he'd left fingerprints in the kitchen. On the counter for sure and probably on the front-door knob. He'd be a suspect as soon as the police found a match.

He needed to get to Teddy first, see firsthand just how rattled the president was. Not that he didn't trust Henson, but as long as Teddy said all the right things, he'd stay in the fold. He drove into the admin parking lot and saw an empty space for the president's car.

He circled back and drove to the football office. In a filled parking lot he found a black Cadillac occupying a designated parking spot for the football coach. Same old Duke. He drove to the end of the lot, to a handful of visitor spots. There: a dark Chevy Impala parked next to two vacant handicapped spots. He stopped. A City of Orlando tag. An unmarked car. *Duke is talking*.

BEFORE ROSSI LAID out the deal, she and Thomas gave Childress details that were going to end his coaching career: computer records of football games, point spreads, money amounts, people.

"You have initials? You don't even have names? You don't have shit," Childress said.

She said, "It won't be a hard connection to make, Coach. We just match up the initials to a name, then match up the name to a bank account, then the bank records to the computer log. It sounds like a lot of work, but it's actually pretty simple. It'll be pretty easy to walk a jury through."

"Jesus Christ," Childress said.

"Here's the way this will go down," Thomas said. And he laid it out: every coach, every player and everybody close to the team would have his cell phone, email, credit card, and bank records subpoenaed and scoured. Home and work. Every booster. Every school administrator. And their wives or husbands.

They'd start with anyone whose initials matched the ones Sean Riggins documented. Once they got a confession or two, they'd push along at a fast clip.

And when he was done, Childress would likely be out of a job, not that the OU job would be worth having at that point. The program would be in shambles.

"But," Thomas concluded, "a lot of this is up to you. Depends how you want to play it."

"I haven't done a damn thing but coach my team and run a clean program," Childress protested. "I'll sue."

She said, "Coach, the program isn't that clean. You know it, and we know it."

"You don't have a fucking clue what you're talking about." Childress pointed a finger at Rossi.

"Maybe you know, maybe you don't," Rossi replied. "But players are getting paid. Not just one or two, but a bunch. We're solid on that. Even if you don't want to help us on the gambling, we know that. That's not something we care about, but we can certainly pass information along to the feds and to the NCAA. They'll care about it. Like he said, depends how you play it."

"You're blackmailing me?" he screamed.

"Negotiating," Thomas said.

"Jesus Christ on a crutch," Childress said, and he rubbed his face with both hands. To Rossi he said, "You used to work our games. You liked this place."

"Coach, one of your players died, and one of your former players killed him. And we think that guy got killed by a man who was involved with your program. So, you know, it's bad all over for this place. There's a lot that needs to be cleaned up. We're not the NCAA. We're not going to wait for you to clean it up yourself."

"What exactly do you want?"

The three of them huddled around a large table in the coach's office. Rossi presented her own spreadsheet, a modified version of one from Sean Riggins's computer. Next to each set of initials, she had matched up corresponding names listed in the football booster organization. There were more than seventy names in all.

Childress knew many of the boosters listed as potential gamblers, but most he didn't know well. Age range, job, and donor level was the extent of most of his knowledge.

"TS," she said. "We think that's Teddy Simpson."

"I have no idea," Childress said. "I'm sure there are a few Tom Smiths in Orlando."

"Does he ever come to football practice?" Thomas asked.

Childress didn't hesitate. "Comes all the time. He loves football."

"Does he pump you for information? Ask about injuries? Ask about the other team?"

"Yeah. Like I said, he loves football."

Rossi nodded at the non-denial denial. She moved to the next initial. "We're pretty certain DH stands for Don Henson."

"I ain't touching that one," Childress said.

"You'll talk about the president but not about a car dealer?" she asked.

The coach replied, "He's good to the school and great to the program. I'm sure whatever you have or think you have, you don't need me for it."

"Coach, this is where we come to the negotiating part. We have information that Henson is paying your players. Has been for a long time. And I don't know how anyone's going to keep that secret much longer. You know how hard the NCAA is going to come down when that gets out. It might be hard to prove that you knew about it, but it won't be hard to make a case that you should have known about it. And, therefore, that you could have stopped it."

Said Childress, "That crap doesn't work with me. *'What I should have known?'* Please. Nobody will buy that."

"Maybe, maybe not," Rossi said. "If that was the only allegation out there, you might survive. But the big picture—boosters paying players, a gambling scandal, a murdered player? You tell us: How's all that going to play? My guess? Everybody looks for another job."

She watched recognition come to the coach in the form of a grimace. He was accepting defeat. "All we've ever tried to do here is the right thing. I didn't give anything to players, didn't tell anybody to give them anything. I didn't kill anyone. I don't gamble. I coach football. That's all I do."

Said Thomas, "Then tell us what President Simpson and Henson do."

Childress finally surrendered. For an hour he purged about his boss and his boss's friends. Most of the details were more background, snapshots into personalities and relationships, and not evidence. He acknowledged an intricate system of compensating players using Hance and others close to the team. A portion of the money came from his own football budget, diverted into nebulous expense categories like equipment and travel.

"Mileage expenses are easy to do," the coach said.

Other money came from donors who liked Childress, including Henson and Ramer.

"There was a time he was a nice guy, very appreciative of others," Childress said of Ramer. "The last six months, he was an asshole."

"Why? What was going on?" Rossi asked.

Childress shrugged. "I heard money was tight at the bank. I never believed it, because he had a piece of every big construction project around here. People told me he was just putting out the word that he was overextended because he didn't want to give any more to the school. I don't know. But I do know he wasn't around that much this season. And when he was, he wasn't pleasant."

She asked, "Did Ramer know David Hance?"

"Tally? Probably. I don't know how well. I'm sure they were both at the same practices, the same games."

She handed him a list of ten names, most of whom she believed could be in the president's gambling group. "How many of them knew Hance?"

Childress studied the names. "Maybe half. Possibly more. There are a few who weren't around when he played. Although a couple knew him from coming to games."

"Do you have any reason to think Ramer could have murdered Hance?" she asked.

Childress shook his head. "He wasn't the kind of guy who liked to get his hands dirty."

She asked, "What did Hance do for you?"

"He did whatever I needed him to do."

"Like go talk to a player in the program who's not following orders?"

The coach shook his head. "That's what I do. I don't have any problem keeping people in line. Tally, he was the candy man. He took care of things. Maybe for a booster but mostly for players."

"How so?" Thomas asked.

"Nothing big, just things that add up. He'd give out gift cards for meals. If I needed to make sure somebody got their cell phone bill paid for, Tally'd handle it. One time I had a player get arrested for DUI and Tally bailed him out. You know: little things."

Thomas cleared his throat. "You asked him to bail a player out of jail?"

"No. The kid's roommate called an assistant coach in the middle of the night, and the coach called me, told me what was going on. The kid asked if Tally could bail him out. The next day, I heard the roommate called Tally and that Tally had posted the bond."

Rossi suspected this was a lie, but it didn't matter. The coach was finished. The details—the things that would end up in the media, anyway— would get flushed through attorneys, police and court filings and a battery of public-relations specialists.

She had a final subject before they were finished with Childress. "What can you tell us about Richie Ferraro?"

"The car guy? Haven't seen him in years. At least three years. He's not on your list."

"Not that we know of," she said.

They picked at the coach about Ferraro, gleaning details to form a bigger picture. Ferraro hadn't been in Orlando for a few years, but he'd made an impression on Childress. The coach loved tough players and admired the same quality in his boosters.

"Was he a big deal around here when you got here, or did he come later?" she asked.

"About the same time. I figured Teddy knew him from politics, but the truth is, I don't know how Teddy knew him. I assumed Teddy talked him into giving money. You know how that works: you give, you get a say. After a while, Ferraro made his opinions known."

"What did he want?"

"Same thing as everybody else: an exciting team that won. He wanted us on ESPN every Saturday. That's what we all wanted."

"That's it?"

"That's all I ever heard. You know the saying: When you win, you're everybody's friend. When you lose, you're all by yourself. Ferraro, he was around for a couple of the hard years. But we got to winning again and everything was fine."

"What'd he do up north? What was his business?"

The coach shrugged. "An investor. Not a Wall Street guy, I don't think, but a middleman. A guy who invests in other people's business and then takes a cut now or a cut later. He was never really that specific. I just knew when we needed money, he had it."

She asked, "Did Ferraro and Ramer ever do business together?"

"I heard Ramer put him into a development that went bust. Put a few guys into that one, in fact. They all lost money."

"Who else? Henson? The president?"

"Other boosters. Friends of his. Nobody on your list."

"That doesn't make sense. If the president and Ferraro were close, wouldn't they do deals together?"

Childress shook his head. "You're talking about a different class of investor. Ferraro, he's got money. Teddy, he's been around a long time, knows a lot of people. He's pretty selective on who he does business with. But I'll say this: if that investment was as bad as everyone says it was, I wouldn't have wanted to be Ramer. Ferraro, he's all polished and clean-cut, but he's a tough son of a bitch. People who take him lightly do so at their own peril. He plays to win. And he doesn't take prisoners."

WHEN THE INTERVIEW was over, Rossi threw the file into the back seat. "We've got all these people we can arrest and we don't have a single one for murder."

"It'll come," Thomas said. "Relax."

"I'm serious. We've got the president. We've got all the gamblers and however many people that ends up being. We've got Childress. We've got Ferraro—although we have to get our hands on him. But we've got none of them for Hance or Ramer."

"I'll give you odds Ferraro had leverage on the banker. Knew about that bad deal. Or maybe he was withholding a signature on a new deal."

"Maybe. But it's just as possible Ramer had something on Ferraro and the blackmail went the other way."

They stared at each other and calculated.

Thomas said, "We're getting sucked into a maze."

She sighed. "Tell me about it." She opened the driver's side door but hesitated when Thomas made no move to climb in.

He popped his hand on the roof. "You know what? I want to talk to Childress's secretaries. We've talked to players, coaches, video people, the president . . . you name it. But I'll bet those ladies in there know a lot." He jabbed a finger at the football building. "I'll bet they knew Tally, know Ferraro, know all the players and where most, if not all, the bodies are buried. Jesus, I'm an idiot."

"Okay, we go back in—"

"No, just me. Let's try a game of slow-pitch. Why don't you check on your new boyfriend at his hotel. Make sure he's behaving."

She flipped both middle fingers at him and opened the car door.

"Glad you approve. I'll see what I can get from these ladies. Give me . . . half an hour. Then pick me up."

39

FROM A PARKING spot on the second floor of a four-story garage, Ferraro watched two detectives, a tall, thin man and a shorter, younger woman with dark, tied-up hair, leave the football office. They stood outside the black car with the Orlando city plates and conversed across the hood. They stood by their doors, and then . . .

Did she just flip him off?

Only she climbed into the car, and she drove off as the male detective walked back into the office.

Ferraro waited fifteen minutes and walked across campus to Teddy's office. It had been four years since he was here last, and it amused him that Teddy had cycled through another set of receptionists. With a fake frown, the blonde one told him Teddy was out of the office for the day. Ferraro thanked her and walked outside.

What did *out of the office* mean? He dug up Teddy's number in his iPhone, pulled out his new pre-paid cell phone, and dialed. No answer. He hung up without leaving a message.

Not at the office. Not with Duke Childress. Not with the police. Not answering the phone at home or his cell. Where was Teddy?

TEDDY WAS HOME. Sat in his home office, blinds pulled, noise-muffling headphones doing their job for "Let It Be." The Beatles worked for him when life turned overbearing. Today, so did the Xanax.

He got no sleep after the detectives left and succumbed to the tossing and turning by making coffee and eating toast. He waited too long to call Valerie. A depressing reality began to set in.

A good part of his life was over. There would be no run for governor. No elected office of any kind, in fact. All those years with lawmakers and lobbyists wasted. He'd have to start over. He had the money. He might not have the time.

He typed out a draft email to his office staff that he'd taken ill, that he was headed to a morning checkup and would spend the day recuperating at home. Then he typed his letter of resignation, saving it to a file in a Dropbox account. Later today or tonight, he'd email the letter to the board of trustees. Not the best way. Then again, it wasn't as if he needed any of the trustees to give him a job recommendation.

He planned to cash out as much as he could here, hop a charter flight to the Caymans and join his money. Not long after, he'd fly to London for another financial exchange. Soon he'd have a more lasting decision to make. He wouldn't have many options. The list of enjoyable countries from which the U.S. does not enjoy extradition privileges was short.

Before any of it, he needed to make sure his accounts were in order. He needed a bottom-line number.

He made a list of to-dos on a legal pad, more than a dozen tasks that would take him all day to accomplish. Once they were done, he'd be ready to fly away. He began to wonder just how many countries carry ESPN.

FERRARO NEEDED TO refuel. Needed food or coffee. Mostly, he needed more information.

He drove north away from campus, spotted a Starbucks, and pulled a quick U-turn. He settled into a cushy chair in the corner, sipped a venti Kona blend doctored with cream and sugar, and began pulling apart a blueberry scone. In his head, he ran down Teddy's lineup of gambling all-stars. Most would never bother him. Others would.

Teddy was brilliant in many ways, stunning in his ability to cut to the chase, make a decision and move on. He was all about the money, and he cared about no one other than himself. And he had that magical tongue. He could barter his way out of hell with nothing but coal as leverage.

Ferraro respected that, even if he did not understand the president. He sometimes wondered if he'd pick up a paper one day and read about Teddy and a history with either teenage boys or a dominatrix. Teddy loved power, control, money, and alcohol in almost equal amounts. Had he not chosen to front for politicians back in the day, he probably would have made a fine one himself in these days of corrupt Florida governing. But it was that damned motor mouth of his that got under Ferraro's skin. Teddy took credit for all his successes and blamed all his failures on others around him. Bad form for a leader. Perfect form for a man who once played politics for a living.

But Teddy held information only a handful of people in the world knew: that Ferraro had a history with the New York rackets that included a fair share of drugs, prostitution, gambling, and violence. A name change fifteen years ago, arranged by an associate who was later killed to keep him silent forever, freed him to move to Florida and join a new industry. And if you asked him, land development in a place with no snow was the preferable way to make a living.

He'd had to threaten Teddy a time or two, and it surprised him when Teddy backed down so quickly both times. It told him that Don Henson had spelled out Ferraro's bona fides well. But instinctively, he knew. *Teddy would give me up in a heartbeat.*

Ferraro needed to deal with that and soon. And with Henson. Don was his eyes and ears in Orlando, and they'd carved out a wonderful dynamic. They'd successfully cultivated the lie about his exit from Florida. Everybody believed the two of them hated each other. They were, in fact, friends. But he knew Don would never trust him when it came to money. Like Teddy, Don would sacrifice him if he had the chance.

He calculated the odds, a long-held talent. They were long, but years of experience with gamblers told him even a hundred-to-one was possible.

Alicia Arsenault needed three minutes to place the face. The length of time for her to see the man and have his venti Kona blend with cream and sugar delivered. Once a big booster, now nowhere. At least, that's what everyone had said. Not that it was a big topic of conversation. The conversation pretty much started as, "You know who I never see anymore?" And today at Starbucks, half a mile from campus, here he was.

She'd studied his features and tried to remember his name. Then he turned away as soon as he caught her staring. He had his phone pushed to his ear, and over the coffee-shop din and mood music she picked up nothing.

And the answer came to her: Mr. Ferraro.

How coincidental was this? A half hour before, she'd spotted the two detectives on the Sean Riggins case leave Coach Childress's office and then had seen the coach walk ashen-faced down the hall. Now, while taking a quick coffee break, this. She didn't believe in coincidences.

She fished through her purse for a business card she'd been given two weeks before. She found it, studied it, and dialed. She wondered if Detective Tina Rossi was still on campus.

40

ROSSI CALLED KEANE, got his new room number, and knocked on the door a few minutes later. He answered and was dressed, but his disheveled hair told her he'd been lying down. She'd started to rag him about napping when her phone vibrated on her hip. She looked and saw UNKNOWN NUMBER and answered.

She listened. "Yes, I remember." And listened more. "You sure it was him? Okay. Is he still there? . . . Okay, thank you."

She turned to Keane. "Ferraro is sitting in a Starbucks just off the OU campus. He's sitting there, eating a scone, drinking coffee, talking on the phone. Like nothing's going on."

"I'm coming," he said. "And I'm bringing my gun."

She called Thomas and filled him in. "I don't want to miss him. I'll call you when I get there." She didn't mention Keane.

Fifteen minutes later, Rossi and Keane rushed into the Starbucks and found no sign of Ferraro.

"He left about ten minutes ago," Alicia Arsenault said. "He's driving a black SUV, if that helps."

Keane thought about it and turned to Rossi. "If he's here, there are only two people he could want to see. Pick one."

"Football office," she said, and dialed Thomas. Into the phone she said, "We missed Ferraro, but we think he may have stopped to talk to Childress. Ask around. We'll pick you up in a couple minutes."

"We?" Thomas asked.

KEANE NODDED AT Thomas after he and Rossi arrived at the football building.

"No one here saw Ferraro," he said.

Keane looked at Rossi. "Oh-for-one. Let's try the president."

A receptionist in Simpson's office ID'd Ferraro, said he'd been there an hour before asking for the president.

"But President Simpson is out of the office today," she said. "That's the truth, and that's what I told him."

"Where is the president?" Keane asked.

"He came down with a migraine. He's home."

ROSSI BUZZED TEDDY'S house from outside the driveway gate. No answer.

"I've done this before, but this time I think there's probable cause, don't you?" Keane said. He exited from the back seat and walked to the back of the property. He ducked through the hedges and opened the gate from the inside. Rossi drove in as Keane hustled to the front door. He spared his shoulder and rang the bell. No answer.

Thomas beat Rossi to the door and nudged Keane away. He knocked, then banged his first on the door. "Mr. Simpson! Answer the door, Mr. Simpson!"

Rossi waited three seconds and said, "Wait here." She darted around the house to the right and reappeared from the left fifteen seconds later.

"I don't see anyone," she said.

Just as she rejoined Thomas and Keane outside the front door, it cracked open.

"What do you want now?" the president asked.

"You're okay?" Rossi said.

"I have a headache that won't end, but otherwise I'm fine."

"Did anyone else call you or try to get you to come to the door today?" Thomas asked.

"No. Like who?"

"Like Richie Ferraro," Rossi said.

"He'd never want to be seen here. Not in Orlando."

"Maybe not, but he's here," she said.

Simpson mulled that over. "Is that all?"

Rossi shook her head. "Can we come in?"

"Not unless you have a warrant."

"I'm worried Ferraro is already in there with you, maybe forcing you to do something you don't want to do."

The president opened the door all the way and stepped aside. "You can't come in, but you can look. There's nobody else here."

Rossi craned her head and peeked. When she pulled back, Thomas looked for himself. Nobody held a gun or anything else on the president.

Simpson said, "Satisfied?"

The three of them stepped back. "You have our number," Rossi said. "Call if you need us."

"I'll be sure to do that."

Keane stopped before they reached the car. "Either one of you ever had a migraine?"

The detectives shook their heads.

"My sister gets them. She says they're awful," Thomas said. "They make her want to crawl under the bed."

"The really bad ones are terrible that when you get one, you don't want to be near any sunlight. Not like our friend back there."

"You think Ferraro is in there?" Rossi asked.

"Doubtful. But something's up. Simpson lied. He's using a sick day as a cover. We have to push this."

Rossi looked at Thomas, who nodded. She pushed speed-dial and said into the phone, "We need more people. Ferraro's here. We just missed him."

She listened for a few seconds and hung up. They climbed into the sedan, Keane again in the back.

Keane repositioned his sling and looked at her eyes in the rear-view mirror. "More warrants?"

She nodded at his reflection and threw the transmission into reverse, then drive. "You look good back there. Like you belong."

Thomas laughed.

Keane reached across his body and held onto his elbow to stabilize his injured arm. "Try not to hit any potholes, huh?"

QUENTIN RIGGINS CONGRATULATED himself for purchasing the GPS tracker. Tracking people with it was so easy, it was no wonder that judges required probable cause for cops to do it.

While Ferraro visited Ramer's, Q had attached the GPS to the right rear wheel well of Ferraro's rental car. And after Ferraro left, Q checked on his handiwork and had been as shocked to see the banker alive as the banker was to see a black man walking through his front door.

He'd kicked Ramer in the groin, carried him rescue-style into the kitchen to get a knife and then dumped him in an upstairs bathtub, where he sliced his throat.

He hadn't planned a spur-of-the-moment killing. But what the hell? It had to start sometime. He figured the odds of escaping at less than fifty-fifty, maybe even as low as twenty-eighty against. Good enough for fighting.

He felt no guilt about using Keane. It wasn't his fault his FBI-agent friend made false assumptions and told him too much. That female cop, Rossi, had called him later to verify an alibi—she didn't say it that way, but he could tell—and Keane had vouched for him.

Then Keane's full-bore investigation of the football coach and the president proved to be a godsend, and his discovery of Ferraro was a welcome development.

Through the years, he and Keane had bonded long-distance about their dysfunctional, messed-up family lives. But Sean's death had given him more perspective. Despite all his recent help, he couldn't help feeling that Keane still needed to pay for years of brother-less sins.

41

KEANE WANTED TO help, but now the job involved paperwork and documentation. He couldn't touch anything.

Sunlight peeking through half-windows dwindled to nothing after dusk, but the fluorescent light in the detectives' room more than made up for the loss. He found an empty desk, got Rossi's nodded approval, and read through his notes. Occasionally, he looked up to marvel at her process. No wasted time. She had files for everything, and she seemed to transfer names, numbers, addresses, and emails from one notebook or computer file to another. Sources on this case who might be long-term sources of hers later for others. Writing down the names of other cops she knew who might be able to fill in a detail or two or provide new information. Once she figured out how better to cope with the internal pressures of the department, especially the politics, she'd elevate. Even now she'd make a hell of a special agent.

He didn't have to sell her or Thomas again on making arrests. More dead bodies meant that they at least needed to protect potential victims.

Rossi wrote up the paperwork. Within an hour, Thomas had arrested three OU boosters for conspiracy, which was another way of saying they'd committed a crime without specifying all the illegal acts that would get spelled out. Rossi would hash it all out later. They would lawyer up, but Rossi and Thomas could hold them for twenty-four hours before they had to file formal charges.

"Who's next?" Thomas asked.

Rossi handed him more paperwork and laid it out.

USING THE SAME route he watched Keane take, Q walked around the back of the house and wiggled through the hedge. He hustled around the long driveway and made his way to the front door and rang the bell.

"What the hell is it now?" came the cry from other side, and Q heard the deadbolt move.

"Who the hell are you, and how the hell did you get in here?" Teddy Simpson asked as he opened his front door.

Q thought: *He doesn't know me.* And then he kicked his way in.

The solid oak door caught the president in the shoulder, and it knocked the fat man back a step. But it was the only step that was needed. Simpson moved his front foot to account for his momentum change, but he tangled with his back foot and he stumbled awkwardly, then fell. Simpson landed square on his back. The back of his head whiplashed against the Italian marble flooring in the foyer.

Q crossed the threshold and closed the door behind him. The president curled up and felt for damage to the back of his head.

"What do you want?" Simpson moaned.

"I'm the man you settle up with," Q said.

"For what?"

"You don't remember me at all, do you?"

"Why would I remember you? We've never met."

"Wrong answer."

Simpson looked at him with a blank expression.

"I've shaken hands with you more than once after a game, usually outside the locker room."

Simpson's eyes narrowed, and then it came to him. "You. You're the father."

"That hard, now, was it?"

"You were running around with that FBI agent. Hell, he was just here."

Q shook his head. "He's running around with that cute cop. I'm here with me."

He towered over the president, who declared, "You're not going to kill me."

Q laughed, reached down and grabbed the president by his shirt collar and yanked him to his feet. He twisted the chubby man's arm, snared a handful of hair, and shoved the man through the foyer toward the kitchen.

He spied the knife block on the far side of the kitchen and steered his hostage toward it. Simpson, following a path that had made him successful and wealthy, chose persuasion over resistance. He walked wherever Q pushed him.

"I'll do whatever you want. Whatever you need, I can get it to you," Simpson said. "You're in a good bargaining position. Hell, you could probably sue the university for not protecting your son and win a couple million. You don't want to do anything you're going to regret."

"I promise you, Mr. University President, I won't do a thing I'll regret."

In one swift motion, Q let go of Teddy's wrist and pulled a long carving knife from the block. He yanked the man's hair hard and pulled his head back. And made a slash from one side of Simpson's throat to the other.

TEDDY DIDN'T COMPREHEND why the white kitchen wall sprouted a strange red pattern. A second wave of liquid hit, and he noticed rivulets forming and being pulled by gravity. He gurgled, and it felt as if he were trying to drink from a straw with holes all along the side. His lungs started filling with fluid. And then he couldn't breathe.

Panic set in. He grabbed his throat and tried to wrestle himself free. He wheezed again, and the only change he saw was more blood. His hands grew slick. They seemed only to contribute to a gathering pool.

A wave of dizziness passed over him. He was enveloped by warmth, then a sudden chill. And then he was falling again.

His head bounced off the floor. This time, he didn't feel it. He came to rest with his chin nestled in a grout line. A second pool of blood formed, this time around his face. His vision began to grow cloudy, then all white.

He thought, *Why? I didn't hurt anybody.*

THERE WAS NO urgency to run. Q had to ditch his bloodstained shirt and his blue jeans, but he had time. Avoiding the blood on the floor, he found a plastic trash bag under the kitchen sink and headed to the bedroom. He hoped that the president had at least one shirt that fit him. He held out no such ambitions for pants.

He put on a blue button-down from Simpson's closet. The arms were too short, so he left the cuffs unbuttoned. All the president's pants were too big for him in the waist and too short in length. He took a black pair of slacks and a belt and made the best of it. He pulled down a pullover sweater and wrapped it around the bloody carving knife.

Satisfied that he looked like an adult who might be walking across campus, Q left through the back sliding glass doors, closing them but leaving them unlocked.

He hustled to his car and drove away. One quick stop and he could resume his GPS-watching.

42

WHILE ROSSI BANGED out more paperwork, Keane dug through his work email for the first time in a week. He'd been surprised that his boss, special agent-in-charge Happy Harding, had not called him in days. Harding had made up for that silence with a succession of increasingly terse emails.

He read them in chronological order and discovered a supervisor who was displeased that he had not called, emailed, or texted a status report back to Tennessee. The emails showed an increasingly frustrated and disappointed boss. Keane thought, *He doesn't know I got shot,* and decided against reporting it. Dombrowski and Cramer would do that for him.

Until now, his relationship with Happy had been solid. It was one of the primary reasons he'd gotten little flak for extending a seven-day vacation into an odyssey with no end date. He'd told Happy "there were complications" with his mother's estate and hadn't leveled with him about Sean or his surreptitious part in the investigation. If it wanted, the FBI could track his cell phone or even his internet usage. Regardless, he had damage control ahead. That much he knew.

He checked his phone and frowned upon finding a new voicemail. He hadn't heard the phone ring.

Q got to the point in his message. "Where are you?"

Why would Q care where he was? They'd talked only a few hours before.

BEFORE ROSSI WROTE up a subpoena request for Simpson's and Ramer's bank records, she called the court clerk and gained another appointment for an arrest warrant. Thomas had lost his argument to put Simpson in handcuffs. Rossi didn't think a judge would be so kindhearted about Henson.

If Childress was right and Ramer had money troubles, they'd need to know why. Maitland Bank was considered wildly successful. Proof to the contrary would be a major turn.

Rossi returned with new paperwork. "Let's go get Henson."

She arranged a quick meeting with Thomas to hand him a subpoena and an arrest warrant, keeping a set for herself. Thomas and a tall, slender detective named Recchi were to gather documents from Maitland Community Bank related to Dave Ramer. Once that process started, they'd make the other arrests.

She hadn't convinced a judge about three other boosters. And even though he was at the forefront of the gambling, Simpson was also getting another pass for now. The judge wanted more confirmation of his participation.

"It's completely politics," Rossi said.

"You should have told him we want to bring Simpson in for his own protection," Thomas said.

"She. The judge is a woman. And I did tell her that. She said it was cop-talk to get around the fact that we don't have probable cause yet."

"She's the one who has to live with it," Keane said. "Did you tell her that?"

Rossi craned her head and gave him the same don't-push-your-luck look from the other day.

FROM ACROSS ORANGE Avenue, Ferraro spied on the executive office suite of Henson Motors. Don's secretary left the office promptly at five o'clock. Thirty seconds after she pulled her Camry out of the lot, Ferraro steered his rented SUV into her spot. That wasn't all that was open. The secretary hadn't locked up.

He took stock of an empty outer office and hustled back to Don's private space. He put on a smile and opened the door without knocking. "Hi, Don."

Henson was on his knees at the foot of the bookcase next to his desk, sorting through files. A short stack of hundred-dollar bills sat on the edge of the desk.

"What are you doing here?" Don said, still poring through a manila file. "What do you want?" Then: "Have you heard about what's going on?"

"Heard?" Ferraro laughed. "You think all this is just . . . coincidence?"

Henson looked at him and dropped the folder.

"You don't think you were just getting lucky, do you?"

"Get out! Get out!" Don lunged for his phone and punched the keypad.

Ferraro rushed at him, grabbed the phone, and ripped it out of the wall. Don let go of the receiver and opened the top right-hand drawer of his desk. He withdrew a .38.

"Any closer and that'll be the last step you take," Don said, leveling the gun at Ferraro's breastbone.

A voice from the other side of the room said, "The same goes for you."

They turned and saw a tall black man in the doorway. The startling look of black slacks that were at least four inches too short was offset by the nine millimeter in the man's hand.

Q LOOKED AT the taller of the men and said, "You're Ferraro."

Ferraro turned and backed up, confused but still managing to create a triangle of people and give the two men with guns clear shots at each other. "Who the hell are you?" he managed.

"I'm the father of the boy this man had a hand in killing," the man said, motioning at Henson.

"Is that so?" Ferraro replied.

"I didn't do any such thing!" Henson protested. "That boy, your boy, just died! And you know that! It was nothing but a goddamn accident."

"It was an accident like this was an accident," he said and pulled the trigger.

Henson shouted as he took a wound to his chest and reflexively fired his gun.

Pain enveloped Q's head. He grasped his scalp with his hands and fell forward. He felt Ferraro beside him, taking the gun from his hand. He reached up to the right side of his head and felt the slickness of blood. He saw a dark red stain forming on the carpet. If the stain grew much faster, he was surely dying.

Ferraro asked, "How do you know my name?"

Q offered no response.

Ferraro wheeled and pointed the gun at Henson, who was on his back clutching his right shoulder. Blood seeped into Henson's shirt but there was none underneath him, which meant the bullet was still lodged.

"Son of a bitch, he shot me!" Henson screamed. "Oh, man . . ."

Standing above him, Ferraro said, "Just relax," and shot Henson in the forehead. He felt both sides of Henson's neck for a pulse. Then he reached into Henson's pants and pulled out a money clip from one pocket and keys from another.

"Thanks, Don," Ferraro said.

Q staggered to his feet and plowed into Ferraro from behind, putting a shoulder into the bigger man's lower back. Light exploded in his head. He drove the man into the heavy desk. Ferraro grunted with surprise and pain. The gun skidded across the desk and tumbled off.

The two of them fell to the floor, and Q pinned Ferraro. Using the side of his face as a fulcrum, he reached underneath Ferraro with both arms, clasped his hands together around his midsection and squeezed. He heaved and squeezed again, driving his balled-up hands into the man's diaphragm. Ferraro writhed and tried to turn.

Q held his leverage and buried his head harder into Ferraro's upper back. He closed his eyes to ignore a building headache. He sensed his blood slicking up Ferraro's shirt. Drops leaked into his right eye, though pressing his head against Ferraro's back staunched the flow.

He squeezed again, as if he were a python wringing the energy and breath out of a victim. Ferraro raised up slightly and tried to break the hold by wedging his hands between Q's arms. Q realized he would lose control of Ferraro if he had to fight on more even terms, and he swapped for a more animalistic approach. He straddled Ferraro and raised the man several inches off the floor. He heard Ferraro groan. He pushed forward and let Ferraro's two-hundred-plus pounds take over, pulling them both down to the floor again. Q's clenched hands, pinned between the floor and Ferraro's body, buried into the man's diaphragm.

Ferraro tried to gasp but could not.

The damage done, Q unlocked his grip and pushed off his prey, surprised at how wet and deep red the back of the man's shirt was. He kicked Ferraro in the head. With no air to carry the sound, Ferraro managed a muted groan.

Q hustled to the other side of the desk and retrieved the gun. He decided Henson was dead. No reason to touch him.

Instead, he said to Ferraro, "I don't know exactly what you did, but you did something bad or you wouldn't be killing a friend of yours."

Ferraro managed another faint groan.

Q used his sleeve to wipe blood from his eyes and retrieved his gun. He left the office and found a bathroom next to the reception area. When he looked in the mirror, he barely recognized the reflection. Henson's bullet had only grazed him, but it had left a burned and bleeding streak on his scalp above his right eye. His head and face had already started swelling, and his eye was nearly closed. Blood continued to leak.

He wadded up toilet paper and gingerly used it as a compress. Merely touching the wound sent a wave of pain through him. He sat on the toilet and rested his head in his hands, using gravity as an aid.

After a few moments he stood and checked the bullet trail. Bits of the tissue stuck to the wound. More blood came out.

He removed his shirt, rinsed off his hands and dried them on his shirttail. He put a new compress on his head and fashioned a make-shift bandana with the shirt. When he determined he could see despite his right eye being almost swollen shut, he went back to the office.

He arrived as Ferraro got off the floor.

FERRARO TRIED REGULATING his breath to minimize the agony. He was certain at least one rib was broken on his right side. Lifting his right arm above his waist was impossible. His shirt felt sticky and wet, but his attacker was gone, leaving a blood trail to the outer office.

Ferraro's gun was gone, as was Don's weapon. Blood pooled behind the car dealer's head, and Don gave no sign of life.

He surveyed the office for anything he needed to wipe down or take with him to help erase evidence of his presence.

Just then, the black man with the short pants and head wound came back.

43

THE MAN LOOKED like he'd walked off the set of a horror movie. His blood-soaked shirt was wrapped around his head and held tight by a knot in the back. Although the bandage staunched the bleeding, it did nothing for the grotesque swelling.

"We haven't been introduced. You said you were the dead player's father," Ferraro said, holding his side to suppress the pain. He guessed Quentin Riggins's body slam at minimum cracked a rib.

The man pointing the nine millimeter at him said, "My name's Quentin Riggins. My son was Sean Riggins, the boy Mr. Henson figured was disposable. And you're Ferraro. The one from Atlanta."

"You don't know me," Ferraro said.

"I know you," Q said. "You're the man behind the curtain. The puppet master. Everybody spending all this time worrying about this guy"—he nudged the gun in Henson's direction—"and worrying about that school president and the rest of them. And all along it was you. Wasn't it?"

Ferraro fought to conceal his surprise. Riggins had shared a good deal of information with his father after all. Teddy had been right to push the kid.

He shifted weight to his left leg to free up his left arm. *Two seconds, tops. At this distance, twelve feet, he'd almost certainly take a bullet. With just a bit of dexterity, he might get lucky with a flesh wound.*

"I asked you a question," Q said, jabbing the gun at him to make his point. "You're the man who pulled the string on the president, aren't you?"

"You're mistaken," he said. He leaned on the desk and wondered how long he could keep up the front before Riggins decided to shoot.

KEANE DIALED Q and got no answer as Rossi weaved through southbound rush-hour traffic on Orange Avenue. She had wanted to get to Henson's parking lot before five o'clock, but now the sun dipped below the horizon.

Keane counted five cars scattered in the parking lot. One of them was Henson's Cadillac, another was a sleek white Ford sedan.

"Henson's here. That's his car," Keane said. "I don't think he's alone."

They both pulled their Glocks, Keane with his left hand, and they hustled against the brick exterior. She shimmied up to the front glass door and waited. Kneeling and cupping her eyes, she peered through the lower third of the glass and got her bearings.

Nothing.

She pulled back and they waited for ten beats. More nothing.

"Ready?" he asked.

Rossi nodded. He reached around her and pulled the front door. It opened cleanly. A good sign, though probably not for Henson.

The receptionist was gone and there were no signs of anyone else. They stood still and then heard muffled voices down the hall. Whoever was here didn't appear to have seen or heard them come in. Keane tapped Rossi's shoulder to get her attention. "I know where he is," he whispered, and he moved in front of her.

He stopped suddenly and pointed at the carpet in the hallway. "Blood." The trail went from the office to the bathroom.

The door to Henson's office was shut, but and two voices were distinguishable. Ferraro and Q. *What the hell?*

AFTER LISTENING TO the voices outside the door for thirty seconds, Keane and Rossi backed away.

"I don't like the idea of going in blind," she whispered. "We need to call for support."

"No time," he said. "Someone could be dying."

They agreed he would go through first, ready to fire on the right side of the room. She'd go through right behind him and cover the left side.

Discussions on the other side of the door were ongoing. He made out the words "car dealer." He took a step back and took aim. He braced his right arm and drove his right heel into a spot right above the door knob. The strike plate gave instantly. Guns drawn, they confronted Henson lying on his back, motionless.

And still the sound of two men talking.

THE VOICES OF Ferraro and Q came from a digital voice recorder on Henson's desk.

"Why did you do what you did?" he heard Q ask.

"People got out of hand. It shouldn't have happened," Ferraro said.

"But it did happen. And my boy's dead. And other people are dead. You bastards decided to take everybody with you, didn't you?"

Q had stood right here minutes ago and questioned Ferraro, probably as he pointed a gun at him. The recording would never be used as evidence against Ferraro, yet Keane was struck by the simplicity of the idea. Q got the man he wanted, got the confession he wanted.

But now he was armed and gone, and that wasn't good news for anyone.

Rossi felt for a pulse on Henson's neck. "He's dead." She stood up and looked around. "This is where he was shot. Nobody moved him here."

He pointed to a blood trail leading out of the room. "We've got another victim."

"Maybe Henson did the shooting?" she asked. She reached into her outside jacket pocket, pulled out two thin rubber gloves, put them on, and grabbed the digital recorder. "This should tell us something."

They listened to ten minutes of the fifteen-minute recording. There were no gunshots, no attacks. Whatever else had taken place apparently hadn't been preserved on the digital file, but there was evidence there. Ferraro admitted to several crimes and to transgressions that would, this time, get him away from OU for a long while. If what he said was true, Teddy Simpson was finished.

Keane kept listening as Rossi answered her phone.

"What?" she exclaimed. "Where? When?"

She listened for a few beats. "Who's working it?"

She hung up and said, "Simpson's dead. He had his throat cut, just like the banker. This time in the kitchen. No sign of a struggle."

He processed this. Ferraro was spotted off campus just before they got there. There was no sign of him when they visited the president a few minutes later. For all he knew, Ferraro had actually watched them pop in on Simpson and then attacked after he was satisfied they were gone for good.

"We should have arrested that pompous egomaniac," Keane said finally.

"Wouldn't have mattered," Rossi said. "He'd have made bail in a day and gotten killed later."

"Bullshit. Stabbings are crimes of passion. Love, sex or else rage or revenge. This guy's on a rampage. First Ramer, now Simpson."

"Ferraro's tying up loose ends. We need to warn the rest of the boosters. They're all targets."

She was right of course, but he went the other way. "We need to find him."

44

Q REPLAYED THE last hour through an aching head. He'd made serious mistakes. He'd gotten shot in the scalp, for one. That scenario hadn't played out in his mind on the drive up to Orlando, but here he was, the shirt taken from Simpson ripped and tied around his head.

Now his blood was all over Henson's office, and Henson was dead. And one of Henson's partners—he had no idea what the relationship really had been—was not. But the man was hurting.

He forced Ferraro, moving slowly, behind the wheel of the rented Navigator. "You should know how to drive this."

Ferraro sat with his right arm in his lap, his left hand on the wheel, and his body arched to the right. "This is a mistake. You don't want to do this."

"Shut up and drive," he replied.

It took them thirty minutes to get through traffic and to campus. "If you're looking for the president, Teddy's not home," Ferraro said.

He smiled at Ferraro. "Oh, he's home. He's just not doing business anymore."

They steered away from the president's house and toward the school's athletic complex.

"You'll never get away with this," Ferraro said.

"Who says I want to get away with anything? I just want you and everybody else in your little gang to pay for all the shit you've caused."

He directed Ferraro to park next to the vacant football stadium. It was unlit except for a small ring of lights along the top of the stadium. He pushed the gun into Ferraro's back, then tapped his rib cage again. Ferraro buckled in pain.

"Nice and easy, and everything will be fine," he said.

"You know," Ferraro wheezed, "you'd better kill me, because if you don't you're a dead man."

They walked, Q nudging Ferraro ahead of him, into the stadium and down the stairs toward the field. They stopped at the front row, where he made Ferraro sit. In the darkness they could see each other, and they could see anything around them for fifty yards. Beyond that it was too dark.

"Tell me how much you won?" Q asked.

His cell phone interrupted them. He looked: Keane.

He answered. "If it isn't the brash and brave Agent Keane," Q said.

He listened quietly and replied, "I'm perfectly fine. But you'll never guess who I'm sitting with."

"WHERE THE HELL are you?" Keane asked. "Are you in danger?"

"I'm not in any danger. Well, hang on."

He pulled the phone away and looked at Ferraro. "I'm not in any danger, right?"

"You are. You just don't know it," Ferraro said.

"I might be wrong, Keane. This asshole says I'm in danger."

Keane recognized the voice, though it sounded weaker than when he had last heard it, thirty minutes before on the recorder.

"Why do you sound like you just got out of the dentist chair?" Keane asked.

"My head is swollen. That asshole Henson shot me. Sonofabitch winged my head."

"So that's your blood all over Henson's office."

"You're pretty fast, Keane."

Keane conjured an image. Head shots, even minor ones, were notoriously bloody. Lots of small blood vessels, not a lot of skin. Q was no doubt already feeling the medium-range effects. He'd be lucky if he didn't have a fractured skull. Even if he didn't, he'd look like part of his head had been attacked by bees.

"Who killed Henson?"

"That would be my man, Mr. Ferraro. I'm sure he'll confess for you."

"And you're with Ferraro. Where are you?"

"Where it all began. And where it's going to end. I'm going to have my new friend here tell me in front of sixty thousand empty seats why he and his so-called friends dragged my boy into their little game. And then I'm going to decide if he's telling me the truth."

"You're on campus? At the stadium?"

"You are good."

"Goddammit, Quentin, this isn't a joke. Bodies are turning up all over the place and you got shot. Did Ferraro get shot?"

"Mr. Ferraro dodged all bullets. But he's probably not feeling his best. I think he might have a cracked rib or two."

"We're on our way. Don't do anything stupid."

Keane relayed the conversation to Rossi as she pushed the car toward campus.

"We have people there already. They're at the president's."

She called it in, saying, "Possibly armed and dangerous, possible hostage situation."

They both knew this was a respond-and-wait situation. With a football stadium as a hostage venue, this was going to necessitate force. And a SWAT team.

45

"WON'T BE LONG now," Q told Ferraro. "The cavalry is on the way."

"I don't have anything to worry about," Ferraro said.

"Well, it sounds like the cops think you killed that guy the other night, and I'm pretty sure they think you killed the president. I don't even know if they even found him yet. But you killed Henson. They did find him already."

Ferraro looked confused. "What guy the other night? Dave Ramer? All I did was threaten him. I never even saw Teddy."

"Nah, I took care of both of them for you. Cut them up pretty good, too. Wasn't like gutting a fish. Blood everywhere."

Ferraro's eyes grew wide with recognition.

"You thought you and your boys were untouchable, huh?" Q asked. "Ain't nobody untouchable." He waggled the gun. "You have anything to explain before they get here? Before I shoot you?"

"You know your son was an accident," Ferraro said.

"People keep saying that. And maybe they're right. He had a bad heart and he could have gone at any time. But he never would have been in that position if it weren't for you and your boys. All that money he had, that nice car, all those friends. He wasn't even the same kid. He used to care about football and school and making a nice life for himself. Then he gets mixed up with all you people, and he's got money and clothes, and he's out clubbing every night. He should have been studying. He should have been close to campus. Not downtown."

Ferraro said, "It was Teddy who sent Hance—"

"I know who sent Tally. The day I heard they suspected it was Tally who was there, I knew it was the president."

"How did you know? Nobody knew."

Q laughed. "Now who has friends in high places?"

"You. It was you who burned down the house."

"When you own a restaurant and you're friends with people who own restaurants and bars, you know a thing or two about how to burn a place down. But I guess I didn't realize house fires don't heat up like furnaces. The bones don't all burn into ashes."

Since Ferraro wouldn't be alive to repeat anything, Q laid out exactly how he had avenged his son's death. How it started by being friendly with an FBI agent with access to inside information. How the FBI agent was immediately suspicious of Sean's nice apartment and clothes, his car. That led to bank accounts, and from there it was just a matter of tracing the money and putting the puzzle together.

"You probably don't know that the FBI guy, Keane, is Sean's brother. Well, half-brother," he said. "Hardly anybody knew, which is just the way their mom wanted it."

"Sounds like you and the FBI man both need to see a shrink," Ferraro said.

Q finished his story about how he'd known about Ferraro's shadow part in the gambling ring. Sean had told him a year before.

"Knew you were out there, didn't know your name," he said. "Keane helped me with that, too."

He told Ferraro how he'd put a GPS tracker on his rental car, how he followed him to Ramer's home, back to the president's house and finally to Henson's office. How he'd begun to work a frame around Ferraro without him even sensing it.

"You'll go down in history," he said.

Ferraro shook his head. "They'll find the bug."

"I wouldn't count on that. One thing I've learned about law enforcement, they pretty much do what they want, when they want. Did you know Keane squatted outside the president's house for a couple hours? Listened to that whole gang of assholes argue about money and blame and what to do next. And then after that, he went right inside like he belonged. Just walked in."

"I'm sure Teddy was in fine form by then. There's no telling what he said."

Q ignored him. "Everybody there, they all bet on games?"

"I assume so. That was the point for most of them. A few of them, like Don, it was a big deal. Teddy, too. He was stashing money away offshore for his retirement, for whenever things blew up."

"And you?"

"I did it for fun. It was just a hobby."

Q shook his head. "Just a hobby?"

"You know what the golden rule is in gambling? Never bet more than you can afford to lose. I never did and never do. These guys, well, not everybody's got common sense."

"Yeah, but they weren't really gambling, were they? I mean, it wasn't a game of chance. They already had the system rigged. Had their players working behind the scenes."

"It was gambling, all right. The thing about a gambler, they don't know when to stop. So, when they lose a game or two, they look for a way to make up the money fast. They double down too fast. They don't really study. They just know they're out of money, and the least they want to do at that point is come home even."

"You talk about it like it's a game."

"Well, it was."

"Fuck that. It was business. And you guys did pretty damned well. I should shoot you just for—"

He stopped when he sensed a movement behind him. He did a half-turn in time to see something move in the shadows. Then he heard footsteps on the metal bleachers above them. Marksmen taking positions. The police had arrived.

46

THEY ARRIVED AT the stadium with lights flashing. They rolled up on sheriff's deputies, no doubt redeployed from Simpson's house.

Keane said as they climbed out of Rossi's sedan, "And you think you guys don't like the FBI. This'll be fun."

Commander Jeff Wiley greeted them with a nod as he talked into a two-way radio clipped to the top of one of his considerable shoulders. Wiley looked like a poster-boy recruit. He stood two inches taller than Keane and carried twenty more pounds on a bulkier chest and a narrower waist. A close-cropped cut of brown hair rounded out a no-tolerance-for-bullshit appearance.

"We've got two inside, both males. One white, one black. Looks like the black one's got a gun on the white one," Wiley said. "They just walked right in. We've another squad coming, and SWAT is on the way."

"I know one of the guys inside," Keane said. "I think I can talk him down."

"Who are you?"

Rossi gave Wiley a thirty-second briefing, told him Keane was FBI and ended with, "We just left another crime scene near downtown that's related to this one."

"Yeah? Me, too. Apparently somebody executed the school president with a knife across the throat. I don't know if this is related or not."

"Safe to say it is," Rossi said. "Fucking mess."

"Fine," Wiley said. "When we're done here you can tie the two together. Right now we're focused on ending this one. We're getting the lights turned on so everyone can see, and then we'll put a stop to this."

To Keane he said: "Which one do you know? The one with the gun or the other one?"

"Pretty sure it's 'with.'"

"Yeah? Well enough to talk him down?"

"Before today, I'd say yes," Keane said. "But now I don't know."

"That settles that."

"Let us go in," Rossi said. "We can defuse this."

"Not a chance," Wiley said. "We're not going to put people in harm's way."

"Fuck this," Keane said and walked away from the group.

"Hey!" Wiley yelled.

Keane waved him off and kept walking. He pulled out his disposable cell and dialed. When the call connected he said, "Two things, off the record. First, you're not terrible at your job. Not great, but not terrible."

Charlie Bone was breathing hard. "Jesus, do you know what's going on? All hell's breaking loose on this thing. They've got cops everywhere looking for—"

"I know. Get to the campus right now. Get to the stadium. You'll scoop everyone. Right now."

He clicked the phone off and pulled out the battery. He dumped the phone into the trash can and pushed a speed-dial command on his primary phone. He walked back toward Wiley as the call connected. "Are you pointing a gun at Ferraro in there?"

"Are you spying on me?" Q said.

"Quit fucking around. Are you?"

A vein in Wiley's neck bulged. "What the hell are you doing?"

He ended the call and looked at the commander. "I'm sorry, you didn't want to talk to the people in the stadium?"

Wiley glared at him. "Fine. You can help us negotiate. But you can't go in. Find out what he wants to end this without anyone getting hurt."

Keane walked away from the group and hit speed-dial again.

"You hung up on me," Q said.

"I'm outside. The guy in charge of all the shooters around you wants to know what the situation is."

Without any emotion, Q said, "I want this asshole in front of me dead."

"You mean Ferraro, or another asshole?"

"Yeah, Ferraro."

Keane nodded a yes at Wiley. "So he's alive. Who else is in there?"

"He's upright, but he's not moving around too well. But it's just us."

"And you've got a gun on him."

"We're just talking."

Keane considered that. "I'm going to give the phone to a Lieutenant Wiley. You need to ask to see me. Tell this guy you'll surrender but only if I come in first."

"I'm good with that."

He walked back and handed the phone to Wiley. "He wants to talk to you."

47

BECAUSE OF THE sling, it took ten minutes to get Keane fitted with a bulletproof vest and a SWAT jacket. Wiley used the time to have OU security turn on the stadium lights. Gradually, banks of fifteen-hundred-watt halogen bulbs came alive. Within three minutes of being energized, six light towers illuminated the stadium. Eleven minutes later Keane was walking down stadium steps toward Ferraro and Q.

They sat on metal bleachers about ten feet from each other. As he got closer, he saw a nine millimeter on a seat next to Q. He barely recognized the man he had spent nearly a week with, maybe the hardest week of their lives. Q's right eye was nearly swollen closed. His forehead had knots sticking out, giving him a caveman look, and his cheek and lower jaw puffed out. Crusts of dried blood clotted in his hair.

Keane easily discerned where a bullet had traveled. A dark crimson groove cut into his hair. A quarter-inch to the left and Q would be dead. A quarter-inch to the right and he'd still look normal. As it was, he looked as if he'd barely survived a heavyweight UFC bout.

He motioned to Ferraro. "This guy shoot you?"

Q shook his head. "Henson."

336 | *David Ryan*

"So you shot him."

"No. That was him," Q said, pointing at Ferraro.

"I told you to go home," Keane said.

"You told me to do what I had to do. And I did," Q said. "You got a gun?"

Keane shook his head, held his hands up, his right hand constrained by the sling, and turned in a circle as proof. When he stopped, he took in the fact Q had taken his advice. His gun was on the metal bleacher in front of him, close enough to reach but far enough from Ferraro that there would be no doubt who would win a chase to it. Besides, Ferraro was crooked to one side and breathing carefully. His left hand held onto the right side of his ribcage as if he were trying to keep a bone from poking out.

"You don't look quite like the smug guy I met in Atlanta," Keane said to Ferraro. "You look like you're in pain."

"Your friend here doesn't fight like a man. He likes to kick people when they're down."

Looking back at Q, Keane said, "You look like you went fifteen rounds with Ali in his prime. And you're still bleeding. You look like hell, and you need to get to the hospital."

"Not until this asshole gets what's coming to him."

"You know, you got my ass in a pretty big sling here. I don't appreciate that."

"I've got to say, you were a goddamned great help. I couldn't have done it without you. I'd say I'm sorry, but I'd be lying."

"So, except for the part where this guy dies, have you gotten what you wanted?"

"Pretty much. Mr. Ferraro here says the president sent Hance to remind Sean what he was supposed to do. What was it you said? 'Send him a message.'"

It made sense. Although Childress had refused to incriminate the school president, he'd signed an affidavit admitting to a number of transgressions that would get him fired. And now that Teddy Simpson was dead, Childress wouldn't be able to back away from anything already in the sworn statement.

"Your man here, he's pretty much crazy. You know that, right?" Ferraro said to Keane.

"I do," Keane replied.

"Hey—" Q started, but Keane cut him off.

"Shut up. The SWAT team out there thinks I came in here to talk you down. But funny as it seems, I came to talk to him."

He looked at Ferraro. "Let's finish what we started in Atlanta."

"Nothing to finish," Ferraro said. "Nothing to say."

"You're finished. Simpson's gone. Henson's gone. It's over. Within a month, the ones that aren't already dead will wish they were. You're all going to prison."

Ferraro tried to chuckle and clutched his ribs. "I don't think so. I'll testify that your pal here shot Don."

"That won't matter. They'll put you at Hance's and Ramer's and Simpson's."

"Put me there for what?" Ferraro looked confused.

"Murder, my friend. A fire, a stabbing and a slashing. And there's shooting me. Firing at an FBI officer is a federal crime, but that'll be the least of it. Quite the repertoire."

"You have me confused for someone else."

"I don't think so."

Q interrupted. "He didn't shoot you."

Keane turned. And then he saw it. It raced through him like a lightning strike. His face flushed with anger. He ticked through a timeline. When, where, how. He'd assumed that not hearing from Q meant he was back in Boynton Beach grieving, setting up Sean's memorial service, taking the necessary steps toward getting his life back together without a son. He'd assumed wrong. Way wrong. And then: "You shot me."

"I'm glad I didn't hurt you."

"You sonofabitch, you kept shooting at me. You tried to kill me."

"I just wanted you to back off."

"You cut the tire before that."

"Just trying to warn you. And slow you down."

"You killed all these people? All for Sean?"

Q nodded and then pointed to Ferraro. "Not all of them. He beat me to Henson."

"Told you," Ferrarro said.

"Shut the fuck up," Keane snapped.

"Tell me, how do you think this all started?" Ferraro asked. "I don't think the mastermind is who you think it is."

Keane said, "First I pinned it on Duke Childress. Then it was Henson, and then I moved off him to the president. Now it's you. A guy who spent a lot of years in New York and suddenly showed up in Florida throwing money around. You're all kind of connected in New York."

"You give me way too much credit. Give all of us too much credit." He looked at Q. "You didn't tell him?"

Q said, "He didn't need to know. And it don't matter now."

Keane crooked his head and frowned. He went through a checklist. These were the power players in the group. Their initials matched up in the spreadsheets. Ferraro had taken care to keep his distance, but he'd have a difficult time contradicting the spreadsheets matched up with either his credit card history or his bank records. If not him, if not them, who? Q?

Keane looked at his old friend. "You?"

"He wishes," Ferraro said.

Keane processed who was left. The only other candidate was Hance. But he'd abandoned that idea days before. The bouncer simply wasn't that smart. He hadn't questioned any of the assistant coaches or the staff members other than the equipment manager. But he had estimated the coaches couldn't do their jobs well and have time to run an illicit side business. Robert Wyndham didn't have the courage. Duke Childress didn't have the time or inclination. Then there was Quentin Riggins.

He worked that over and decided: *Plausible*. More than one bookie worked out of a bar. And then: *No*. Anyone who needed help from his son to make sound business decisions couldn't pull this off.

A chill ran through his spine, from his scalp to his feet. "Oh, God."

Sean.

"There it is," Ferraro said.

Keane sat on the bleachers and looked at Q. "You said he was smart. Simpson said he would have been a millionaire. You knew because what he did for your restaurant he was doing here."

Q did his best to nod.

"Jesus," Keane said. Now all of the spreadsheet numbers made sense. Sean didn't track booster winnings to build up evidence. He tracked them because that was good business. To make sure he got paid.

Sean had motive and he had opportunity. Access to all the players, all the coaches, the biggest boosters, and even the president. But not big enough in the end for a hidden health condition triggered by a gofer who wanted to take the arrogance out of him.

Ferraro smirked. "He was brilliant. He had everything figured out. He had help, but it was all him."

"How? Why?" Keane asked.

Ferraro looked at Q. "You want to tell it?"

Q didn't move, said nothing.

Ferraro talked, and the tale was both fascinating and businesslike. Just like Sean. Shortly after he arrived on campus, booster payments started. Unlike his teammates, Sean squirreled his money away, where it mounted up over time but generated little to no interest.

"He bitched to Teddy about it once, and Teddy told him if he wanted to grow his money, he'd have to invest like everybody else. He told the kid to buy stocks. Sean came up with more of a sure thing."

Throwing football games and betting on them.

"Gambling's never a sure thing," Keane said.

"It is if you have enough control to manipulate the outcome and the score," Ferraro said. "He pulled in enough teammates to make it go. But he made a mistake. He couldn't keep quiet."

Ferraro recounted how Sean had recruited teammates for his venture, and then one night, they all got drunk at a party. Sean slipped. Tally Hance was there and coaxed most of the salient details out of him. Sean and Tally talked for an hour, Sean outlining everything, Tally taking it all in. Tally calling it foolproof.

"And then Tally told Teddy," Ferraro said. "He left out the part that it wasn't his idea, but Teddy was smart enough to figure that out. So Teddy called the kid in. Didn't even tell Duke about it. Sean was smart, but Teddy was smarter. Teddy sat back and let the kid sell him. And the kid laid it on thick. Explained how to gamble online, how to throw games. But Teddy saw the potential. How to fund it with big money. That way, Teddy told him, they could pay the players more money. Everybody was a winner, and there were a lot of incentives to keep it going. Eventually the kid was pissed that Teddy was going to use his idea, but that didn't dawn on him at first."

Keane considered the brother he didn't know at all. Sean was charismatic and enjoyed rafts of friends. It stood to reason he could be a strong salesman among his peers. But selling a university president? And a school trustee? Recruiting hired hands? That was almost incomprehensible.

"What was the catch?" he asked.

Ferraro said, "One school throwing games and one game a week don't add up to enough cash, and it makes things too concentrated. Too easy to spot if you're in Vegas or if you're watching the betting lines really close. Too much chance of unwanted attention."

Keane nodded. He knew where this was going.

"Teddy worked a deal with a handful of his president buddies around the country. Ten or twelve of them, anyway. They were all big football fans, and they all agreed to share inside information on their football teams. Teddy talked to them all every other day during the season, getting all the real information about players who were injured, guys who would and wouldn't play, suspensions that hadn't hit the papers yet. All the things that, if they were made public, would move a point spread this way or the other way."

"That was their edge. Nobody else was throwing games."

"One other school, Memphis Tech. Believe it or not, their president is more corrupt than Teddy."

"But that's not what brought it all down. What went wrong?"

"What always goes wrong. The players got greedy. At first, there was a small group of people, one for all and all for one. And a lot of money. That's what made the whole thing worthwhile. But then he expanded, went for volume. Smaller dollars maybe but more people. Pulled in the fraternities and other organizations on campus. Everybody but the Student Government Association. It got to be a lot of people. That's a hard business model unless you're McDonald's. And, of course, just like he told Tally about it, at one point he told his old man about it."

Keane stood and looked at Q, and then at Ferraro's smirk. "Jesus. Of course. And all this time, Hance was just a middle man."

"Hance was a gofer," Ferraro said. "He ran the money. Sean transferred money from account to account. Tally dealt in cash. He made sure everybody got what they were looking for. He worked for Sean, he worked for us, he worked for other boosters. He was the candy man. But then he fucked up."

"He killed Sean."

"Who knows? But he was there when the kid's heart gave out. Either way, the golden goose was gone. The heat was coming. And the whole thing was over."

"Why not just find somebody else to help run it? Why not keep going?"

Ferraro gave him a confused look. "You don't get it, do you?"

Q interrupted. "Sean was too good at his job."

"Hell, he was the Pied Piper," Ferraro said. "He told everybody what to do, how to do it. He'd recruited a raptured audience of players willing to fake injuries and stumble and fumble almost at will. My God, he was a natural leader. Just about everybody on the team did exactly what he wanted."

"And yet you guys sent the gofer to muscle him," Keane said.

Ferraro took a long, labored breath and blinked away the pain. "Big mistake. Incredibly dumb. Biggest mistake Teddy ever made. Teddy had a soft spot for Hance, but he shouldn't have trusted him. Teddy should have handled it himself, but he didn't think he could risk it." He looked across at Q. "Your son went off the reservation, and he was putting us all at risk."

"He just wanted a fair cut," Q said.

Ferraro had no response. Keane let the silence linger, and then his brain clicked. "He was going on strike for the bowl game." He looked at Ferraro. "Sean was maybe going pro after the season, so you had one more game to make some money. And Sean said no."

"Never a smart thing to tell a syndicate," Ferraro said. "When Don told me who was at the bar that night, I figured the players were talking about how they were going to hold us hostage, get a bigger share."

"How did Coach Childress have no clue? How's that possible?" Keane asked.

"Shit," Q said. "Childress only cares about football. The president, he made sure Tally stayed close to the coach so that if there were signs the coach found out or got too close, the president would take care of him. I mean, he wins some, but it's not like the guy's popular."

Realization tingled the top of Keane's head and ran down his neck and into his shoulders and arms like a fast-working painkiller. Shame washed through him as his mind raced. He thought about all the spreadsheets on Sean's laptop, the volume of . . . *revenue* that he had generated. He thought about what Q said about Sean days ago, how he'd suggested changes to his restaurant operations that would save money. And yet even as Q had said it, he was in bed with his son on an illegal gambling operation.

He said, "I can't believe Sean was responsible for all this."

"You would if you'd known him at all," Q said. "But you didn't know anything about him. Didn't even make much of an effort."

"You know better than anyone the reason why—"

"Too late for that," said Q. His swollen head made his face impossible to read.

"When did you find out?" he asked.

"Pretty much right away," Q said.

Ferraro said, "It took him a year to get involved."

Keane shook his head. "You knew all this time. You asked me to find out why this all happened and you already knew. Why'd you even ask?"

"I had no idea Sean dying and his . . . business venture were connected. But once you told me about Tally, I knew. After that, well, I couldn't bring all these people down by myself."

Keane said, "You had to know I'd bring you down too. And you ended up getting them anyway. You just did it the wrong way."

Q turned. "I wanted to make sure they stayed down. These guys have been covering their tracks the whole way. Nobody would touch them. But I touched them. It's solved."

"Okay, fine. It's solved. You've gotten your revenge."

"Not all of it. And you. You don't accept any blame, do you?"

"What are you blaming me for? You used me as a pawn."

Q shook his head and spat on the bleachers. "You know, at some point after you left home, you became a grown-ass man. One that could have stood up to his crazy mom and done exactly as you pleased. I think you tried once or twice to stay close to Sean, but your mom, she got in your face and you just backed down. Tucked your tail and ran. Didn't even try after that. Finally, Sean gave up on you. I held out hope that you'd turn things around, learn how to be a real brother, but you never came through."

"I'm sorry," Keane said.

"You were never there for Sean, for me. All those years when he was a kid and you let it all happen. You had a job, a career, a little bit of money. Jesus."

"I wish I could go back."

"How sweet: a family reunion," Ferraro said. "You guys should find a couples therapist."

"You asshole," Q said. He moved to his side and reached for the gun. "You're never—"

"No!" Keane screamed. He took one step toward Q and drove his arm upward to divert Q's aim. The shot never came, but Keane was a half-second too late.

He heard a faraway *pop-pop-pop* and a loud clang, lead hitting metal as the air in front of his face exploded with red wetness. Q's nose and jaw disappeared in a pink mist just before Keane tackled him. He rolled down one row in a heap, pulling Q with him.

His shoulder screamed in pain as he hit, and he felt the stitches rip. They ripped again when Q, lifeless, toppled onto him.

Seconds later, he heard the sound of boots clanging down the metal bleachers. He heard the yelling of commands and felt nothing. Then his ears were filled by a voice yelling at Ferraro to get on his face.

Keane scrambled from beneath a bloody corpse and rolled Q over. Keane took that in just as a SWAT team member drove a hand into his back and pushed him face-first onto the bleachers.

48

ALL THE NETWORKS aired stories for three days after the sheriff's marksman did his job. One anchor linked OU to Kent State, Virginia Tech, and UC-Santa Barbara, universities inexorably tied to campus shootings. Never mind that Q threatened no students and that the only person to pull a trigger on campus was a member of law enforcement.

The stories, though, focused on the myriad of questions that had no answers. School officials were scratching their heads about why their president was packing several suitcases when he was killed. President Simpson had announced no vacation plans.

Only the fact that there were no students on campus prevented a full-fledged media frenzy. Professors had already turned in their final grades and had left for their holiday break. There simply wasn't anyone on campus for reporters to inflame.

But shock gripped the university and the city. A killer had taken the president, one of the university's trustees, and one of Orlando's well-thought-of businessmen. The governor appointed an interim president to replace Teddy Simpson. The media floated the name of a prominent Winter Park lawyer as the permanent choice. Keane recognized

the name from his research of Sean's spreadsheet.
He didn't doubt its veracity one bit.

STATE CRIMINAL INVESTIGATORS, plus Dombrowski
and Cramer, questioned Keane about everything
he'd done since he flew to Florida. They wanted
details of his three-way conversation with Q and
Ferraro and what the two of them shared about
their earlier confrontation with Henson. They spent
more time on Henson's death than Q's, tipping
their hand on which they considered more
important. When Q reached for a gun, he more
than justified a sharpshooter pulling a trigger.
Standoff over, gunman dead, everybody else safe.
Job well done.

Q would gain the title of serial killer, staining
both OU and Orlando for years to come.

Rossi and Thomas took their turn with Keane
next. They sat in the same interview room he'd
shared with them and Q the day after Sean died.
This time, the detectives pushed harder, and they
expressed no condolences.

Rossi had pulled her hair back in a bun and had
been generous with her makeup, but she couldn't
hide the bags under her eyes or the heaviness of her
shoulders. "I went back and looked at video from a
7-Eleven in Colonialtown the night Hance was
killed. Quentin Riggins was on it. Just before
midnight, he bought a liter bottle of soda and a two-
gallon gas can. He drained the soda bottle and filled
up the gas can. Makes for strong evidence for the
fire at Hance's."

"Circumstantial unless you have the bottle or the
can," Keane said. "I assume they burned up."

Neither of them answered, but Keane
understood. Their case wasn't air-tight, but it was

solid. Sean's accounting would see to that. He wondered but didn't ask if they second-guessed themselves for not securing the video immediately. It was a shot in the dark, but if they had, it's possible Q's killing spree never would have happened.

Keane let out a long sigh. "I should have seen it. He was right in front of me, and I didn't see it."

They told him Ferraro had secured a high-priced attorney, talked sparingly, admitted nothing, and figured to walk away a free man.

"He'll get his eventually," Keane said.

After four hours of interrogation, Thomas finally looked at Rossi. "Good?"

She nodded. "Give me a minute." The detectives left the room, and then Rossi stepped back in and sat. "We're not recording. This is off the record."

Keane sat up. "I was wrong about a lot of things. I made a lot of bad assumptions."

"I won't disagree with you there," she said.

"Are they going to investigate you? About pulling me in to help you?"

She patted the back of her head as if to make sure her bun was secure. "There's going to be blowback, but I'll be okay. I'll stay on homicide, same grade. It'll take me longer to get promoted."

"They know if they dig around hard enough, they'll find out things they really don't want to know about. How you told me things you probably shouldn't have and how I did things I probably shouldn't have. They just want it to go away."

"They have enough problems. There's enough for everyone in this one."

Keane tapped his hands on the table. "There's a lot more than they know. I figured out the spreadsheets."

Rossi uncrossed her legs and scooted back into interview position. "We think we have it figured out too. Sean wasn't just *a* bookie. He was *the* bookie on campus. He had whole fraternities as customers, and a few faculty members."

He nodded. With the volume of initials on Sean's spreadsheets, it made sense. "When's it going to come out?"

"Maybe over the summer. Maybe never," she said. "Everybody is ready to move on."

"What about OPD?"

"Brass is right there with them. You know how that goes."

She looked him in the eye. "There is something we can't figure out."

"What's that?"

"Once we picked through Sean's laptop, we found he was placing his bets through a company in the Cayman Islands called Blindside.com. You ever heard of it?"

"I saw it on the same computer you did."

"I'm sure. Anyway, it's the strangest thing. It turns out Sean closed his account."

"What's wrong with that?"

"He closed it a few days ago. After he died. How do you suppose that happened?"

Keane weighed his response. "I don't have an answer for that."

"We're thinking maybe it went to the father or Simpson or one of his friends in his circle, but we can't find anything on their end yet. Maybe we'll get lucky, catch up to it in probate. If it ends up in there, we'll get it."

"I didn't realize that," he said, but knew the money would never show up on a probate record.

"You didn't ask how much."

He paused. "Okay, how much?"

"Eighty-six-thousand, five-hundred and sixty dollars."

"Jesus. Lot of money for a college kid."

"A lot of money, period."

She pursed her lips. "I almost hope it doesn't leave a trail. I'd rather not know."

He nodded. "I know what you mean." He wouldn't risk documenting on future tax returns his latest charitable contributions. He'd scheduled five-figure gifts to Gamblers Anonymous and the American Heart Association from a bank based in the Caymans.

KEANE PACKED FOR his flight home and then typed out a letter of resignation. He emailed it to Happy Harding and cc'd himself. Then he texted his boss to let him know he'd show up in a couple days to set up his interviews with the disciplinary board.

When he finally arrived at his condo six hours later, he soaked under a shower long enough for his hot water to run out. He was drinking a beer and going through his mail at the kitchen table when a delivery from FedEx arrived. He signed for it and looked at the sender, a law firm in Stuart, Florida. The letter inside looked official. So did the accompanying documents, one of them a letter from Jacob Johns, Esquire. *I am writing to inform you that you are among the named beneficiaries of Quentin Marvin Riggins. Mr. Riggins bequeathed to you The Tides bar and grill. . . .*

He re-read the letter and looked at the documents. They were the formal documents of a title change. If he signed, he would own The Tides. Technically, he owned it now, but this would put him on the hook for property taxes and liability insurance.

A second envelope clipped to the restaurant title documents was addressed to him in an awkward scrawl. A signed, handwritten, one-page letter matched the shaky penmanship.

Keane,
I hope you end up getting this. This is just us.
I'll never understand why you spent all those years so far away when you could have done so much good down here. You could have reached out more than you did, but you decided to stay away.
If you're reading this, something bad happened to me. If so, I don't regret trying to keep Sean's name clean. I hope you can make things right.
If I had money, I'd leave it to you. All I have is The Tides and the car. I hope you don't sell them. Sean liked them both.
Stay out of trouble,
Q

Keane walked to the living room and let the light in. He could barely manage his life. Now he was being asked to manage the lives of at least a dozen others, plus a business—if the business was still open.

If he were to salvage it, he'd need to get back to Florida as soon as possible and take stock. Best case, a new career beckoned. Worst case, he could keep the Tides running until he found a buyer.

He dug out a legal pad and began a list. When he finished, he re-read it, and then added a final item. *Invite Rossi to dinner.*

ACKNOWLEDGEMENTS

Katherine Adams couldn't pick me out of a police lineup today, but my heart-felt thanks go to her, a writer and teacher once upon a time in Knoxville, Tennessee, now in New Orleans. She taught me the value in letting a story breathe.

This particular one, however, would not have started if not for the kindness of Henry Pierson Curtis, who connected me with Barb Bergin, who nudged me in the right direction of homicide detectives and their ways of life. The late Charlie Bone told me endless anecdotes about his time in the FBI, and younger agents clued me into today's bureau.

Bianca Prieto, Amy Pavuk-Gentry, Sarah Lundy Cecile, Jim Leusner, Rene Stutzman, Susan Jacobson, Greg Miller, Kevin Connolly, and Walter Pacheco answered cop questions without rolling their eyes. If there are any mistakes in this book, they are all mine.

Peter Brown and Skip Lackey were great encouragers and served as sounding boards. Mike Huguenin, who has read more crime novels than any person his age, found holes and made suggestions that proved pivotal to the final story when it appeared all was lost.

Truth-teller John Cherwa delivered tough news early on and, much later, threw in a last-second save, as did Kim Borwick. My friend Bruno also blew me away with his proofreading skills.

Greg Dawson and Wynter Daniels, two vastly different authors, delivered to me the ABCs of publishing business, and Tim Dorsey allowed me to leverage an old friendship for advice. Lyn Davis, Barrie Byron and Bit Shaw survived early drafts of this tale and still showered me with love, food, wine and good vibrations.

Micki Browning shared this journey long-distance as she wrote her first novels. Micki, I owe you chocolate and wine. Similarly, Ray Flynt, the best Ben Franklin you'll ever see on stage, never let me surrender.

Finally, Christie Davis endured too many versions of this book, mediocre and otherwise. Thank you for never saying move on.